Dying
to
Know

Dying
to
Know

A Gumshoe Ghost Mystery

TJ O'Connor

MIDNIGHT INK
WOODBURY, MINNESOTA

First Edition
First Printing, 2014

Book design and format by Donna Burch
Cover design by Lisa Novak
Cover illustration: Jesse Reisch/Deborah Wolfe Ltd.
Editing by Connie Hill

Midnight Ink, an imprint of Llewellyn Worldwide Ltd.

This is a work of fiction. Names, characters, places, and incidents are either the product of the author's imagination or are used fictitiously, and any resemblance to actual persons, living or dead, business establishments, events, or locales is entirely coincidental.

Library of Congress Cataloging-in-Publication Data

O'Connor, T. J., 1960—
   Dying to know : a gumshoe ghost mystery / TJ O'Connor. — First edition.
      p.   cm.
   ISBN 978-0-7387-3950-2
1. Murder—Investigation—Fiction. 2. Murder victims—Fiction. I. Title.
   PS3615.C596D95 2014
   813'.6—dc23   2013030624

Midnight Ink
Llewellyn Worldwide Ltd.
2143 Wooddale Drive
Woodbury, MN 55125-2989
www.midnightinkbooks.com

Printed in the United States of America

ONE

DYING IS OVERRATED. MURDER, on the other hand, is not.

Trust me, after fifteen years as a detective, I know a lot about both. Like death and murder are always complicated, but not always related. You can have death without murder, but not the other way around. That's what I used to think anyway. I changed my mind after an episode of my recurring nightmare. I'd been having it for years and it always turned out the same. While chasing a bad guy in the dark, he turned and shot me. I was about to die when something always pulled me from the nightmare.

This time, it was Hercule's hot breath.

My four-year-old black Lab was standing beside my bed alternating between low growls and a tongue-lashing. Both demanded my attention. When my eyes first opened, he lapped at my face and nudged me with his big, wet nose. I forced my eyes open wider and at the same time realized that Angel was not snuggled beside me in bed. She was standing across the room and listening at our bedroom door.

"Angel, did you hear something again?" She always heard things late at night and always felt compelled to share them with me. "Are you sure?"

"Yes, Tuck. Herc can hear it, too. Wake up, will you? What kind of detective are you?"

"The asleep-kind."

"Just get up. Please?"

Hercule froze, nose down, staring at me as we both heard creaking floorboards in the downstairs hall. I rolled sideways and sat on the side of the bed. Hercule crept away and crouched near the door. For the third time, something interrupted Angel's sleep. The first two times were just our old house's creaks and groans, and both failed to wake Hercule out of a stone-cold sleep. Now, after summoning me, he was poised for homeland defense.

I got to my feet and gathered my clothes littered in a strategic path across the room. I nearly toppled over slipping on my jeans and a black tee shirt, and did manage to trip over my running shoes.

Angel motioned for Herc to return to the bed. To me she whispered, "Hurry up."

"Look, if I'm going to get killed tonight, I don't want to be naked." I grabbed my 40-caliber Glock from the nightstand and checked the chamber. Then, I retrieved a .38 revolver from our walk-in closet and handed it to Angel. "Just in case."

"Okay. Be careful."

"Keep Herc close, babe. If it's your imagination, stay awake and lose those pjs. If it's trouble, give me fifteen minutes—then lose them."

Even in the dark, I could see her eyes roll. "Just be careful."

At the door, I listened but heard nothing. I winked at Angel and Hercule on the bed and whispered, "I love you—you too, Angel."

Hercule wagged his tail.

In the hallway, I waited for my eyes to adjust a little more to the darkness. I shifted them to use my peripheral vision, looking for any telltale movement. Still nothing. From the top of the stairs, I could just make out the foyer below and did not see or hear anything. There were no wispy shadows, no running feet, and no creaking floorboards. Yawning, I eased down the stairs with my Glock out in front of me. At the bottom landing, I stopped.

Darkness and the grandfather clock greeted me—it chimed two.

The downstairs was quiet and I checked the front door. It was still locked and there were no signs of splintered wood, broken glass, or other forced entry. The only sound I heard was my own breathing. The only curious sighting was the half-dressed, frumpy guy in the hall mirror who looked tired and irritated.

Maybe Angel would be losing those pjs sooner rather than later.

I started with the kitchen and worked my way around the first floor, searching room by room—all five of them—ending in my den. Nothing. The most dangerous thing I found was Hercule's squeaky frog that scared the crap out of me when I stepped on it. I felt foolish and decided to head back to bed.

It hit me when I reached to turn off my desk lamp.

The light shouldn't have been on. I looked around. My briefcase wasn't in its ritual place on my credenza. It was on my chair and the contents strewn over my desk. Everything was dumped out—my gold detective's badge and I.D., several files, a notepad, tape recorder, and my .380 backup piece.

No, the Walther wasn't there—the holster was empty.

"Angel..." I bolted to the stairs and looked up.

Floorboards groaned above me. A door opened in the darkness beyond the landing. Movement—a shadow.

Somewhere above, Angel called, "Tuck."

There was a flash at the top of the stairs... a shot.

I lunged for the third stair. A figure stepped out of the darkness twelve feet above me.

Another flash.

"Angel!"

TWO

THE NEXT MORNING, I realized how much in common I had with my heroes. They were, of course, some of the greatest detectives in history. I'm speaking of Doyle's Holmes, Christie's Poirot, and Bigger's Charlie Chan. I could add Scooby and Shaggy, but they're cartoons and don't count. The others are fictional characters, too, but they're legends nonetheless. I'm not saying I'm a legend. I'm saying they're all dead.

So am I.

Being dead is not intuitive, mind you. In fact, it's downright confusing. Disappointing even. There were no trumpets, billowy clouds, or bright beacons of light—not yet anyway. On the bright side, there was no horny guy with bad breath and fire everywhere either.

No, the revelation of my fate began with me sitting at my desk, dazed and confused. I felt as though I'd touched a bare electric cord while taking a bath. Images swirled around me. My eyes didn't focus at first, and my body felt edgy and uncontrolled. It took a long time to realize where and who I was. The pictures on the den wall were at first empty frames. The books and knickknacks were foreign and without a story. Nothing seemed familiar.

Until I saw the evidence in the hallway.

A body. My body.

The lightning hit me again and I exploded in a kaleidoscope of memories. My life hadn't passed before me last night after charging for the chairs. It waited until now—just now—and the rush of forty years poured over me. All of them, every memory, left me aching and afraid.

My house was alive with murmurs and police radios, rushing feet, and crime scene technicians taking photographs. They vacuumed the carpets for evidence and dusted fingerprint powder everywhere. Their meticulous search for clues left nothing untouched.

All the proof I needed was on the foyer carpet just outside my den.

My body lay crumpled where it fell just after two this morning. I'd never made the third step before the bullet struck my chest and ended my life. It was gone before I hit the floor. I didn't recall any trauma, any pain, or any fear.

Just a flash.

When I opened my eyes, it was over. I watched my body being processed for gunshot residue, fibers, and time of death. A crime lab technician bagged my hands to protect evidence. Someone else kept snapping photographs and took measurements. I'd performed those procedures dozens of times over the years. Watching, they now took on a new meaning. So did homicide. It had been my job and an important one, and I tried never to let it get personal.

Now it was personal. Very personal.

My body and I shared the same forty-year-old exterior—five-eleven and about one hundred ninety-five pounds with short brown hair and three day's growth of beard. My body was barefoot, wearing a blood-stained tee shirt and jeans. Luckily, spirit-me had enough class to have on a blue blazer and my running shoes—my customary detective attire. Even my gold detective's badge was clipped in its customary place on my belt.

Not that wardrobe matters to the dead, but I'd hate to spend eternity half-naked.

I looked at my body and saw the crime scene technician signal someone in the living room across the hall. A petite, dark-haired woman wearing a sweatshirt and jeans emerged. She stood in the doorway looking down at my body.

Helen Sutter was the captain of the sheriff department's detective squad and my boss. She knelt down beside my body and the hum of commotion from a half-dozen cops quieted. A few tears touched her cheek and she wiped them away. She cussed a few times, bit her lip, and waved at one of the technicians.

"Carl, no mistakes. I want everything by the numbers. Do it all three times. The one who screws up my evidence dies a slow death."

Carl shrugged. "There is no evidence."

"Don't give me that shit. There's always evidence. Find it."

"Yes, ma'am." Carl looked back at my body and threw his chin at two other deputies nearby. Feet started moving again, orders spat, cameras chattered.

Captain Sutter lifted her radio and stood up. "Spence—Sutter. Give me an update."

The radio chirped and sputtered. "Ah, yeah, Captain … nothing. Not a damn thing. We've talked to everyone on both sides of the street for two blocks …"

"Then make it four blocks. And cover the side streets—then you can damn well do it again."

The radio chirped again but no voice followed.

"Braddock," Captain Sutter bellowed. "Braddock."

My front door banged open and a mountain walked in. He was two hundred sixty pounds of rock and muscle. His hair was short cut and his face scruffy and stained with emotion. Powerful muscles strained against his golf shirt matted with dark stains—blood stains. My blood.

Detective Theodore Braddock—Bear to most—stopped inside the doorway. Bear Braddock was not an emotional man, not by any means. We'd been partners since the police academy twenty years ago. Since then, I'd seen the brute pick up body parts after a horrific traffic accident without a twitch. He could clear out a bar fight and take a beating without losing his temper. Not too long ago, I'd seen him at his own brother's funeral and he never shed a tear. He wasn't a cold man, mind you, just hard and tough. Maybe he was really a wussie-boy underneath, but no one—including me—ever saw that side of him. No one ever suggested it was there, either.

Now, he raised his chin and refused to glance at my body. "Yeah, Cap?"

"Give me what you got."

"Nothing new."

Captain Sutter took his arm and dragged him into my den, stopping beside the desk where I was still rooted. As she did, Bear sidestepped my body like a child afraid to step on the cracks. "Then give it to me one more time."

"Yeah, right, again." Bear went to my brown leather chair in the corner and dropped into it. He leaned forward, burying his face into his meaty hands. "Got the call from Angel at two-oh-five—I know 'cause that's the time on my cell. She was upstairs, locked in her bedroom. She said Tuck got shot—maybe dead—someone was in the house. Tuck went to see and…"

She was nodding. "And you?"

"I arrived about two-thirtyish. Came straight in and found him—he was already…"

"Got it." She looked back into the foyer. "You two were supposed to be on surveillance all night, right?"

"Yeah." Bear cleared his throat. His eyes were red and his face puffy from an onslaught of emotions. "It was going nowhere. Nothing happening at the warehouse so I called it an early night."

"How early?"

He thought, then said, "Eleven, I guess. Maybe a little after."

"So…"

"I went straight home. Tuck said he was going to do some paperwork at the office for a few hours. Angel didn't expect him home, so he was going to catch up." Bear's face angered. "I already went through this, Cap. Give me a break."

Sutter gave him a moment. "Okay, after you found him and called it in, then what?"

"I searched the place. Outside, too. Nothing. Uniforms arrived five minutes later."

"Do we have anything to go on?"

In one violent rush, Bear got to his feet and closed in on my filing cabinet. He slammed two brutal blows into its side, denting the metal and sending several framed photographs tumbling to the floor.

"I guess not." She waited until Bear straightened himself. "Motive, clues? A friggin' guess here? Come on, Bear, give me something."

"Motive? Give me a break, Cap. We've been chasing the man for a week now. You know that. We pay him a visit and try to connect the dots back to the guard's murder and wham—Tuck's in a body bag. What more do you want?"

Helen Sutter might have been small for a cop, but she was feisty. At forty-five, she still had a youthful, pretty face that hid the steel character inside. Small and girlie were deceiving; Helen Sutter would out-shoot, out-drink, out-cuss, and out-smart most of the cops in the county. Now, she drove an iron finger into Bear's chest and backed him all the way to the dented filing cabinet.

"I want evidence, Bear. Speculation and revenge won't impress a courtroom. Get me fingerprints, witnesses, or a frigging microscopic fiber. Link this to him and I'll drag his mobbed-up ass in myself. Just prove it. Only a fool or a desperate man hits a cop."

Bear straightened himself again and had to look down in order to find her eyes a foot below him. "Yeah, yeah. I got that. But if not him, who?"

"Find out. There's no forced entry—nothing taken, nothing ransacked. Nothing, nothing, nothing." She walked to the open den door and looked out at my body. "We rarely get two homicides a year—let alone in a couple weeks. The crime boys have diddly shit. Tuck's backup piece is gone. It's probably the murder weapon. Son-of-a-bitch."

Bear moved beside her and, for the first time, looked over at my body. His voice was guttural. "It was either someone who knew the house and how to get in and out..."

"Or it was a professional hit."

THREE

CARL CALLED FOR CAPTAIN Sutter. She went to the doorway and spoke quietly with him. When she turned around, her face was white and drawn. "Okay, Bear. They're taking him out."

"Oh, shit," Bear said, turning his back on the door. "I can't, Cap. I just can't."

"Right, okay. Listen, why don't you finish in here. I want all his files in the cabinet taken down to the office and gone over by the entire team. Maybe something in one of them will help. Take care of that, will you?"

Bear nodded. "Okay. Close the door, Cap. I don't want to watch."

She did and the voices in the foyer became a muffled drone I couldn't discern. Moving a homicide victim's body was one thing; moving a dead cop's was another.

Bear stood in the middle of the den and listened. When the front door banged shut, his eyes closed, and for a second, I thought he was going to pummel the filing cabinet again. Instead, he did a very odd thing.

He went to the den door and quietly locked it. Then, he returned to my filing cabinet and slid open the top drawer. He rifled through the files until he found a thick manila one. He opened it, scanned the pages, and nodded.

Instead of returning it to the drawer or placing it in one of the cardboard boxes stacked alongside by the crime scene technicians, he went to my bookcase and slid it behind a series of law journals. He stepped back and surveyed his work.

"Bear?"

"Huh?" His head twisted around and he looked back at the door. "Shit, what's wrong with me?"

He again went to the filing cabinet, but this time began removing files from the drawers and laying them into the evidence boxes. His movements were slow and lethargic as if he had a mechanical arm mindlessly performing the task.

"Bear, did you hear me?"

Nothing. No nod. No eyebrows rose. Nothing.

I leaned forward in my office chair and found myself staring at a photograph of Angel and me. We were dancing at last year's police ball. My Angel was beautiful. She has flowing, auburn hair, green eyes, and a curvy, sexy figure that, at thirty-five, puts most twenty-year-olds to shame. Her short, black evening dress showed off her wonderful curves and her smile stole all the attention around us. Taped to the side of the frame was her black lace garter belt that had my full attention later that night.

I reached out and touched the garter.

Lightning.

Firecrackers ignited inside me. Every nerve exploded all at once. A rush of emotions poured over and through me. I was crying, laughing, aching—depression collided with exhilaration—every emotion I ever felt grabbed me all at once and twisted.

A blur swept before me.

It happened again. The cascade of memories swirled around me like a tornado. They were fleeting wisps of faces and feelings—loves, friends, and strangers. My life's story whirled by like a train at a crossing—glimpses of the past, people I knew, places and things. Life.

My memory was a child's—immature and vague.

Then it stopped just as it had earlier. I was crying. The photograph held my eyes while Bear stood across the room filling his boxes in total oblivion. Whatever had happened to me had done nothing more than show me what I'd lost and how I'd ended.

It was abrupt and violent.

I felt woozy but stood and went to the doorway. I gripped the knob and tried to open the door but nothing happened. My fingers didn't feel the cool brass knob or the hard oak doorway as I pounded on it. There was nothing. The simple task of opening my door was as impossible as my being in that room at all. I was trapped in my own den, in my own three-story Victorian.

Returning to the desk, I tried to pick up the photograph that had taken my breath away but my fingers closed on nothing. I couldn't open the desk drawer or lift a pen to write. Nothing moved for me, nothing lifted in my fingers. Nothing would obey my commands. Nothing.

Something tingled inside me and I felt myself aching for my life back. Earlier, as an onlooker to my own crime scene investigation, I felt nothing—no emotion, no fear, no despair. Now, all those feelings were welling up inside me and heaviness began to consume me.

I stood in the middle of the floor and took in all the photographs, knickknacks, and bric-a-brac. Flashes of memory congealed and formed my past. I closed my eyes, trying to recapture every second of my elusive life.

The whirl of light and pictures began again.

I let myself go—let myself drift along in the feelings that were sweeping over me. There was the smell of coffee and the aroma of a thousand dinners I'd never taste again. The grandfather clock in the hall chimed and I remembered Angel's thirtieth birthday— that was ... five years ago. Our home was awash with emotions that made me ache and laugh at the same time. The smoky scent of smoldering fireplace logs surrounded me and the rich, sweet taste of expensive wine wet my lips. Angel's laughter tickled my ears and her passion took me.

When I opened my eyes, I was alone and staring at our wedding photograph on the bookshelf. Twenty years of memories roared into me—one after the other, churning and twisting, all of them jumbled and slamming into one another—into me. The visions were dizzying. I felt lifted and euphoric. Colors swirled and pictures coalesced—flashing images of my life. College, the police academy, Angel—the beautiful doctoral candidate who traded me a speeding ticket for a date. Passion, love, darkness. Handcuffs on my bookshelf showed me a foot chase through Old Town and my first felony arrest. A plaque on the wall—Bear and me getting our gold detective shields—laughter, bourbon, hangovers. Long nights on stakeouts. Long nights with Angel. Aching for sleep, praying it never came.

The memories settled into their rightful places inside me and I calmed again. I was standing outside the den door where my body had been lying. It was gone now and so were the army of cops and crime scene technicians. It was still afternoon, but darkness enveloped me—and so did the rush of questions that thrust into me like needles.

The first answer spun me around and made me dizzy.

I looked up to the second floor balcony as I'd done a million times. This time, something was different. Strange fingers grabbed me and drew me backward and off balance. A dull ache overcame me. Something sharp thrust into my chest and my breath exploded. Above me, there was fading light and below, black ooze that should have been oak hardwood. I heard Hercule barking wildly before collapsing onto the floor.

It should be near four in the afternoon, but the grandfather clock chimed two. It was happening again ...

∞

... Angel was standing over me and in her hand was a gun—the .38 I'd given her. She dropped to her knees beside me and pressed two fingers against my throat. Her eyes went wide and the gun slipped from her grasp. Tears welled in her eyes and she brushed them away as I heard a low, painful moan from the top of the stairs. Her hand slid over my eyes and closed them. Without a word, she jumped to her feet and ran up the stairs.

Somewhere in the distance, voices yelled and a siren grew louder.

Before I slipped away, Angel's voice cried out, "Oh, my God, Bear."

… light.

I understood. It was clear now, painfully clear.

Someone killed me—murdered me in my own home. I shouldn't be, but I was still here among the living but not one of them. There could be only one reason.

Detective, solve thyself.

FOUR

THE GRANDFATHER CLOCK CHIMED four and I was back.

So was Hercule. He grumbled at me from his perch on my recliner in the corner. When I went to him, he churned in the chair. His tail was in overdrive and as he started to get down, he groaned painfully and stopped half in, half out of the chair. There was a swath of torn hair across the top of his head and a bandage adorned parts of his scalp. I bent down and calmed his gyrations long enough to examine him. His hair was ... *singed*?

Someone shot Hercule. The bastard didn't just kill me—he shot my dog.

"Herc, I'm so sorry. You saved Angel. Good boy. It's steak tonight."

Woof. Wag. Double-woof. Hercule was not modest.

I heard the front door open and someone came in. The crime scene boys and everyone from the department were already gone. Were they returning? Hercule barked and his tail returned to happy mode. He meandered around the room, found his favorite hard-rubber ball, and positioned himself at the ready.

Bear walked in.

"Hey, boy, how you feeling? You look okay. You saved the day, Herc. At least part of it."

Hercule moaned and flipped the ball from his mouth, letting it bounce across the floor to Bear's feet. It was good to know the big Lab wasn't going to let my murder spoil his day.

"Later, boy," Bear said. He looked around the den with a long, slow sweep of his eyes.

Then he did a more curious thing than hiding the folder in my bookcase.

Instead of heading for the bookcase liquor stash and a taste of my best Kentucky bourbon—that's what I'd have done—he went out into the hall and climbed the stairs. I followed him to the second floor. There, he began a systematic search of my home, room by room.

"Ah, partner? Didn't you already search the house? The crime boys left."

He started with the spare bedroom at the far end of the hall. I stood in the open doorway and watched him explore every square inch. He went through everything—the dresser, closet, bookshelves, even under and between the mattress and box spring. It took him twenty minutes, and when he was done, he started on the other spare room next door. I knew every move he was making and had done so myself a thousand times at crime scenes. This time, though, this crime scene was mine.

Whatever he was looking for, he was a hound on a hunt—no offense Hercule.

By the time we were done, it was two hours later and he had exhausted two spare bedrooms, our storage room, two bathrooms, and a large walk-in hall closet. When he emerged from the latter, his hands were still empty. The last place he vanished into was our bedroom. This time, he closed our door behind him.

I was locked out. "Dammit, open it."

Nothing.

Thirty minutes later, he emerged, empty-handed. Whatever he was looking for, he had not found it. He went back downstairs to the kitchen.

Hercule and I followed him out the back door that he left ajar. Bear went straight to the garage. There, however, he stopped Hercule and bade him sit and stay in the yard. He entered through the side door, closing it behind him.

"Well, Herc, we're stuck. I wonder what he's looking for. He sure is acting weird. First the file, now this."

Woof.

Bear was taking his time inside the garage so Hercule and I returned to the kitchen. Just inside the door, Hercule froze. He lowered to a spring-loaded crouch—hair up, tail straight, and teeth bared. He inched across the kitchen toward the hallway and stopped. He looked back at me waiting for orders.

"Easy, boy. Easy. It could be neighbors with cookies and meatloaf. Let's go see."

We reached the hallway. Faint footsteps descended the stairs and went into my den. Hercule raised his nose and lowered himself again, taking two slow, deliberate steps—it was not Angel.

There were two low voices in my den. We heard desk drawers open and close, books being pulled off shelves, and my filing cabinet open. Someone, like Bear, was looking for something.

Hercule crept down the hall beside me and we peered into the den. Across the room was a tall, thin African American in a dark suit. He was rooting through files that Bear had packed in boxes and set on the floor. The other man, a short, wiry, white man of about thirty, was rummaging through my desk. This man was going bald, and what blond hair he had was short. His narrow face and dull eyes always made me think of a snake waiting for prey.

I knew them—all too well—and they were both nemeses.

The African American was Calvin Clemens from my detective squad down at the county sheriff's office. He wasn't the brightest bulb in the box, but not a bad guy overall. His Achilles' heel was his partner, Mikey Spence. Spence's mouth and limited common-sense were often at odds. I was professional with both men, but not friends, and we worked together when required. Bear and I always made a point to stay as far from their caseload as possible—crap tends to stick to you even when it's not yours.

Spence and Clemens always seemed to be involved in crap.

I watched Clemens continue his foray into my files. Spence moved to my bookshelf and began pulling books off the shelf and breezing through them. A strange nagging touched me—I felt like I knew what they were looking for. It was there, just out of reach of my thoughts. It nagged at me, but I couldn't get it to focus into a readable script in my head. Confusion, it seems, is a byproduct of death; it was like goo stuck to my shoe. Memories swirled around me and some were taking their time landing. It was starting to piss me off.

I knew what they were looking for—yet I didn't know what it was.

Spence stopped fanning through books and noticed a picture sitting on my bookshelf. It was of Angel and me at her doctoral commencement. She was wearing an alluring knee-length black dress that showed off her legs and other lovely parts.

Truly, though, her mind attracted me. I swear.

"Spence, I may be dead, but that's still my wife." I put my hand on his shoulder and squeezed. "Paws off."

"What?" His eyes peered around and settled on Clemens. "What'd you say?"

"Nothing, why?"

The two exchanged dumb glances. Spence said, "I thought I heard something."

Grrrr—Hercule pounced in and posted in the center of the room. He let out a low growl that sent both men against the wall.

"Easy, boy," Clemens said. "Easy, Hercule. It's your pal, Cal. Calm down."

Hercule was crouched in launch mode and growled again.

"What in the hell are you doing here?" Bear's voice boomed from the doorway. "Crime scene's done."

"Oh, hey Bear," Clemens said. "We thought we'd give it another go. You know, looking for anything missed."

"Bullshit." Bear was edgy. "Crime guys worked this place all night and most of the day."

"Sure, yeah," Spence said, pointing at Hercule. "No offense. How about having him back off? I don't think he remembers me."

"He remembers you." Bear leaned down and patted Hercule. "It's all right, boy. If they act up, I'll shoot them."

Herc walked over to me and lay down. He kept his eyes fixed on Spence.

Clemens asked, "Where's Angel?"

"That's Angela to you. Or better yet, 'Doctor Tucker.'"

"She home?"

Bear ignored him. "What are you looking for?"

"Nothing." Spence patted the air. "Just checking around."

"We're done here. Captain Sutter says so. Angela's over at Professor Stuart's place for the night. You two leave her alone. She needs rest."

"Sure, sure." Clemens went to the file cabinet and shut the open drawer. "How are you doing, Bear? You okay?"

"Cut the crap, Clemens. This is my case."

"It was," Spence said. "The captain pulled you this afternoon. You can't run the case since you were Tuck's partner and Angel's... *friend*."

"What the hell does that mean?"

I knew exactly what that meant. So did Bear.

"Gee, I wonder," Spence said, winking. "You're here, aren't you? Keeping the pretty widow company?"

"You little shit." Bear took a dangerous step toward him. "She's not here. You better watch yourself, Spence."

23

"Yeah, well you better, too." Spence waved the photograph of Angel that he was admiring. "We're on this case, pal. We need to question Angela again. But, sure, we'll wait until tomorrow."

"Angel had nothing to do with this."

"Yeah?" Spence tapped a finger on the photo. "Ninety-five percent of all homicides are committed by the spouse."

I said, "No, you moron, that's not right."

Bear rolled his eyes.

"Ah, Mikey," Clemens said, "you sure of that?"

Bear grabbed the photo from Spence. "You two hit the road. I'll straighten this out with the captain."

"You do that, Bear. Cal and I are through—for now. I can't wait to chat it up with Angela. Funny, you don't look all that upset, Bear. If my partner here was killed, I'd ..."

Detective Mike Spence may have been a little dense sometimes, but he didn't lack survival instincts. Before Bear could reach him, he and Clemens made a tactical withdrawal through the front door and down the walk. From the safety of the outer gate, Spence turned and threw a wave back to Bear, now standing on the front porch.

"Hey, Bear, we gotta take care of Tuck's case. We'll let you get back to taking care of his missus."

FIVE

WHILE BEAR WASHED DOWN his bad attitude with my fifty-year-old Kentucky bourbon, I went wandering around the house. He'd left the doors open and I moved from room to room uninhibited. This was handy since my current state of existence seemed to limit my physical abilities like opening doors.

Hercule strolled with me. He dropped his ball on the hardwood floor and watched it bounce here and there whenever I stopped to reflect on some photograph or knickknack. We were on the second floor balcony overlooking the foyer when Hercule got bored and headed down the stairs. He stopped three stairs down, withdrew two. He let out a low, mournful growl that was half warning, half fear.

He had good reason.

Below us, the foyer had disappeared. In its place was a murky darkness that congealed as we watched. A strange breeze rustled through autumn trees. The scent of musty, freshly turned dirt grew heavy as shovels sliced into the earth. Then I heard the rumble of two men's voices, but could not understand them.

"Holy crap, Herc. Stay here. I gotta see what this is all about."

Hercule liked my plan.

I crept down the stairs but did not land on oak hardwood. Instead, I was standing in tall field grass above an earthen pit surrounded by crumbled stones and mounds of freshly piled dirt. The breeze brought a crisp taste to the air that reminded me of autumn's changing leaves.

The two men dug in weary, slow-motion effort. A lantern that sat on the side of the pit above their heads cast a dim light that battled with their shadows. I couldn't make out their faces, but their features were dark and hard, and their work clothes grubby and sweaty. The mound of earth told me they had been working for a long time. Grumbles said they were unhappy with the labor.

One of them threw himself against the edge of the pit and dropped his shovel. "¿Qué? Madre de Dios, mira."

The other man looked on but didn't move nor speak.

The first lowered his head and ran a solemn finger from forehead to chest and shoulder to shoulder, muttering a prayer that I didn't need translated. Then he bent down and retrieved something from the dirt, holding it in the light for inspection. When the light touched his left arm, something just below his rolled sleeves caught my attention. It was a dark tattoo in the shape of a cross with a halo atop it.

"¡El hombre será feliz. Apúrate!" The tattooed man whispered. "Date prisa. Cavar más rápido."

With a fever, the two attacked the pit again. After several moments, the tattooed man used the lantern to survey their work.

"¿*Qué?*"

The other man bent down and retrieved a fistful of earth. He cleaned something in his fingertips and held it to the light. A round piece of metal, perhaps a coin, caught the light, and both men smiled. The find renewed their enthusiasm.

The tattooed one said, "Dig. Dig. *Hay más.*"

I found my footing in the loose dirt and stone and moved closer to the pit. "What do you have? Who are you?"

The tattooed man jolted upright and spun around, holding the lantern in front of him shining it toward the top of the pit.

When the light touched me, it snapped dark and Hercule barked behind me. I turned to find him creeping down the stairs. When I looked back at the pit, it was gone. My front door was in its rightful place. The oak landing was beneath my feet. There was no pit—no men digging in the night. Their discovery was gone, too.

Perhaps my sanity followed it.

Hercule stood halfway down the stairs, uneasy and unsteady. He looked around and raised his nose to smell the air. He moaned in a low, worrisome tone and looked up at me.

"Hell no, boy—no clue."

SIX

BACK IN MY DEN, the images confused me, and yet I was not afraid or unnerved. Had my home turned into a nighttime treasure hunt when I was among the living, I would have checked into a hospital or a nearby bar. Now, however, the vignette was no stranger to me than having no reflection in the hall mirror. Dying was far more complicated than I imagined.

Angel was one of the many complications. She was at the top of my list. I had to find her. I had to know she was all right. My eyes fell back onto her garter belt and an empty feeling of remorse consumed me. The ache built and her memory drove nails into my heart. In a slow, churning boil, desperate feelings rose inside. I had to find her. I had to go to her.

But where?

Ernie Stuart, of course—Bear said as much. Ernie was her university superior, her dearest friend, and lifelong mentor—a role he'd assumed when she was still a child. He was never far away. He'd be close now.

The garter belt had triggered a cascade of emotions. Perhaps it would again. I touched it again, closing my eyes, trying to find her—to see her, reach her, touch her. I felt dizzy like a child twirling with outstretched arms, spinning in a playground game. I twirled, too, until the smoky scent of a fire reached me. I opened my eyes and let the lightheadedness subside. Familiar surroundings greeted me. I was standing in a large room with a grand fireplace and high crown-molding ceilings. An expensive Persian rug covered part of the hardwood floors. Shelves of books lined the room, and Civil War antiques were displayed everywhere.

Professor Ernie Stuart's living room.

Ernie lived on a twenty-acre, nineteenth-century farm on the northwest corner of the county. His farmhouse was miles from the nearest neighbor and he preferred it that way. He was reclusive and always had been. Acres of rolling fields shielded him from whatever he loathed—and his demeanor suggested that was most things. Angel was not among them.

She was curled up on the couch. An empty brandy snifter rested on a nearby end table as she dozed on a billowy pillow. Her face was a mixture of anguish and alcohol. There was a large, purring gray tomcat on her lap and her hand rested on his back, unconsciously petting.

Boy, Hercule wasn't going to like that. He hated cats, Ernie's the most. Truth be told, Hercule hated Ernie more, but the cat suffered his wrath.

"Dear? Angela?" Ernie was standing near the fireplace sipping a drink. He was a distinguished, striking man in his sixties—tall and strong. He had wide shoulders and an athletic build. His face sported a "professor's goatee" and immaculate silver hair. He presented a thoughtful, analytical demeanor born from two doctorates and a university professorship.

"Huh?" Angel stirred and sat upright, rubbed her eyes, and turned her attention to the tomcat. "I'm sorry, Ernie. I dozed off. What were you saying?"

"I was saying that you must get some rest. It's been a long and trying day."

"Yes, yes. You're right. But I have so much to contend with. First…"

"No first." Ernie set his drink on the mantel and folded his arms like a parent about to discipline. "You get rest. Everything else will wait until tomorrow. I'll take care of everything—well, André and I, of course."

"Thank you, Ernie. I don't know what I'd do without you two."

Ernie was always near in difficult times. During her childhood, he was a close family friend. When tragedy took her parents, he assumed the role of uncle and never ventured far. He helped mentor her through her doctorate and secured her professorship at the university. Since then, he's been a fixture in our home for holidays and summer barbecues. Her choice, not mine. But, since she made three times my cop salary, Old Ernie could hang around whenever he wanted. Ernie was a mixture of doting uncle, persnickety mentor, and pain-in-the-ass houseguest.

Thankfully, he was nearby now.

"Angel," I said. "Are you all right?" I slid onto the couch beside her and sent the tomcat bristling from the room with hisses and growls.

Did I do that? "Angel, it's me. Can you hear me? I'm all right—I'm okay."

She looked after the cat before turning toward me. I thought she was going to reach out and touch my face, but she dropped her chin and cried instead.

"Angel, I'm okay."

"I hope so," she said, and the words startled both of us. "Tuck?"

"No, Angela." Ernie crossed the room and sat down between us. "No, dear. He's gone—I'm so sorry."

Angel blinked, rubbed her eyes, and scanned the room. Her face paled and she leaned back onto the pillow. "No—yes, of course. But for a moment, I swear I heard him."

"No, I'm here." I slid off the couch and stood, looking down at her. "Listen for me."

She looked at Ernie and smiled a faint, embarrassed smile. "You're right. He's gone."

"No, Angel. Focus on my voice. Listen for me. I had a dream ... a vision."

She cocked her head and closed her eyes. Her eyebrows rose and she bit her lower lip as she did when concentrating.

Was it working?

"Angel, listen. There were two men digging in our house—but it wasn't our house. They found something important. One of them had a cross tattoo. It must have something to do with my murder ... that's why I saw it ..." Even dead, I tended to ramble.

"Tattoo?" She sat upright. "A tattooed man? Digging?"

Ernie suddenly stood and returned to the mantel, draining his drink. He stole a glance at her and retrieved the crystal decanter, pouring a healthy refill.

"Angela, you're dreaming—confused—grieving."

"What tattooed man?" A voice said from the doorway. André Cartier—officially, Uncle André Cartier—walked into the living room with a tray of sandwiches. "Someone was digging? Where and for what?"

"She has to get to bed, André. Leave the dream alone."

"Dreams are funny things—manifestations of our subconscious. Especially at a time like this." Dr. André Cartier was a professor of history and anthropology and a senior director at the Smithsonian Institute in Washington D.C. His accolades were long, but he coveted no greater role than as the former guardian of his sister's only child. "Besides, she has to eat first. We all do."

Ernie lifted his glass. "I'll drink, thank you."

André and Ernie could easily be brothers. André had distinguished gray temples and a presence of confidence and intellect. He shared Ernie's athletic build and ageless appearance. André, however, wore round, wire-rimmed eyeglasses perched on his nose, preferred to be clean-shaven, and had ten or fifteen pounds on Ernie.

Ernie was an uncle by choice, André by birthright. Both shared Angel's devotion.

"I didn't dream, André." Angel stood and folded her arms as though unsure of what to do next. "I heard Tuck. He was talking to me. He saw a tattooed man digging. It had to be a dream. Right?"

"See, André, a digging tattooed man. This is nonsense …"

"Nonsense?" André threw Angel a wink that drew a smile. "How would you know about digging, Ernie? In all these years, I've never seen your hands dirty."

"I'm a history professor, not a laborer."

"And a snob." André let a thin smile dull the jab.

"And you? You are a typical Washington bureaucrat."

"Perhaps." André laughed. "But I've done more historical excavations this year than you have in your life."

"Oh, you have?"

André threw his chin. "With more hours in the field than you have in the classroom."

Did I mention they were competitive?

Ernie dismissed him with a huff and returned to his brandy. The glass stopped halfway to his lips when André spoke again.

"You don't suppose this tattooed man has anything to do with Kelly's Dig?"

Angel sat upright. "Kelly's Dig? Why would that involve Tuck?"

"Oh come now," Ernie said, snorting. "I don't see a connection. After all, it's just a dream."

André said, "Dreams are funny things—but yes, enough said."

Ernie agreed with a nod and took a long pull on his brandy.

"Kelly's Dig," Angel mused, curling her legs beneath her. "I want to get working there immediately. It'll be good for me."

"Now, Angela," Ernie said. "I think work should wait a few weeks. I've arranged …"

"No. I need to work. It'll keep my mind off … Tuck. Kelly's Dig is not the day to day at the university. That'll help."

André caught Ernie's eye and nodded. "I agree with Ernie. The university has already given you ample bereavement time. I can handle the dig. You don't need distractions. You need to grieve."

"Distractions?" Ernie sprang to the middle of the living room and thrust an angry finger into André's chest. "Distractions? Kelly's Dig is the key to the county's historical future."

"Please, Ernie," Andre whispered. "Not now. Think of Angel."

"If Tyler Byrd gets his way, he'll pave over our entire legacy. You Washington bureaucrats only understand money."

"Now hold on." André met him nose to nose. "I work for the court, too, Ernie. And my Washington credentials are why."

"Ernie," Angel said, "you know very well he's the expert we need. Shame on you."

"Yes, yes, I'm sorry." Ernie patted the air in surrender. "Of course it's your Smithsonian credentials. Kelly's Dig frustrates me. I'm sorry."

"I'm sure it does," André said. "I'm not saying you're wrong. It's just not the time to be discussing Civil War cemeteries and nineteenth-century skeletons."

"Oh, dear." Ernie looked at Angel and his eyes softened. "No, of course not. Forgive me."

"It's all right." Angel forced a smile. "But, Ernie, the time off from the university will be good for me to work on Kelly's Dig. You understand—a new project and all. I'm not ready to face all the faculty and students yet."

André said, "We can talk about this in the morning—all of us. Why don't you run up to bed, Angela?"

"Yes, all right."

"Do you need anything?" Ernie asked.

Angel tried to smile but failed miserably. "Bear is taking care of Hercule. He said they're done with the house—the crime scene people I mean."

"Shall I bring Hercule here?" Ernie asked. "Would you feel better?"

"No, he's fine—recuperating. Bear's looking after the house."

"All right, dear." Ernie hesitated before holding up his hand. "There is one small thing."

"What is it?"

"About Kelly's Dig." Ernie moved close and placed a gentle hand on her shoulder. "I called the local medical examiner's office about their final report on the skeletal remains. They sent it and some artifacts they unearthed to you. I was unaware that the artifacts existed. I'd like to see them."

"No, I don't have anything," Angel said. "Where did the M.E. send it?"

"Where?"

"To my home or office?"

He shrugged. "I assumed your home. We agreed you wouldn't involve the university."

"Well, yes we did. But the court sends papers to me there."

"I see." Ernie nodded. "You think it's at the university then?"

"I don't know."

André said, "I'll get it for you, Angela. I can swing by your office tomorrow. I'll have Carmen find it."

"That won't be necessary." Ernie waved his hand and gave Angel a squeeze. "I'm in the same building. I'll speak with Carmen in the morning. She'll be calling about you anyway."

André shrugged. "Fine, I'll be at Kelly's Dig then. I'd like a copy as well, Ernie."

"Certainly."

André stepped between them and gave her a long, comforting embrace. Ernie huffed and retreated to the mantel again. André said, "Now, get some sleep. No more skeletons, Kelly's Dig, or tattooed men."

"Good night to both of you."

"Dear," Ernie said in a soft voice. "I hope you know that I was very fond of Oliver."

I hated that name. It reminded me of that sniveling little vagabond from Oliver Twist. I am more a Raymond Chandler or Mickey Spillane kind of guy. I lost the name "Oliver" in the first grade after my third playground fistfight.

"Tuck," Angel said. "He hated being called Oliver."

Ernie grinned. "I know."

SEVEN

I SAT ALL NIGHT with Angel trying to talk to her, to reach her, anything. Sometime after three in the morning, her tears succumbed to exhaustion and she fell asleep. I don't know if I'd reached her, but I wouldn't stop trying until I did.

The next morning, I left her sleeping and went for a walk.

Strolling down Ernie's half-mile gravel road, I stepped through the looking glass back into my den. Hercule was nowhere around so I assumed he was up on our bed basking on my pillow. That was his preferred place whenever I worked late at night.

A disheveled blanket and pillow lay on the couch and I found Bear sipping coffee in the kitchen. He checked his voicemail and the sheriff's dispatch, then he poured more coffee. He penned out a note to Angel telling her Hercule was okay and that Captain Sutter had released the house back to her. She could come home. Crime scenes take time, but when a cop is killed, things move faster. It also helps to have ten extra cops working the scene and being a priority at the crime lab.

For the third time in two days, Bear startled me.

On my front porch, he reached into his pocket and withdrew his key ring. With a key I never knew existed, he locked my front door. Then he walked to his cruiser outside the front gate and drove away.

When did Bear Braddock get my front door key?

I felt the dizziness churn in my head again. Before I realized it, I was sucked from the house onto the spook-express. I'm not sure what happens when I'm pulled from here and sent to there—wherever "there" ends up being. I seemed to go into time-out. Sort of like when kids are bad. It was "time-out" and off to their rooms. For me, it was an empty, dark place where I was very, very alone. This time, however, it was momentary, and when the light surrounded me again, I was standing next to Bear's cruiser.

He was nowhere around.

I recognized the parking lot of the Shenandoah View Fairways golf club. It was ten in the morning and a chilly fall day. There were about five cars in the lot. Since Bear didn't play golf, he was up to something.

What?

I found him standing beneath a rain shelter along some trees three fairways away. He was arguing with a large man beside him. The man seemed familiar but I couldn't place him. His face was round and puffy and he was built more for sumo wrestling than golf. He had powerful, burly arms, and his bulky body was stuffed into golf slacks and a sweater—his girth exceeding his belt in the front. His features were tinted with a dark, Mediterranean complexion. His hair was black and his eyes shadowed by a thick, perpetual eyebrow. He reminded me of an old movie thug collecting overdue debts. Mr. Sumo—for lack of a better name—was part wrestler, part bagman.

Bear jabbed a finger at Mr. Sumo. "I told you to drop that. I don't want to hear that shit again."

"Sure, sure, Bear," Mr. Sumo said. "Whatever you say. But, listen, I'm just saying what's on the street."

"Forget rumors. I want your boss. I want him now."

Mr. Sumo threw up his hands. "Fagget it. You know the rules. I don't give him up like that."

"I want him. I need something to take the edge off. Funerals make me grouchy and I got a big one coming."

"He's clean on that. I swear."

"I don't give a shit."

"No, listen. The Man ain't gonna whack no cop. Especially one snoopin' around him already. You nuts?"

"Did I mention Tuck? I'm talking about the other one."

"Him? No way, man." Mr. Sumo looked around the fairway. "The Man's worried you cops are thinkin' that. He's clean. Clean on both. He's retired, for Christ's sake."

Bear laughed. "Bullshit. Guys like him never retire."

"Listen, please." Mr. Sumo pointed a finger at him and squinted. "You gotta be careful. The Man ain't playin' around, Bear. He's retired, but he ain't dead."

"Meaning?"

I stood there, listening and watching. Frustration set in—who was this guy? His face was a nagging, deliberate memory trying to form in my head. It was there just out of reach. The conversation wasn't helping either. Faces and questions with no names. Another murder—the other murder? Damn, damn, damn.

"Look, Bear, I got somethin' else."

"What?"

"The Man says someone is runnin' stuff around here without his blessin'. He's pissed. I heard him talkin' to New York. A heavy's in town and the Man don't like it. He told them this town is off-limits. Ya know, he gotta live here."

"Who's the heavy? What's he here for?"

"Dunno. Could be about Tuck." Mr. Sumo leaned closer to Bear and poked the air. "Like I told you, Bear, street sees things different. You know, like maybe you and the lady professor did him—or got someone to do it for her. Maybe the heavy."

Bear knocked away the man's finger, grabbed his shirt, and slammed him back against the rain shelter wall. "You bastard. I told you to drop that. Who's talking that shit?"

"People, just people. Don't go bitin' the hand that feeds you. I never said it—but it's out there. Somebody's diggin' around on that, too. Somebody wants your ass, *paesano*."

"Digging around?"

"Yeah, digging around on the lady professor and you, Bear. Now settle down. I'm tellin' you this for your own good. Somebody's askin' questions and making it sound like you and the wife, you know, gotta thing."

"Who's spreading that?"

40

Mr. Sumo shrugged.

"Find out." Bear tapped his watch. "Time's ticking. Get me the name or I come for your boss. *Capisce?*"

"Sure, sure. But I'm tellin' ya, he's not playin' in this one. Back off."

Bear reached into his pocket and pulled out a wad of bills. He tossed several at Mr. Sumo. "You find out who's talking about Angela and me, Tommy. Find out fast. And you better start proving your boss is clean, too, or he's going down. The easy way or the hard way."

So, Mr. Sumo's real name was Tommy. Tommy was now more familiar but not quite a recollection yet. Bear turned and headed for his golf cart.

"Yeah, yeah. And hey…"

Bear stopped and turned around.

"Watch your ass, Bear. If you get it next, who's gonna keep my parole clean?"

EIGHT

When Bear left Tommy on the fairway, he seemed angry and frustrated. He mumbled he was late for a "thing," abandoned his golf cart in the parking lot, and drove off. He took his frustration out on the gravel driveway.

Whatever his "thing" was, I didn't want to be part of it.

I decided to let him cool down and headed for home on foot. I strolled along trying to conjure up the magic words to launch me onto the spook-highway and materialize in my den, but nothing was working. Unable to find the formula, I settled on a five-mile fall hike to contemplate what my life—or lack of it—would now be.

I never made it a mile.

"*Oliver—go to Angel. Go now.*"

Oliver? Who said that?

Fear gripped me. It squeezed my thoughts in a fist and twisted. It was confusing, disorienting—I wasn't afraid ... Angel was. She appeared in front of me as her terror reached out and seized me. She was bracing herself against an unseen attack. Her thoughts were flustered and whirled in circles searching for protection, somewhere to hide and find safety. Her voice echoed in my head, calling me, begging me to help her.

"*Dammit, Oliver, go to her. Follow her.*"

The voice burned into my head. It was loud and commanding but it wasn't from anyone near. It came from inside. Then I heard Angel again, begging me to reach her. *Follow her* ... Yes. Like a distant light in the darkness, I followed her voice and it led me to her.

She was pressed against a highboy dresser, fighting to slide it across the floor against the bedroom door. She was crying, but her teeth were clinched in determination. Something was terrifying her and she was barricading herself in.

"Angel, what is it? What's happening?"

I recognized the room from the photographs on the wall. They were all Civil War monuments from throughout Virginia. This was one of Ernie Stuart's guest rooms. The Monument Room, as Angel called it, where she slept last night.

"Angel, I'm here. What's wrong?"

For a second, she stopped and looked around as though searching for my voice. Then she attacked the dresser again. The highboy stuck on the heavy corded rug. She grunted, tried to lift it free, but failed. She ran to the window and looked out. Whatever she saw—or didn't see—calmed her, and she went to the door and pressed herself against it to listen.

"Angel?"

Her face paled and she returned to the highboy. This time, she succeeded in inching the dresser across the rug and against the bedroom door. For a second, she leaned against the wall, head cocked, straining to hear what I was sure she would not.

I was wrong.

Footsteps in the downstairs hall tromped to the foot of the stairs and stopped. Then they moved away, lighter this time. Seconds later, something crashed and rolled across the floorboards. Then one glass—then two—shattered on the floor. The footsteps retreated farther and went silent.

"No, no, no." Angel's eyes flooded and she pressed all her weight against the highboy, leveraging it tighter against the door. "Please, go away, please."

I tried to slip into the hallway to see who was in the house. With the door shut, I was as much a prisoner as she. Twice, I tried to will myself from the room, but each time, Angel's terror chained me to her. I couldn't feel anything, sense anything, except her pounding heart and her grip on me, holding me fast, keeping me near.

Whoever was downstairs, I was helpless to seek them out.

The footsteps began again. This time, they grew louder in the downstairs hall and climbed the wooden stairs, clacking up the hardwood to the upstairs landing. A door down the hall from us opened and closed. Then another.

Angel stiffened. She tried to muffle in a gasp but failed when the footsteps stopped outside her door.

"Go away. Leave me alone, please."

"Dear?" The voice boomed outside the door, and for an instant, it startled both of us. "Angela? What's wrong, dear?"

Ernie.

"Ernie? Oh, God, it's you."

It took all her might and Ernie's shoulder to force open the door and push the highboy clear enough for Angel to slip out. When she did, she crashed into his arms.

"Angela?" He looked around her and through the half-open door. "What on earth are you doing?"

"I was so scared."

"Dear? Scared?" He relaxed his embrace. "What's all this?"

"Someone is in the house."

Ernie turned and looked down the stairwell, then back to her. He shook his head but stopped when she began to cry. "Angela, it was me. I was cleaning up and dropped the tray of dishes and wineglasses from last night."

"No, before. I saw someone."

Ernie held her at arm's length and tried to calm her with his best Uncle Ernie smile. "No one is down there. No one passed me on the main road or my private road. The front door was locked. There's no one here."

"Yes. I heard someone. I saw a man."

"Angela. You've been through a lot. Maybe…"

"No. I know what I saw."

He watched her, silent.

I stood beside Ernie. "Hey, go take a look around, Ernie. She's scared—terrified. Just look around."

"Ernie, I …" Her hands flashed up and wiped away the fear and confusion raining down her cheeks. "I know I saw someone."

He eased her hands from her face and held them. "All right, dear. I'll look around."

"Hurry, and be careful."

She followed him through the house, room by room. With each door he opened, she withdrew and her body tensed with anticipation. Nothing but dusty bedspreads and a sink of breakfast dishes waited. One of Ernie's cats lay sleeping in the living room atop the couch, unthreatened by any intruder or their search. A dustpan of broken glass and china waited on the coffee table. At the front door, Ernie bade her lock it behind him and went outside.

"I'll go with him," I whispered. "It's safe, Angel. Everything is all right."

She never even flinched.

Outside, I followed Ernie around the house in a haphazard inspection of windows, doors, and gardens. Angel shadowed us from inside, peeking out each window, racing to the next room until we navigated the house and returned to the front door. We found nothing. No scratched door latches. No jimmied window latches. No footprints or scuffmarks in the gardens. There were no signs of forced entry. Nothing. If there had been an intruder, he was more ghostly than I was.

When Angel opened the front door, she was trembling.

"Nothing." Ernie slipped his arm around her. "No one, my dear. All is as it should be."

"Are you sure?"

"Yes, very. Nothing has been disturbed. As I've said, the door was locked when I returned—I forgot some meeting notes and came back. There were no other cars on the county road for miles. No signs of anyone on my driveway."

Angel's tone was shallow and uncertain. "Maybe they came through the woods. Maybe from another road."

"No, dear."

"Maybe …"

"No, Angela. No." Ernie guided her to the kitchen and into a high-back kitchen chair. "No one was here. You've had a very tough couple of days."

"No."

Ernie sighed and went about making tea. I sat at his kitchen table beside Angel. She gazed vacantly out the breakfast nook windows, shaking her head in slow, almost imperceptible movements. She was pale and her eyes dull with the battle between self-doubt and disbelief. When Ernie placed the steaming cup in front of her, she took it and sipped it.

"I know what I saw and heard, Ernie. A man—a tall man—was trying to get into the house. I heard someone moving around outside, rattling the windows. I thought it was you or André. When I looked out, I saw a tall man."

"Can you describe him more?"

She shook her head. "No, I just saw him walk around the corner of the house. I couldn't see much from the window."

"Well, I suppose it could have been André. I left earlier this morning and he was still here. His car is gone now. I can find out when he left if you like."

"It wasn't André." She peered into her cup and the memory seemed to scare her again. "When … when I went to the top of the stairs, I heard someone in the living room. I called out but no one answered. I got frightened. When I turned to go to my room, I caught sight of someone passing through the foyer."

I leaned in close to her. "It's okay, Angel. There's no one here."

Angel turned and looked right at me as though she could see me. The thinnest of smiles edged the corners of her mouth. She glanced down; perhaps embarrassed at any whimsical notion I was close.

"I saw him twice. I'd swear …"

"Did you phone the police? Bear?"

She shook her head. "No, my phone is in my purse in the living room. There's no phone in the guest room."

"Yes, yes, of course." He sipped his tea, reaching out and taking her hand. "Angela, perhaps—just perhaps—it was a bad dream. Perhaps you were thinking of the other night. You said a man was in the foyer. Just like when Tuck …"

"No. Call Bear. Please. First Tuck … now someone was here. Maybe …"

Ernie shook his head but didn't respond.

"Listen, Ernie," I said. "Call him. It'll make her feel better."

Angel's eyes glistened. "Please."

He relented. A few moments later, he was repeating the story for the second time. When he quieted to listen to Bear, he went into the living room to finish the call in private. Five minutes later, he returned to the kitchen. He poured himself more tea and sat down beside her.

"There. We had a good chat. He'll come over, but he felt there was no rush. He believes it's stress."

"No rush?" Angel frowned and went to the sink with her tea mug. She was biting her lip and swirling the remnants of tea in her mug—a sign she was confused and questioning herself. The fear was passing and anger was filling the void.

I didn't see any intruder or feel any danger when I'd found Angel. It was her fear—her terror—that summoned me. Perhaps her hold on me blocked any other sense or sight I might have had. Her fear was real enough to her—real enough to reach from her world to mine and pull me to her.

The reality of fear is that it need not be justified. Fear is fear. If a tall man was in Ernie's house—for whatever reason—he terrified Angel. If no man rounded the corner of the house outside, if none passed through the foyer, if it were all a manifestation of shock and trauma, Angel was just as terrified.

At that moment, I doubted any of us knew the truth.

NINE

"I've got deputies checking the neighbors," Bear told Angel, pulling into our driveway. "There's not a house within a mile. We'll be lucky if anyone saw anything."

"Do you believe me, Bear?" Angel didn't look at him. "Ernie doesn't."

"It's not that. He thinks you had a bad dream. We both think it's stress. I can relate to that."

Angel opened her door and stepped out, glaring at Bear over the hood of his cruiser. "So you think it's all in my head."

From the backseat, I said, "I don't." Neither cared.

"Honey, listen. There's no trace of anyone getting into the house. Nothing. If my deputies find someone, I'll let you know right away."

"Forget it," she snapped, and ran into the house.

We both watched her go. I said, "Can't say I blame her. Something scared her. Dream or not. Something scared the hell out of her."

He peered over his shoulder as he climbed out of the cruiser and walked to the house. "Shit—right, it's just stress."

Angel's cry reached us as Bear shut the front door. He looked up to the second floor landing just as she slammed a closet door in our bedroom. "Damn. Damn them."

"Bear, hurry," I yelled.

He took the stairs three at a time. On the second bound, he tugged his handgun free. At the top of the landing, he pivoted, scanned the hall, and ran to the bedroom door and hesitated.

Hercule was standing beside the door, wagging but refusing to enter. He'd been around Angel before when she was mad. He took a defensive position, just watching.

She was standing in front of her dressing table. Her hands were folded across her chest. "Someone's been in here."

Bear looked around. "What's wrong?"

"Someone's been through my room." She waved her hands in a flutter. "All my drawers have been rifled. Even my closet and clothes drawers. Someone's dug through everything."

"You sure?" Bear said. "It looks all right to me."

"I just know." She gestured to her notebook computer on her dressing table. "That was in my briefcase. It wasn't strapped in and it was replaced upside down. I never leave it that way. Someone was snooping in my computer."

Bear holstered his handgun. "Maybe you left it that way in a hurry. Things have been crazy."

"No, and stop telling me that. Someone's been through everything since I left yesterday."

I watched Bear snoop around the room. He checked the closet, nightstand, and pulled one or two of her dresser drawers open. "Crime scene boys might have . . ."

"No. I straightened this room up before I left. They were done in here."

Now, why wasn't he coming clean? As he disappeared into the walk-in closet for a second time, Bear-The-Detective didn't seem like Bear-My-Partner and best friend. We never kept secrets from each other. At least I didn't think so. Now, he was playing his cards very close. Just today, I learned he had my house key, and Tommy, a snitch I never knew. And earlier, he'd searched this house top to bottom. That was apparently a secret, too.

Were there others?

"What's on your computer?" he asked. "Anything, you know, that shouldn't be?"

I hoped he was referring to porn, evidence she was a serial killer, or perhaps the missing Watergate tapes. Deep down, I knew he wasn't.

"No, of course not." Angel went to her dresser and checked each drawer, opening them and examining the contents. She did the same with both our nightstands. "Someone's been rooting through these, Bear. I'm sure of it. Everything's moved."

"Crime lab."

"I told you, they were done up here." Angel's face paled. "Or maybe not."

"Don't worry, Angela. I'll take care of it. I promise."

I went to him. "What's going on, pal? Tell her you searched the house. Tell her about Spence and Clemens, too."

He didn't. "What's on your computer, Angela?"

"Nothing. Just office work, emails, and some household bills. I do bills online. Tuck couldn't figure any of that out, so I do it."

"Yes, I could. I chose not to." Even dead, Angel was needling me about the bills. "I'm a cop, not a computer geek."

"Are you sure?" It was not a question. "Nothing on there that might get their little brains churning in the wrong direction? You know what I mean?"

She nodded. "Of course I understand."

Understand what?

Whatever their little secret was, I wasn't in on it.

Bear slid an arm around her shoulders. "Don't worry, I'll take it up with the captain."

"Am I a suspect?" Tears filled her eyes. "Am I?"

"You have to understand. A spouse is always on the suspect list—always." Bear kissed her cheek. "Forget it for now. You've had a rough morning. You okay?"

She nodded. "You do believe me about Ernie's house, don't you? I mean, I'm not imagining things."

"What matters is that you believe it."

"And what about this? Do you know who went through my things—my computer?"

He shrugged. "Let it go, Angela. It's all part of the investigation."

"That's not an answer."

No, it wasn't. And when Bear shrugged and headed for the stairs, it was all she was going to get.

The question was "why?"

TEN

AFTER BEAR LEFT FOR the office, Angel began straightening the house. She cleaned fingerprint powder from the stair railings and doorways, bits of tape from the floor, and other crime scene remnants littered everywhere. Captain Sutter's team tried to straighten things up, unlike most crime scenes, but Angel knew every out-of-place nuance of the house.

She went into my den, stood in the middle of the floor, and closed her eyes. I thought she was going to cry again, but instead, she inhaled long and deep. She did that several times, then turned around the room in a slow-motion pirouette.

I stood beside her, watching a smile emerge in the corners of her mouth.

"Angel?"

"Oh, Tuck," she said, dropping into my leather recliner beside Hercule. "I cannot believe this had to happen."

Hercule groaned his disapproval and sank onto the floor.

"I can still smell you, Tuck. You're here."

She was talking to me, but the question was, did she know I was listening?

"Yeah, babe. I'm right here. Close your eyes. Listen for me. I'm right here."

She did but her patience didn't last. "No, dammit. You weren't supposed to die." She stood and headed for the door.

"No. Angel, wait." Frantic, I tried to find a lure. "Wait."

Hercule did. He jumped up on the recliner and barked, standing like Rin Tin Tin and commanding her attention. He barked again and Angel turned around.

"What, boy? Do you smell him, too?"

Woof. Wag. Woof. Hercule looked right at me standing in front of the bookshelves and moaned. He barked again and glanced back and forth between Angel and me. He moaned that low, grumbling moan that meant he was frustrated with our failure to understand. He saw me. He knew I was right there. He didn't understand why she didn't, too.

She looked at him. "Herc?"

"Angel, listen to me…" Wait, I had it. "Look in the books; behind the leather law books."

Herc barked at me again. Angel took a step toward the bookshelf, hesitated, and looked at Hercule. "What is it boy?"

Hercule pointed his nose at me and moaned.

"Angel, behind the books. Bear hid a file. Get it for me. Please."

Woof. Groan. Wag.

"Herc?" Then Angel startled me—perhaps both of us. She came to the bookshelf beside me and ran her fingers across my collection

55

of mysteries and old collectables, then reached out and touched one of the leather law journals. Her eyes welled up as she slid one of them forward, taking it from the shelf and fanned it in a slow, deliberate motion.

"I gave these to you years ago, Tuck. Did you ever read them?"

Did she know I was right here, within arm's reach? Did she know I was listening? No, she didn't.

She sighed and started to slide the book back into its place. She stopped and reached behind it, withdrawing the thick manila file Bear hid there. "What's this, Herc?"

Holy Agatha Christie.

"Bear put it there. He hid it before the crime scene guys got in here. Technically, that's obstructing justice, but I won't tell if you won't."

She went to my desk and fanned the file. Pages fell out onto the desktop. When she looked down at them, she cried, "Oh, Tuck," and burst into tears. She ran from the room and a second later our bedroom door slammed.

Hercule leapt from the chair and jogged after her. At the door, he turned and barked at me. He wanted me to follow.

I looked after them but the scattered pages on my desk called me like whiskey to a drunkard. I was torn. The file pulled at me but when I looked down at the collage of pages, all I could see was Angel lying on her bed, sobbing and shaking. No, the file would have to wait.

At our bedroom door, I could hear her anguish inside. When I tried to go in, I couldn't. Doors were starting to irritate me. I could poof around golf courses and spirit from here to there, but one closed bedroom door and I was powerless.

Hercule stood beside me. He sat wagging his tail and shifting his eyes side to side. He stuck his big black nose against the door as if to say, "Go in dummy, she needs us."

"I know, Hercule. I know."

Inside, Angel was gushing with pain. I needed to hold her and stop her sorrow. If I could let her know that I was all right, that I was close. Just a few seconds of comfort. I ached to reach her—ached to make it stop for her—ached to touch her. There had to be a way...*please.*

I focused my every thought on turning the knob, moving it, grasping it. Nothing. Then I concentrated on moving through the door. Nothing. I tried again. Again. Again.

Nothing. Not even a creak from the stubborn latch.

Closing my eyes, I could see her curled up on the bed with tears streaming down her face. Please...please...something...Why was I here? Why was I held back from wherever? The only reason had to be Angel. *Just let me inside, please.*

Warmth.

A shiver of warm, rising emotion trickled in and began to fill me. The silky heat rippled inside as my thoughts exploded rhythmically like tiny lightning bolts one after the other. The hall light dimmed and for an instant, everything around me vanished—or perhaps I did—and darkness enveloped me. A strange, soothing tingle enveloped me, drawing me in.

Angel, I'm trying. Reach for me, babe, reach.

The journey lasted an eyeblink.

I was beside Angel, standing next to the bed where she lay.

"Angel, I'm here." I reached down and touched her hand. Her skin's softness and her scent flooded me with memories. I could feel her as though life was still between us. I dropped onto the bed beside her and fought back my own tears. My finger closed around hers.

Shazzam.

An emotional tsunami swept over me, through me ... into me. My fingers quivered and my face felt like July sunburn. My body shimmered with sorrow and pain—Angel's pain. I felt her loss—my loss—and began drawing it, commanding it to leave her and fill me instead. Waves of grief washed through me and for an instant consumed me. Tears flowed from me and my body weakened from despair. I was in a whirling, dizzying swell of misery that weakened my knees and scattered my resolve. The emptiness swallowed me and I was helpless to defend myself.

Then something new rose. The waves of grief receded and my longing ebbed from me into her. Something extraordinary drew us together and melded our emotions, one by one. The cold void of pain simmered into a brew of memories and love.

Angel sat up on the bed and looked around the room, settling her gaze on the bed where I sat. For an instant, she reached out and touched the comforter beside me but shook her head and withdrew. She stood up, walked to the bedroom door, and let Hercule in. He bounded past her and to the bed, standing in front of me and barking. He turned to her, barking again.

He knew. He wanted her to know, too.

"No, Herc," she said. "It's just me."

Woof. He stood in front of me and lifted his paw to shake. The gesture made Angel gasp and choke back tears.

"Angel, it's me."

"No, Herc." She went to her dresser and gazed for a long time at the pictures there. They were of our honeymoon—pictures we'd both stopped noticing long ago.

Hercule bounded to her, barked at her, and then bounded back to the bed. He scooped up his ball from the floor and jumped up, landing just inches from me.

Hercule's ball stole her heart.

He flipped his head and the ball popped from his mouth to my lap—or the bedcovers from her view. He barked and pawed at me, jabbing his snout at the ball demanding I take it and give it a toss. He'd done this a million times and demanded one more.

"Oh, Herc. Stop."

"I'm here. Think, Angel, think about me. I'm right here. Herc, tell her."

Moan—he grabbed the ball, flipped it again, and resumed his demand for a catch.

Angel's face flushed with that devilish smile that often emerged just before our bedroom light turned off. She laughed and tears glistened.

"Tuck, you jerk. You weren't supposed to die. What am I to do—talk to myself the rest of my life?"

I leaned close, gently touching her cheek with a long, slow, fingertip. Her eyes closed and she smiled. She reached for her cheek, but her cell phone rang and wrenched her back to reality.

I withdrew my hand and slid from the bed.

"No. Don't go. Come back!"

ELEVEN

ANGEL LAY ON THE bed, alternating between tears and laughter as she spoke with some family friend on the phone. They'd been chatting for ten minutes before I became bored and headed downstairs. It was time to start investigating the most important homicide ever—my own. It would begin with one of the first unusual things I could remember since rejoining the living.

The file.

Whatever it held, it was important enough for Bear to break the law by tampering with my crime scene. That was going to be a problem, though, because when I looked at the pages scattered across my desk, nothing made sense. Pages of scribbled handwriting—mine—were as unintelligible as chicken chow mein, without the fortune cookie. If this were a case file, there should be crime scene photographs and investigative notes. Instead, I found a macramé of jumbled words and foggy images. It was all unintelligent blurs as though my brain had Dyslexia and Alzheimer's all at once.

Words were a clutter of meaningless smudges and I couldn't read anything or see the slightest coherent image in the photographs. Nothing. My autofocus was busted.

"So," a familiar voice said, "are you figuring things out?"

A man was watching me from my doorway. He was dressed in old, green surgical scrubs with a stethoscope wrapped around his neck. He looked to be in his sixties with gray hair and deep blue eyes. His face was dark with stubble as though he'd just completed a double shift of weary surgery.

"Are you getting settled, Oliver?"

Oliver again? His voice was ... yes. He had called me earlier—summoned me to go and help Angel. I didn't know the voice then, but it felt familiar now. His presence didn't startle me or concern me at all. He was no more physical than I was. That is to say, he was dead, too. It was as though he'd been with me all along and yet I'd never seen him before.

"Call me Doc—Doc Gilley."

When he said "Doc," the name flirted with memories too distant and unclear to retrieve. It was like déjà vu but without the trepidation that often comes with it. I was nodding and wasn't sure if it was because of the ease with which I accepted him, or the strange feeling that I knew him.

"Okay, Doc. You sent me to Angel, right?"

"Yes, of course." He came in and stood across the desk from me. "I know you're not sure of what to do or how to do it. You have to come to terms and fast. There's a lot at stake."

"Terrific." I leaned back in the chair. "I've got a million questions. Let's start with what happened to Angel. Then let's talk about the two guys digging holes in my foyer and why it wasn't a foyer at the time. Then…"

"No."

"No?"

Doc shook his head. "I cannot give you those answers. It's better to learn for yourself."

"Great." I waved a hand over the file. "And this? How am I supposed to learn for myself if I can't read?"

"You can't read?"

I shook my head.

"Hmmmm, interesting." He grinned. "Give it time. You've done okay so far. Be patient."

"How am I going to find my killer if I can't read or get through doors? Aren't I…"

"Maybe you're not supposed to. Maybe this is about something else; something more important."

"More important? Like what?"

"How do I know? This is your death, not mine. You figure it out."

Great. I get a guardian angel and he's a smartass. "Come on, Doc. Help me out."

"I can't."

"Why not? Isn't that why you're here?"

He sighed. "Oliver, I didn't just simply appear. You just now noticed me. You have to focus."

"I'm trying to…"

"No. By focus, I don't mean thinking. I mean doing. Being there. It's connecting to where you need to be and what you want. Just be there."

Connecting? "I don't get it, Doc."

He shook his head like Angel's done millions of times. Okay, like everyone does. "Oliver, listen, you're dead. You don't have thoughts. You have emotions, what you used to call your gut. You have *being*."

I thought about that and wasted my time doing that. "Yeah, being there. Got it. And hey, who are you? How do you know me? I think I should know, but I don't."

"In time." He went to Hercule and the big Lab moaned and went twenty-toes up. "I like Hercule. He looks like my old Jed. He's seen me for a while now."

"Really?"

He nodded. Hercule moaned.

I went on. "None of this dead stuff is right. Like the whole light thing. When I first got back here, right here, I didn't see any light or anything."

"A light?"

"Don't I get a light?"

He laughed. "I never got one. Be happy you're here. There are worse places. Well, at least I think so. And if there are, you certainly would be a candidate."

"What the hell does that mean?"

"Exactly."

Yup, a smartass guardian angel. I watched Doc milling around as though he were a guest admiring my etchings. He was a strange, yet familiar man. All I knew was that he belonged somewhere in my life, years before. Where and when, I had no clue. At the moment, however, it was comforting having him to talk with.

"Are you an angel? You don't act like one. And you sure as hell don't talk like one."

"How does one talk?"

"Well, you should be giving me sage advice and showing me the way to my maker and all that. You know, be worldly or heavenly or something. For Christ's sake, show me a light. At least I'd know I wasn't going to hell."

"Ah, I see." Doc scratched Hercule's neck. Herc wagged up a storm. Obviously, they were old pals. "I'd love to help you out. But it doesn't work like that. I'm no angel—at least not that I know of. And you're not going to hell."

"If you're not an angel, how do you know?"

"Because you'd be there by now."

Well, that was good news. "Okay, that works for me. So, why are you here?"

"To help you get settled. There's so much you have to do."

"Like solving my murder?"

"Yes, that too."

"No light?"

Doc laughed again. "Will you forget the light? This isn't television or the drive-in flicks. You're still here, so there has to be a reason."

Yeah, that's right. I remembered a ghost movie I saw—actually, every ghost movie I ever saw—about spirits hanging around because they had unfinished business.

"Yeah, Doc. I have to find my killer. Then I'm gonna kill him. So make them a reservation."

"No, no killing." He went over to my bookshelf and admired my collections. "Not bad, Oliver. Nice collection—I approve. Spillane was my favorite. You remind me of Hammer."

"Thanks, some were my grandfather's—a few first editions. It's the only stuff from my family I got."

"Yes, yes." He turned and threw a lecturing finger at me. "Killing is not in the playbook. You don't have the power to kill or hurt or anything of the sort. You are a bystander, a witness, not a participant. In time maybe a little more. No killing. That I know."

He put down a volume of Agatha Christie as his demeanor changed from kindly spirit to divorce lawyer. "Are you sure about Angela?"

What did he say? "No way, Doc. Not Angel. She loves me."

"Good for you." A thin smile etched his lips. "If you're sure."

"She didn't kill me, right?"

"What about Bear?"

"What about him?"

He rolled his eyes—people do that a lot with me. "Do you trust him?"

"He's acting strange, I'll give you that. But he saved my life three years ago. He took a bullet for me."

"Yes, that was a mistake."

"Are you saying..."

"No." He turned around as his face began losing clarity. I watched him become little more than a wisp of himself. "All I'm saying is this is entirely wrong. Nothing is as it should be. It started with Bear. And it's not over yet."

"Wait, dammit." I watched Doc vanish. "Did he change things? Should I have died before?"

He was just a voice. "You have a lot to do. Remember … just be there."

"Yeah, yeah. I'll just be there."

"And you'll have to come to terms with everyone you thought you knew. You may find you don't know them at all."

"How am I gonna figure all this out?"

"I don't know, Oliver, but things are going to get crazy."

TWELVE

"GOING TO GET CRAZY?" I turned to Hercule. "So, Herc, you've been holding out on me. Doc and you are old pals."

Woof. A second later, his eyes closed and he was asleep.

"Thanks for the help, pal."

Doc seemed surprised I couldn't read the file, so I returned to it on my desk. The pages were still spread about where Angel had left them. On top were blurry photographs, and with them, my yellow legal pad of notes. I concentrated on the top photograph. The image looked like a man. The face was indiscernible and his surroundings unclear. Sparks flickered in my head and the nagging feeling of recognition struck me. This man was important.

Think, Tuck, think...

Nothing. I touched the image. Sparks tickled my fingertips as one by one they moved over the image.

Be there.

Like striking a match, the sparks ignited and flames singed my fingers. An image swirled in the print as if developing before me. A thin, shallow face with haunting, powerful eyes emerged. The face was aged and showed a man worn by more than years.

This face was no friend.

Poor Nicholas Bartalotta.

Poor Nic was not poor at all. In fact, he was one of the wealthiest people in Frederick County. He was also the county's most notorious, albeit only, gangster. Poor Nic was retired from the New York City mob families. Newspapers, being as fond of notorious mobsters as they are of bestowing silly names on them, dubbed him "Poor Nic" from his lavish lifestyle. The *nom de guerre* followed him to Winchester.

"Hi, Nic. I bet you thought you were rid of me."

I laid my hand on the photograph and a manic episode exploded in my brain. My thoughts lost focus and melted. Needles pricked me everywhere. I tried to get control but a jolt of electricity shot through me like a cattle prod to my brain. Lightning burst through—synapse by synapse. My eyes shuttered closed and the current swept through me.

∞

When my eyes opened, I was standing in a luxuriously furnished, two-story great room. There were antiques and expensive trappings and I could have been in an English castle amongst lords and ladies. There were paintings, sculptures, and fine art of every variety. The room exuded wealth and power. Across from me, in front of the story-tall double oak doors, two muscular men stood guard. But they were not watching me, they were watching ... the other me.

The other me?

Bear was there too, sitting in front of a battleship-sized mahogany desk, right next to *the other me*—the me that had been alive, in this room, working a case with Bear. The details were as hazy as the file on my desk. Across from us was the now familiar man in the photograph. In person, he was short and thin, with silver hair recently trimmed and combed back. He looked seventy despite his younger age. Wear and tear caused battle scars but he held himself with starch and power.

This was Poor Nicholas Bartalotta.

Bear was questioning him. But I recalled it was more an interrogation. "Listen, Nic, lawyer or no lawyer, I want those records. If you're innocent, show them to us."

"I think not." Poor Nic sat stone-faced and played with a large gold coin. He rolled it in his fingers and fondled it like a lover. A smile traced across his boney face and that unnerved me—both of me. "Detective, you don't have a warrant. You get nothing. Now, leave my home."

Alive-me sat next to Bear and leaned forward, tapping the desktop. "Listen, Nic. Give Bear a break. You don't have any donuts. What he means to say is, if you don't cooperate, you'll be in our office later today. You'll be answering questions and it will be really unpleasant. Give us the records and we're out of here. You know the warrant is just a formality."

"Then get one."

"Come on, Nicky, do the right thing."

"My men will show you out." Poor Nic motioned for his two bodyguards and continued fondling his good luck coin. "I've told you, I had nothing to do with that guard's death. He worked at my warehouse—that's all. Now leave."

This was frustrating. I'd come in on part of the conversation—the part I remembered—and the missing part left me blank. "Damn, will one of you just say the dead guy's name?"

"Have it your way." Bear stood and shot a gun-finger at the two bodyguards. "Sit, boys, or I'll shoot you."

As I stood there, just a foot from myself, a mind-meld sizzled through me and everything fell into place. This was Saturday morning more than a week ago. Bear and I had been working a homicide that led us to Poor Nic Bartalotta. After the crime scene, we headed straight to this house. Poor Nic was, as previously mentioned, our local—albeit retired—mobster. He had his finger in everything from land deals to labor unions in his time with the New York crime families. So why not here? Bear was convinced he was involved in our case, but I couldn't remember why. The victim was ... nuts. I couldn't remember the name.

"Nic," alive-me said. "Get your lawyer and be at the office by noon. If not, we'll come back with two warrants—one for your books and the other for you. *Capisce*?"

"Be on time, *gumba*," Bear added. "Got it?"

Poor Nic glanced at his men and they closed in. Bear turned and brushed past them on his way to the door. He threw an elbow into one of the bodyguards that made the big brute stagger backward and cough.

Alive-me followed, but stopped at a grand bookcase near the door. On the center shelf was a lighted mahogany and glass case. Inside were a dozen or more mounted coins of varying sizes and distinctions. I knew less about rare coins than I knew about space travel, but I could tell these were valuable. In the very center of the display's mounting apron were several empty, circular holes.

"Hey, Nic. You have a robbery?" Even alive-me had wit.

One of his bodyguards stepped in front of me and blocked my view.

Nic said, "No, Detective. I'm a collector. Those are family heirlooms—the pieces are 1881 Twenty-dollar gold pieces—without mint markings. They are very, very rare and valuable."

"You're missing a few."

Nic stood up. "Good day, Detective."

When Bear and Alive-me were gone, I was surprised that I didn't follow them or evaporate into nothing again. Instead, I stayed behind, standing in Poor Nic's great room. I felt locked inside as though the memory held me tight. That rattled me. But hey, what was this old gangster going to do, kill me?

Actually, he did something much, much better.

He picked up his phone and dialed.

When I was here the first time—alive—I left with Bear. What was happening could not be from memories. Bear and I left together. I didn't stay behind eavesdropping on the phone call as I was now.

I liked this part of being dead. It didn't require a warrant.

"It's me," Poor Nic said, jabbing a finger toward the door that sent his two bodyguards from the room. "Frederick County's finest just left. Get your sorry ass down here and bring your list of friends. We have an appointment with them you have to cancel."

Okay, so being here was cool, but it had its limits. I could not hear the other half of Nic's conversation. Maybe Doc would show me the Texas-two-phone later. For now, it was frustrating. I'd failed to watch Poor Nic dial the phone so I had no clue what number he called.

Lesson learned.

Poor Nic went on. "I don't give a damn. Tyler made promises and I expect him to keep them. Now get down here."

He began nodding and cursing—more the latter. When he laid the phone down, his face was tight and angry. He rolled his good luck coin in his fingers and tossed it in the air, deftly catching it. Then he laughed and slapped it down on the desk beside his phone. He turned in his chair, striking a pose of heavy thought. He closed his eyes and began mumbling.

I studied the coin and tried to make out the engravings on its face. It was thick and heavy and looked like solid gold. It had to be an antique or perhaps something rarer—maybe one of the twenty-dollar pieces from his display case. Whatever the coin was, it didn't flash any memory or turn on warning lights. So, for now, it was just a gold coin.

I reached out to touch it but Poor Nic spun in his chair and slapped his hand atop it. His eyes flared and darted around the room in freeze-frame snapshots as though searching for a spy laying in wait.

Kaboom—I left into nothing.

THIRTEEN

I LANDED IN THE Frederick County Detective Squad room on the outskirts of Winchester. Bear was there, too, sitting at his desk rummaging through a stack of files and plastic evidence bags.

For more than a decade, I sat opposite him. I'd witnessed that big ugly mug happy and sad, asleep and pumped on adrenaline, and even so angry he'd overturned his desk. Bear could have a rather broad-brush stroke of emotions at times. Now, though, I was looking at a man I hadn't seen before. His face was dull and eyes bloodshot. His clothes were wrinkled and dirty from wearing them more than thirty-six hours. His hair was uncombed, his shirtsleeves rolled up at different heights, and his tie was undone and dangling from his neck. Generally, he looked like shit.

"Cheer up, Bear," I said, slumping into my chair across from him. "I may be dead, but I'm not gone. But there are a few things we need to talk about first. I don't like your secrets, pal. After that, I'll help you solve this case."

He rubbed his eyes. Then, he opened a large flex-file on his desk and dumped the contents out, sorting through the items one by one. Inside were a pen and some loose change, a pocketknife, assorted pieces of paper, and a white envelope. He pulled out a notepad and began making an inventory list of all the items. He recorded all but the loose papers and stopped. One of the papers wasn't a paper at all but a business card. He turned it over and dropped it on his desk. When he did, I saw several numbers scrawled on it. The numbers weren't familiar and there was no name.

"Ah, Bear? You look like you could use some coffee."

"Yeah, coffee." He frowned and rubbed his eyes. "Shit, I'm losing it—again."

A cup of black coffee later and he was back at his desk. He picked up the folded papers, read them, logged them on his list, and set them aside. Then, he picked up the business card and read it. Something on the card struck him and he began nodding. Instead of recording the card on his list, he slipped it into his shirt pocket.

"Bear? You can't do that. It's evidence."

Nothing.

"Braddock, what the hell are you doing here?" Captain Sutter emerged from her office and startled us both. "You should be home, sleeping."

"Sure, Boss. I'm just sorting some things out."

"Go home." Her voice left no room for negotiation. "Now."

"Yeah, yeah, I'm going." He stuffed the folded pieces of paper back into the envelope and slipped it into his pants pocket. "Boss, what's the idea of putting Clemens and Spence on Tuck's case?"

Captain Sutter came over and leaned against Bear's desk. "I have to have a clean investigation. One wrong move and any defense attorney could have a field day. You were his partner—let alone anything else. You can't investigate this one, so stay clear."

"What 'anything else?'"

"You know what I mean."

"No, I don't."

"Spell it out, Captain." Bear watched her with curt, angry eyes. "What 'anything else?'"

"You're too close to Angela. You can't be objective. Plain and simple."

"Come on, Captain." He pounded a heavy fist onto the desk sending papers to the floor. "No way in hell she's involved."

"That's my point. Everyone's a suspect, Bear—including her. When a cop goes down, even the frigging dog is a suspect."

"Hercule has an alibi," I yelled.

She changed the subject. "What about this break-in at Professor Stuart's house this morning?"

He shrugged. "No break-in at all as far as we know. Stuart's convinced it's all in her head. Our boys didn't find anything. I think Stuart's right."

"Can't say I blame her. She's been through hell."

Bear agreed.

"How about that security guard killing?"

"Salazar?" Bear didn't look interested. "He was found shot dead ten days ago just down the road from where he worked at Bartalotta's warehouse. Tuck and I went to see Bartalotta but got nowhere. No witnesses. No evidence. No leads. All corpse and no clues, boss."

Raymundo Salazar—my last case. His name belonged on that strange file back home—the file Bear hid in my den.

"Anything new on Tuck?" Bear's tone was flat and oozed contempt. "Spence and Clemens are acting like there is."

"No," she said. "Leave it alone, Bear."

He softened. "Okay, Cap."

"Look, we have no evidence. Someone got in and left no trace behind. The hit was clean and fast. If it weren't for that dog, Angela might be dead, too."

"That's right, the bastard shot my dog." I pounded my fist on the desk, but despite my assault, not even Bear's coffee rippled. "Hey, Bear, tell her about Tommy at the golf course."

Bear went rigid, but then shrugged and looked embarrassed. "Sorry, Cap. I get a buzz in my ears now and then. It's driving me nuts. I'm just tired."

"What the hell, Bear? Tell her what he said about the New York heavy. What's up with you?"

Captain Sutter crossed her arms and studied him. "You need to go get some sleep."

"Sure, Cap."

"First thing tomorrow, I want the entire Salazar file—everything."

"It's all here, Cap. Everything."

No it wasn't. "Ah, Bear, what about my file at home? The one you hid?"

"Including everything at the house?"

He nodded.

"Okay then, get it all logged in and cataloged tomorrow. Every damn page."

"Right, Cap." Bear stuffed the files from his desk into the filing cabinet and slammed the drawer closed. As he disappeared through the squad room doors, Captain Sutter was in her office doorway on her cell phone.

"He just left. My bet is he's heading to get drunk. There's something just not right with him. Find out what it is."

There were several "somethings" that were not right with Bear. There was the hidden file, my house key, and a secret gargantuan informant. Now, he was stuffing evidence in his pockets. Since my death, Bear's secrets unnerved me and sent a chilling question through me. Were his secrets because of my murder or the reasons for it?

FOURTEEN

"I'M SORRY. I DRANK too much to drive." Bear sat back in the kitchen chair and drained his second cup of coffee. When his cup hit the wood tabletop, Angel refilled it.

"Stop it," she said. "I'm glad you didn't drive. You should have called me. I would have picked you up."

When he arrived an hour ago, he startled Angel with his ragged and red-faced appearance. He'd walked five blocks from Old Town Winchester to our front gate, muttering and fuming the entire way. Several times, I'd swear he was talking to me, but unlike his reaction at the office, he didn't respond when I spoke. The walk was laden with angry outbursts of self-deprecation and unintelligible comments, several times stopping and turning back toward town. Each time, he returned to the path to our front door.

"Walking helped." Bear gulped his coffee. "Damnedest thing, honey. I swear someone was following me, too. Maybe it's the booze—maybe I'm getting paranoid."

"Or …" Angel sat down at the end of the table. "Maybe it was him."

"Him?"

"Tuck."

He snorted and sipped at his coffee.

I leaned over and touched her hand. With every ounce of emotion I could muster, I glided a finger across hers. I'd done this a million times and I knew now that I'd taken that feeling for granted. The thought punched into me. As I caressed her hand, a warm tickle etched down my fingers until it disappeared into hers. Her eyes closed and her breathing slowed—almost stopping. She began to smile as moisture glistened from her eyes and she sighed.

"Angela? What is it?" Bear's eyes fixed on her.

She jolted up, blushed, and swiped a strand of hair from her eyes. "I'm sorry."

"What's wrong, Angela?"

"You won't understand. You think I imagined what happened at Ernie's. You'll never believe this."

"I always have an open mind."

"It's Tuck." She stood up and went to the sink. "He's here—with us now. I can feel him."

"Oh, shit. Don't start that."

"Yes, listen. I can feel him. Don't you?"

"No." He went to her, put his arm around her, and kissed her forehead. "Angela, I know you want to believe he's here. But he's not. Sometimes I get this buzzing sound—even hear things—and I want to believe it's him. It's not. It's just guilt."

Guilt? "Ah, partner, what does that mean?"

Angel lowered her eyes. "No, Bear. No guilt. You promised me. Let it go."

"It's my fault. I never should have let this happen."

This? What "this"?

"Bear," she slipped from his arm. "I can feel him. I'm telling you the truth."

He looked down at the floor, shaking his head. "Angela, I can't do this. He's dead. I'm going for a walk. I have to get away from it."

"Bear, wait..."

It was too late. He disappeared into the hall. The front door opened and closed.

"Damn you, Bear." Angel dropped back down onto her chair and buried her face in her hands. "Damn you."

I was helpless to console her but I tried anyway. I stroked her hair and tried to reach her with a fingertip caressing her cheek. After several minutes, she wiped tears from her face and a hand went to her cheek. It lingered there as though responding to my affection.

"Oh, Tuck. I want to believe. I'm sorry this happened. I wish I could change it all."

"I know, Angel." If only she could hear me. But, deep down, I knew she couldn't.

"Damn him." She dug into her jeans pocket and withdrew her cell phone. She hit speed dial 2—Bear's number—and sighed when it went right to voicemail. "Please, Bear. Try and understand..."

A hungry rush of anxiety gripped me. It was...

"No—get down. Down!"

Hercule erupted into a deafening bark. He lunged across the room and drove Angel out of her chair just as two shots shattered the kitchen window. He pinned her to the floor, shielding her beneath him. A steady, deathly warning reverberated through his clinched teeth.

"Stay boy," I yelled.

Several long, heavy moments passed.

"Angela?" Bear crashed through the front door and down the hall. He burst into the kitchen with gun drawn. "You all right?"

"I, I ... yes."

"Stay here. Call 911." He disappeared out the kitchen door into the backyard darkness.

Without thinking, I was in the backyard, standing in the darkness, looking for Bear. I turned in circles and searched. I felt nothing—no presences, no fear, no danger.

I caught up with him in front of the house. He was standing near a bush beside our front gate. He looked up the street where a streetlight bathed parked cars and the street disappeared over a knoll. Several times, he threw a look over his shoulder toward the house, then moved into the street and began a slow advance toward town. When he reached the cone of light arcing down from the streetlamp at the corner, he stopped crouching and stood upright, heaving a breath.

No shots rang out. No shooter ran for an escape.

A block ahead of us, I heard shuffling feet and the sound of a barking dog.

"Easy, Bear. Take a breath. Someone's up ahead but it could be anyone. Don't drop your guard now."

He hesitated, looked back to the house, and then continued up the block. At the next corner, he stopped behind a parked pickup and rested. He started to move forward again, edging out from behind the truck.

"Bear, wait. I'll check ahead."

He stopped and backed into the shadows. I don't know if he heard me, or that buzzing in his head made him think twice of the danger, but either way, he stayed put.

I left him and ran up the street, dodging behind parked cars until I realized how silly it was. No bullet could hurt me nor could any shooter see me. I sprinted to the corner and was about to jog farther when a faint voice jingled in my head—not one, but two.

What I saw across the street began a new chapter in my dead-detective saga.

Two young girls stood beneath a tall, broad oak tree near the opposite corner. They were outside the cone of two streetlamps, on the hazy periphery of their light. I could see them—almost. They were out of focus and little more than silhouettes with vague hints of detail. And they were … they were waving to me. *Me.* I didn't know what to do. So, like any warm-blooded man when pretty girls beckoned, I waved back.

At least it wasn't two guys digging holes in my foyer.

The girls gained focus and coalesced into dim figures just light enough to see. They exchanged words, laughing and cajoling each other. One of them beckoned me to join them but I didn't move— I couldn't. My legs were frozen in place like a freshman at his first dance.

One girl beckoned to me again. She was pretty—of that I was sure. She seemed young, not a teenager but not yet a woman. Her companion was pretty, too, and shared her youth. Their images were incomplete, unclear—photographs still developing.

Who were they? What did they want with me?

I managed to walk to the curb and stopped twenty feet away trying to see them clearer in the streetlight. Something was pulling me again, willing me to join them. I had to go—to talk to them. They were like me—bound here for some unknown reason. Yet every instinct said they had been here for much longer. They were in my world or I was in theirs.

I had to talk to them.

As I took that first step forward, they waved and faded. I heard the jingle of youthful giggles and they were gone.

A shiver ran through me. Can a ghost be haunted?

I returned my focus to Bear. He was behind me, somewhere back down the street in the dark. The girls sidetracked me, and now the shooter could be anywhere.

I jogged down the block in time to see Bear walking down the middle of the street, gun holstered, strolling casually back toward my house. He seemed oblivious to the possible danger that could be waiting nearby. He was muttering to himself.

His cavalier attitude made me mad as hell.

Someone shot at Angel—tried to kill her. The shooter, unlike the two young wraiths, was bone and muscle, and very, very dangerous. For the second time, someone violated our home. And for the second time, I was helpless to stop them.

A disturbing thought pushed through my emotions and settled into the detective part of my brain. There were three common elements each time someone came to my home to kill. The answer, I feared, was secreted among them.

Angel, Bear, and me.

I didn't have any secrets—did they?

FIFTEEN

THE CRIME TECHNICIANS FINISHED their work just after midnight. Their hunt for bullet fragments and shell casings started at the house and finished in the yard. Much to my displeasure, Spence and Clemens arrived at ten. Of course, it took more than two hours to complete their endless and mindless questions.

Most of Angel's answers were, "I don't know, I didn't see anything," and "How would I know, I didn't see anything."

Bear's answers were not as polite.

When they left, I followed Clemens down the front sidewalk. Spence was there, talking with a uniformed cop assigned to guard the house for the night.

Spence said, "Yeah, you have to stay the night. It's all bullshit, ya' know. My money says the only one shooting up the place was him."

Him? The little turd thought Bear shot at Angel.

"Come on, Mike, what are you saying?" Clemens leaned on their car, eyeing the uniformed cop beside Spence. "You think Bear did this?"

"Maybe," Spence said. "Maybe he's trying to make Tuck's murder look more convincing. You know, get the heat off him and Angela."

"No way," Clemens waved the uniformed cop away. "Bear's straight—least I think so. What makes you think someone didn't come back for something?"

"What makes you think they did? Angela didn't see anything—just the shots. Bear claims he only heard the shots. Neighbors saw him heading up the street with a gun. Maybe Bear did the shooting to make it look like a stalker."

"Oh, come on, Mikey. That's a lot of maybes." Clemens made some notes in his pad. "Why go through all that?"

"Why do you think? Dr. Angela Tucker is smart, gorgeous, and has money. The oldest motive in the world. Sex and money."

"Bear?"

"Bear."

"No way." Clemens scribbled in his pad before he changed the topic. "He was pissed about her computer. Was it you? I never touched it, I swear."

"Nope."

"You sure?"

"Nope." Spence's face lit up in a big smile. "But he sure is worried about it, isn't he? Maybe we should take a look."

"Ah, shit. Come on, Mikey. Lighten up on them."

Clemens was a good guy, deep down, but handicapped by Spence. The problem was that Spence was the senior detective and that meant Cal Clemens had to follow his lead—even if that was over a cliff.

"Cal," I said. "Bear's innocent. Angel is innocent. Spence is full of shit. Jesus, man, you have to know that."

Spence climbed into their cruiser and started the engine. Clemens stood there, leaning against the fender watching the house. The last thing he did before climbing in beside Spence was to rip the notes from his pad and shred them into confetti.

"Not Bear," he whispered and tossed the papers into the street.

Angel watched from the front door as the detectives drove away. I followed her to the kitchen where Bear was pouring coffee. For a man who just survived a shooting, he didn't look fazed. But then again, it took a lot to faze him.

"I don't like those two," Angel said. "I don't like their questions, either."

"Relax. They will never solve this. I'll take care of it."

I slipped onto the chair next to Angel and touched her hand again. "Ask Bear about your computer. Ask him about the file in the den."

She sat very still, barely breathing, watching her coffee cup. "Bear, I hear him again."

"Don't start that—Jesus."

I leaned over, whispered into Angel's ear, and touched the side of her cheek. On cue, she said, "Oh, don't forget that file Sutter wants. The one in the bookcase."

"What did you say?"

"The file."

"Oh, shit, Angela." Bear's face twisted as if he bit into something sour. "How do you know that?"

"I don't know, Bear. I don't know … never mind, I'll get it." Angel disappeared down the hall. When she returned, she was carrying the file. "Here. I found it earlier in the bookshelf. You hid it there. Why?"

"How'd you know?" He took the file in one hand and her shoulder with the other. "Shit, Angela, I just, well, I wanted to see it before anyone else."

She cocked her head. "But why?"

"Just because. You know, in case there's a good lead. I want it before Spence gets his paws on it." Angel was thinking about that when Bear changed gears. "Do you have anything else of Tuck's I should take?"

She shook her head and when she took his hand, a twinge of jealousy stung me.

Bear was somehow different from the man I'd known for years as my best friend and partner. He was hard—harder than I re-membered—and suddenly detached from my murder. People react differently to pain and loss, but if it were the other way around, I'd be kicking in doors all over town hunting his killer. Maybe it was the booze. Maybe it was the stress. Maybe it was something else.

Maybe.

"You don't need to watch over me tonight," Angel said. "Captain Sutter has that deputy outside. I'll be fine."

Bear looked at his watch. "Okay, I'm heading out. I'll check in with the cap first." He pulled out his cell phone and punched a key. "I have messages. Let me check."

"One's from me…"

"What the?" The phone skidded across the table as Bear shuffled back, colliding with the sink. "Jeez, no way. No…"

"What is it?" Angel asked. "Who called?"

He tapped the air with his finger and pointed at the phone. "Your voicemail."

"What about it?" Angel picked up the phone, hit the speaker button, and replayed the message. "*… Please try and understand…*" Angel's voice was clear but it was not what made her replay the message three times. Then she cried—happy tears—as a smile blossomed on her face. Suddenly, without hesitation, she believed. Bear, however, shook his head and muttered guttural denials as he replayed the last words.

It was all captured on the message. All of it. There were Hercule's frantic bark and the two gunshots. Even before that—before Hercule knocked Angel to safety—were my muffled, near indistinguishable words recorded in the mayhem.

"*No … Get down … Down …*"

SIXTEEN

THE UNIVERSITY OF THE Shenandoah Valley is tucked into a small valley—a hollow as many locals call it—just outside Winchester where Frederick County begins its climb west toward the Appalachian Mountains. Just off State Highway 50, the university sprawls among rolling hills and picturesque farm country. The campus is right at home in the country setting. Its mixture of turn-of-the-century Americana and modern academia is captured in the campus's brick, stone, and steel architecture. Despite its mid-twentieth-century construction, it still manages to exude old-school charm.

The drive was relaxing and Angel seemed at peace with things now.

Last night, it took Angel and Bear two hours to reach an agreement on the voicemail. They agreed to disagree. He decided my voice was a leftover message from an old call, somehow electronically merged with Angel's message. She knew that was bunk. She went to bed with a smile; Bear went to his apartment and erased the message. I sat vigil beside Angel, watching her sleep. It seemed restful and undisturbed. I doubted Bear's was the same.

When we pulled into the campus drive, a very strange thought began to nag me. Angel was the brains in our family. I was, or had been, the other part. Now, that had changed. I was gone—at least, as far as everyone was concerned. I had to think about Angel in a different way—a less selfish and sentimental way. Sooner or later, I'd have to face the possibility of Angel moving on and finding some eager young historian or equally interchangeable brain to while away the years with her. She was young and had so much life left. Unlike me.

The thought of someone else's feet propped on my desk choked me. Perhaps I'd have to learn about good, old-fashioned haunting. Of course, when that time came, I might just go searching for the ghost of Marilyn Monroe or Jayne Mansfield. Two could play that game.

I followed Angel through the brick and glass entrance of the John S. Mosby Center for American Studies and up to the senior faculty offices on the third floor. A dozen or more professors and staff stopped to greet her, each passing along sympathies and all manners of condolences. It was a gauntlet of well-wishers, and after two floors, Angel lowered her head and dashed to her office.

"Thank God," she whispered and dug in her handbag for her key. But, the door was unlocked and she pushed it open. "Carmen?"

Carmen Delgado was the department administrator and a long-time family friend. Angel and I both expected to find her inside, filing, checking budgets, or doing any number of tasks in Angel's absence. It was not, however, the lovely Ms. Delgado rooting through Angel's desk.

"Ernie?" Angel's voice was thick with irritation. "What are you doing?"

Ernie looked up and dropped a stack of mail as if it were on fire. "Oh, my, Angela, you startled me."

"What are you doing?"

"Out with it," I said. "What the hell are you doing in here, Ernie?"

"I was handling your mail so you wouldn't worry about work. I wanted to make sure nothing urgent went unattended."

"That's very kind, Ernie," Angel said, patting his shoulder. She walked around behind her desk and dropped her backpack onto it. "I already spoke with Carmen. She'll take care of my mail. I came in to pick up some things."

"Of course," he said. "We've covered your classes for two weeks; longer if you need it. I may take them myself."

"I appreciate it, Ernie." She sat down in her chair and picked up a handful of mail. "Did you find the M.E.'s report you asked about?"

"Well, no, now that you mention it."

She shrugged. "I'll check at home, too. Maybe Tuck…"

"Yes, maybe he did," he said. "Have you decided on the arrangements?"

"No, they're still holding his body." Angel's faced paled. "I have to wait a couple more days. Bear is pushing to get him released, though."

"I see. Please let me know if I can help in any way." Ernie went to the door, but stopped and turned around. "There is something else."

"What is it, Ernie?"

He looked thoughtful, perhaps hesitant. "I noticed a note from Tyler Byrd—of course I didn't open it. That disturbs me."

"Oh?" Angel asked, shuffling through the mail until she found the pre-printed address label that read, "Byrd Construction & Development." She slipped it into her backpack. "I'll see to it that my mail concerning Kelly's Dig is delivered to my home."

He raised an eyebrow. "Yes, I suppose it should. But since it wasn't, may I inquire about its contents?"

"I'd prefer not."

"Really?"

"I'm sorry, Ernie. It wouldn't be appropriate. After all, it's your historical foundation—not the university—opposing him. I'm impartial. I'm interested in history, not politics. That is, after all, why I'm a 'friend of the court.'"

"Well, perhaps." Ernie's pucker-factor hit nine. "But I do speak for the university."

"Forgive me, Ernie, but you don't."

"Now see here…"

"Please." She smiled to soften the blow to his ego. "When the dean approved my assignment to the court, he was very clear. He pointed out you spoke for your foundation. Only the foundation.

The university has no position on Kelly's Dig. I'm an independent consultant with no ties back here."

Pucker-factor nine-point-five and climbing.

I laughed. "You tell 'em, Angel."

"We all have a stake in this," Ernie snapped. "Byrd is destroying this county. He's a thug."

Tyler Byrd was perhaps the largest and most powerful of the local Virginia developers. He had been for as long as I could remember. Nevertheless, I'm not sure "thug" was fair. At present, he was hip-deep in the development of a highway bypass around northeastern Winchester. The project would take years to complete, and with the other projects around town, it would leave Tyler filthy rich. He was, after all, only dirty rich now.

"Be reasonable, Ernie. After the human bones and artifacts were unearthed at Kelly's Dig, all the rules on Byrd's project changed. You were one of the first to see them. You know what this discovery might mean to his project."

"I hope it means his demise."

"Oh, Ernie, stop. This is too important for you to be so one-sided. Please, think about that."

"I do think about that, Angela. Every day. And there is too much at stake to make any mistakes. The county is spending millions on that project—millions to Byrd. No one seems concerned about the local heritage at stake."

"It's only been a few weeks." She folded her arms and leaned back in her chair, watching the anger swell in Ernie's cheeks. "And you're wrong. The county does care. That's why the judge assigned me the research."

"Byrd's project is a disgrace to this county's history. Why, our Civil War heritage—some of the deepest in the state—is at risk. Byrd has no respect, he may..."

"I know that, Ernie, but..."

"Some of Mosby's Rangers are buried here. General Jackson and countless others left their marks, too."

"I know, I know, Ernie." Angel waved her surrender. "No one disputes Winchester's history. But, you know the rub. Every time someone wants to dig a hole, the historical societies charge in and try to protect the land. The courts have to get involved. Ernie, people are frustrated on both sides."

"You don't sound like a historian, Angela."

She recoiled. "Why, because I think there has to be a balance between history and development?"

"Balance? The developers are destroying our history and the newspapers put it on the back page."

"Well, not this month."

"That's right. Kelly's Dig accomplished that."

Kelly's Dig, officially Kelly Orchard Farms, is a swath of land in the northeast side of the county. The farm dated back to the Civil War and it had at least two known battlefields within its boundaries. The land changed hands dozens of times over the last century. Several years ago, a small parcel of it was quietly sold to the county. Then, two months ago, Tyler Byrd broke ground on the highway bypass project.

Then the war began anew.

Ernie and the Virginia Battlefield Historical Preservation Foundation—one of his favorite charities—tried to stop Byrd. They failed. Roads and jobs, as it turned out, were in higher demand than another battlefield historical marker. Ernie couldn't stop the bulldozers.

Nineteenth-century skeletons and artifacts could, however.

During Byrd's initial excavation, a crew unearthed the fragmented remains of two human skeletons. Along with them, uniform paraphernalia, remnants of munitions and weapons, coins and other historical artifacts, too. Something appeared to have happened at that site—something historically important. Within hours, shovels and hardhats were ushered from the site to make room for the medical examiner and sheriff. The Civil War paraphernalia convinced the coroner it was not a twentieth-century crime scene, but a possible Civil War gravesite. Then the real battle started.

The newspapers called it a fluke. The judge called it, "cease and desist."

The court ordered Kelly's Dig protected as a possible historical landmark and interment sight. Kelly's Dig, the skeletal remains, and the dozens of Civil War artifacts unearthed became the ward of the Virginia Historical Society. So said a dozen state and federal laws. Lawyers marched into battle and their legal cannons raged. Counter-claims and motions piled up. Bulldozers and dump trucks sat idle.

Tyler Byrd began sweating thousand dollar bills.

"Angela," Ernie said. "I'm sorry. I'm being difficult."

"Well, maybe just a little." She smiled. "The District Judge wants my assessment on how to protect the site and continue the project—

at the same time. That means working with Tyler. That's all. André is doing most of the work anyway."

"Of course you have to work with Tyler." The way Ernie said "Tyler" suggested Angel was giving aid and comfort to the enemy. "I'm rather emotional about these matters—forgive me. My foundation can't match Byrd's financial power."

"It doesn't have to. That's why the judge assigned me."

He nodded. "Yes, I know."

"You have to trust me, Ernie."

"I do." He changed the topic. "Dinner later in the week? Perhaps stay at the house for a few weeks?"

"No, I'm fine, really."

"I'm worried about you, Angela," he said. "I understand your loss. I do. But you've been acting rather odd—and Braddock has, too."

Angel's face reddened. "Odd?"

"I'm sorry, I don't mean to offend you. But sometimes you act as though Oliver isn't gone. And Braddock, well, he acts like he doesn't care."

SEVENTEEN

As soon as Ernie left, Angel folded her arms and pouted. Then with a few mumbled words, she launched herself into a torrent of work. I sat watching her sifting mail and throwing files around her desk. She was angry and hurt and would need to exhaust herself in work until it abated. That could take hours.

I got bored after five minutes. So, I did what I would have when I was alive—snoop around the department and see what I could find to amuse myself.

I found what I was looking for down the hall.

Low murmurs from the conference room sounded like trouble to me. Nosey as ever—that's what made me a good cop—I stuck my head in and found the missing Carmen Delgado.

Carmen was an attractive woman. She was Angel's height, with dark Latin features and a friendly, though sassy, personality. She was nearing forty, but that didn't stop the students who frequented the office from flirting. Heaven help any of them who dared to make a play—she was hell on wheels and could draw, cut, and quarter you without getting her makeup smeared.

If I weren't married to Angel ... well, it's too late anyway.

Carmen was sitting at the end of the conference table opposite Detectives Spence and Clemens. Both men were stone faced and sipping steaming paper cups of coffee. Spence scribbled on his notepad. Clemens sat idle.

Carmen did not look happy.

"Detective, I can't help you," she said. "I have work to do. Can I go?"

"Sure, sure." Spence leaned forward in his chair and tapped his pen against his temple. "Now, Miss Delgata ..."

"Delgado."

"Yeah, Delgado. Why would someone suggest that Angela wanted her husband out of the way?"

I couldn't believe what I was hearing.

"They wouldn't." Carmen slapped her hand on the table. "Detective, let me set you straight. Dr. Tucker is an honest and hardworking woman. She's admired on campus. She is, er was, crazy about Tuck. He was a good man, too. She's devastated. Anyone who ..."

"Please understand," Clemens interjected, "we're trying to find his killer. We have to run down every lead."

"Yeah, every lead." Spence made more notes. Then he pulled his cell phone out of his pocket. To Carmen, he quipped, "Listen, we have to know if there was anything going on with Angela. You know, any foolin' around or any juicy gossip. Seems like her secretary ..."

"Department Office Manager," Carmen corrected. "No. There was nothing Dr. Tucker was doing that should interest you."

"What about Braddock?" Spence asked. "You know him well?"

The question seemed to startle Carmen and she flushed. "You're not suggesting…"

"Miss Delgado, please," Clemens said. "You know Braddock, right?"

"Bear and Tuck were partners—best friends." Carmen folded her arms. "Bear is a great guy. Everyone loves him."

"Oh, really? Everyone?"

She flashed him her death eyes.

Spence wasn't fazed. "Bear ever come around *without* Tuck?"

She didn't answer.

"Come on, you know what I mean." Spence took a long sip of coffee and watched her over the rim of the cup. "Has Angela ever met him elsewhere?"

"Well," Carmen's face flushed ever so slightly. "Email here and there—we all do. And, yes, I think they met sometimes for coffee and such. But that doesn't mean…"

"Where—here or somewhere else?" Clemens asked. "When?"

"I'm sure it's innocent. Angela always tells me how wonderful Bear is and what a good man he is. They were best friends, they would never…"

"Did they ever meet for lunch or dinner?" Spence pressed. "I mean, you know, as friends?"

"Sure. Lunch a few times—I joined them quite often. I'm going through a painful divorce and they're my good friends."

"Oh? How good?"

She ignored him. "Sometimes Bear would come by late if Angela and I were working evenings. We both worked late hours at the end of semesters. Bear sometimes came by—so did Tuck."

"How cozy." Spence didn't look up as he jotted on his pad. "Everyone is such pals around here."

The little twerp was irritating me and I wanted to see his notepad. When I did, I couldn't make out his handwriting, but I didn't have to. Spence was digging away at his favorite motive—Angel or Bear killed me. Now, Carmen fell into his trap and gave him enough to chase his theory. Angel was now his prime suspect.

Clemens asked, "How close were they?"

"Well…"

"How close?" Spence demanded.

She shrugged. "Ask her."

"I will," Spence said. "Anyone else ever hang around Angela—a lot I mean?"

"Well, maybe." Carmen was hedging and doing a bad job of it. "Professor Stuart, but he's her boss. And Tyler Byrd's called several times. A few times Angela went out afterwards. You need to talk with her. She asked me not to discuss it with anyone—especially Professor Stuart."

Oh, really? Angel never mentioned that to me. Spence was scribbling again, and when I looked over at Carmen, she was watching him too, anxious that he was taking so long making notes. As much as I hated to admit it, Spence was learning things I never knew.

"I'm sure it was nothing," she added.

"Interesting," Spence said, "another suitor?"

"No, Detective. You have it all wrong."

Clemens held up a hand. "Now, Miss Delgado, let's get back to Bear. Did you ever know him and Angela to do anything unusual? You know, secretive or anything?"

"You're saying they're having an affair?" Carmen wagged a finger at him. "They aren't."

"Maybe they are, maybe they aren't."

Spence's cell phone rang. He took the call and announced where he and Clemens were. Then he added, "And Miss Belgada suggested that Bear may have been involved with Dr. Tucker. Interesting, huh, Cap?"

"You bastard." I grabbed the cell phone in his hand and tried to wrench it free.

Rage overflowed from me. My fingers tingled and I felt them grip his cell phone. I wrenched Spence's hand and phone away from his ear. Energy surged through me. The rush felt like I'd mainlined a hundred cups of coffee with a five-pound sugar chaser.

Spence's face flashed surprise and he twisted toward me, unseeing, at the same instant I let go of his hand. For that instant, our eyes met but he recovered and returned to his call.

His voice was edgy and uncertain. "Yeah, yeah, Captain. I'll get back to you." He put the cell on the table.

"You bastard." Carmen was on her feet. "I never said that. You twisted my words."

"Did I?" he said. "We never said 'affair.' You did."

Clemens frowned. "Come on, let it go, Mike."

"Go to hell, the two of you." Carmen was done. "Leave or I'll call security."

Spence laughed. "We're the cops, sweetie. Security can kiss my ass. I'm not through with you yet."

"Yes you are." Carmen nearly ran out the door.

"Fine, Miss Delgado," Spence called after her. "Have it your way. We'll be back."

"You better lighten up, Mike," Clemens said. "She's pissed."

"Mark my words, partner. She's hiding something. She's covering for Angela—or Bear—I'll bet you anything."

"I think you're out of your mind, Mikey. You better hope Delgado doesn't tell Bear about this."

"Screw him." Spence winked at Clemens and started dialing his cell phone again. "Let's see if Professor Stuart can spill on Angela, too. She seems to be a real popular girl around here. Real popular."

Enough.

I grabbed his cell phone with one hand and slapped his coffee cup sitting on the table with the other. The cup flipped forward and dumped its steaming contents into Spence's lap.

"Son of a bitch." He jumped up, swatting at his crotch. "What the ..."

"How did you do that?" Clemens roared.

I went to the doorway and watched Carmen throwing office supplies around her desk. Her answers to Spence's questions bothered me. Her body language suggested something I didn't like—deception. I didn't want to admit it, but Spence was right about one thing.

Carmen Delgado was hiding something.

EIGHTEEN

Woof.

Hercule? When I turned around to see what Spence and Clemens were doing, Hercule barked again. Instead of the conference room, I was back in my den. Herc was sitting in the center of the room, head cocked and tail wagging.

He moaned and lay down. My popping in and out was unsettling him. It was unsettling me, too.

"Sorry, pal. I'm trying to get the hang of all this."

Woof.

He followed me into the kitchen where I sat at the table and considered Carmen Delgado's interrogation. She had worked for Angel for years and her loyalty was unquestionable. Still, she was concealing something. That bothered me. After all, this was a murder investigation. What was so secret that she felt compelled to hide it now?

I went to the kitchen sink and gazed out the window. It was sunny outside and a faint breeze was blowing through the half-open window. The air smelled crisp and fragrant with the musty, almost sweet smell that came with fall. It was my favorite time of year. The curtain fluttered and I noticed a pair of Angel's earrings on the windowsill. She was forever leaving her jewelry lying about. Twice her wedding ring fell from the sill into the sink drain and I had to pay a plumber for an emergency job. Not to retrieve the ring, but to repair my retrieving the ring; I'm terrible with tools.

The earrings now on the sill were gold hoops with two garnet stones affixed at the base. Each had a small diamond set between them. I didn't recognize them. While not unusual, Carmen's recent interview sent a tickle of doubt into me. The earrings were strangely alluring as the sun glinted off the diamonds and sent strobes of glitter into my eyes. When I reached out and touched them, they seized me.

The room began to close as the diamond's glitter flowed over me like a river of light.

The familiar tingle of electricity grew inside me. Before I could warn Hercule, the room spiraled into darkness and was gone. The journey was not the comforting one I was growing accustomed to. Where the strange, flowing euphoria had filled me before, dread did now. As the room disappeared, a vacuum drained my energy—weakening me, drinking every drop of strength. The glitter exploded and was gone, leaving me swallowed in darkness. Ahead of me—at least I think it was ahead of me—was a round, brilliant beacon. It grew from a pinprick in the black veil to a blinding aurora. The light was driving straight at me like a freight train. Then, just as it reached me, it burst in a brilliant flash.

It was gone—extinguished. Blackness returned.

I sensed the rain first—musty dampness of evening showers. I looked around but couldn't get my bearings. Cars and trucks surrounded me—rows of all makes and models. Not far away was a streetlamp that bathed the vehicles in cones of opaque, rain-streaked light. Farther away, silhouettes of buildings and tall trees looked like a strange, evil skyline. The panorama was dreamlike—faint, hazy images surrounded by nothing but the feeling that I didn't belong.

I was standing in a parking lot. A dark, rainy, unrecognizable parking lot. It was night and I had no idea which day or place. Something told me it was not the "when" I left moments before either. The only thing that was certain was that I was alone. Not just alone, but isolated and vulnerable. That unnerved me—unnerved me as it hadn't since my demise.

My limbs wouldn't respond. They were frozen in place. Unable to break free and find a familiar landmark, doom washed over me. An eerie, penetrating cold touched me. I looked around as a faint, almost benign sense of familiarity ebbed in. Terror followed it.

I saw him.

A figure, obscured in the trees beside the far edge of the parking lot, edged toward the buildings a hundred yards away. The figure was tall with broad shoulders, but I couldn't see more than an outline. The movements were a man's stride and boldness. As he passed near a street lamp, he pressed back into the trees and hid from discovery. He emerged near the building's courtyard where it emptied into the parking lot. He stopped and melted into the trees again. I lost him just beyond the fringes of light.

I knew he was there. I could feel him. I could feel his danger.

Fear tightened its grip and I felt sick, helpless, and weak. I tried to move but my roots seemed more firmly planted than ever. When the second figure appeared out of the courtyard, I knew my role.

A witness.

The second figure came from somewhere in the courtyard and walked into the parking lot with short, quick steps. For an instant, I saw the dim outline of a woman's face before she pulled her raincoat hood tighter over her head. She stopped for a second and studied the parking lot, then hurried into the first lane of cars. She hesitated under a streetlamp, perhaps believing the light was safety. My senses burned and recognition singed my nerves, sending alarm bells raging in my head. Her coat was a tan, double-breasted English trench coat. I knew the coat. I knew the shop in Old Town where I'd bought it just a year ago. It was Angel's coat.

The earrings brought me to her. But brought me where? When? No—*why*?

"No. Angel, go back. Go back inside."

Her pace quickened along the front row of cars. At the fourth car, she stopped, looked down, and fidgeted inside her coat. She was digging for her keys. I'd told her a million times to have them ready—ready to get into safety. A key protruding from the fist can stop an attacker if thrust and slashed into his face. Angel didn't have her keys ready. She never did.

She shifted her raincoat and leaned forward. Her hand pointed to the door to activate the electronic lock.

That's when he struck.

He lurched from the darkness before she knew he was there. He struck from behind, driving her into the car door. She staggered back. He pounced again, gripped her neck and hair, and slammed her into the doorframe—once, twice. Her body slumped.

"Angel, no. Stop, you bastard. Stop!"

It was no use. Rage vibrated through me—arching and churning to escape my shackles. "No, please, no. Leave her alone."

It was over.

He stuffed her into the car and followed. A second later, the engine started and the car disappeared into the drizzle and darkness.

No one saw. No one helped. No one witnessed her abduction. No one but me.

"No. Please … no. Doc, help me!"

The aurora of light swallowed me again. This time, the journey was empty. No electricity charged me. No welcome tingle of anticipation warmed me. I collapsed into a chasm of hopelessness. When the light took me, I had no desire to leave the darkness I was in—no will to escape. Perhaps it was the darkness—my darkness—that held me firm. Perhaps this was what death was for me now.

I was lost. Hopeless. Alone.

I'd been unable to manage doors and office files. I had little control of movements. There was nothing I controlled—nothing. Yet, I had to find a way. I had to be more than a spectator, more than an onlooker. Nothing was more important. Perhaps this is why I was back—why I never left.

Doc told me I was only a witness, a bystander—no killing. I had to prove him wrong.

Somewhere, sometime in the future, someone was going to take my Angel.

NINETEEN

"No."

"No?" I opened my eyes to Doc Gilley. He was standing behind my recliner where Hercule sat enjoying a petting. "'No' what?"

He frowned, raising his eyebrows like the answer was too obvious. "I know what you're thinking, Oliver. You can't change it. You can't stop it. It'll be whatever it will be."

"You know where I've been? What I saw?"

"Yes."

"Then tell me. Where is Angel going to be attacked? Who takes her? Tell me when."

He shook his head. "Slow down. I don't know. I know what you know—perhaps a bit more. What's important is that you were there for a reason—and it's not to change things. Didn't you ever see that flick? You can't change events."

"Bullshit." I sat behind my desk and studied the ceiling for answers. They were hiding elsewhere. "I also saw the movie from the forties about ghosts solving crimes. Don't give me that crap about changing time. Nothing makes sense; my being here makes no sense."

"It will."

"Tell me what to do, Doc. Please."

"No. I couldn't even if I knew. All I do know is that you cannot change what happened."

I caught that. "What happened? It already happened? How? I just saw Angel this morning."

"No, no." Doc came to the front of the desk. His lips tightened and he looked down, gathering his thoughts. When his eyes rose to mine, his face was sad and dark. "It hasn't happened yet. You saw it for a reason. Find the reason."

Oh, Christ—riddles. "What for?"

"You saw it like a movie, right?"

I nodded.

"Then watch the movie. Play your role."

Huh? Oh, yeah. "Right. Be a detective and investigate."

"Yes, but don't trust your eyes. Use your gut. Question everything—everyone."

"Right. Everyone's a suspect."

"Everyone should be."

TWENTY

ANGEL'S ABDUCTION CHURNED TERROR inside me. Doc's insistence that I couldn't change things was damning. I had but one thought on that—*bullshit*. I had to try. And I could think of one way—Jeremiah Dempsey.

When I was a young deputy a year out of the academy, I happened upon a fugitive outside of town during a routine traffic stop. It was purely accidental, mind you. He was sitting near the main post office when I rounded the corner heading his way. He tried hard—too hard—not to look at me. When he couldn't resist any longer, he squealed his tires pulling away. I pulled him over. Jeremiah Dempsey was wanted for murder in Pennsylvania— four murders and suspected in six others. Two homicides were the Pennsylvania State cops who last tried to apprehend him. Jeremiah Dempsey vowed not to be taken without a fight and he'd already left a trail of bodies to prove it. My shotgun sticking in his left ear convinced him to fight another day. The newspapers said

I'd saved lives by capturing him. No one knew how many more he would have murdered had I not stopped him.

A serial killer only stops by capture or kill. Jeremiah wanted the latter.

I had to stop the killer before he could strike. Whoever killed me was now after Angel. Maybe she saw more than she knows that night. Perhaps she knew something beforehand. Perhaps the killer wants to be sure.

Jeremiah Dempsey was the answer.

Four people could help me. First of course, was Angel, who I'd have to try to keep away from dark, rainy parking lots. And there was Bear, who was technically off my case and who these days had checkmarks in both the plus and minus columns. I could shadow Bear anytime and Angel would be even easier, so they'd be last. No, I'd start with the last two, Spence and Clemens. They were assigned my case and might trip over clues. It would be an accident, of course, but I'll take any help I can get.

I found them sitting in the corporate offices of the Bartalotta Industrial Storage Corporation. They were smarter than I thought. While they were supposed to be investigating *my* murder, they were here investigating Raymundo Salazar's. Even those two can add one and one and get two. I guess they figured the best motive for my murder was my connection to Salazar's. Two cases, twice as many clues. All they needed was a suspect.

So far, there was none.

The Bartalotta Industrial Storage Corporation, or BISCORP, was the last place Raymundo Salazar was seen alive. He worked as a security guard on the three-to-twelve shift. An hour after he left work one night, his body was found beside his car along the country road heading back to Winchester. As previously noted, there were no leads, no witnesses, and no motive.

Just like my case.

Oh, I should mention that BISCORP is owned by one Nicholas Bartalotta—my old pal Poor Nic.

The facility was a huge tract of warehouses twenty miles southeast of Winchester. There were five main warehouses and a smaller, two-story corporate office building. A well-guarded, fifteen-foot chain link fence surrounded the premises. From a distance, it was often confused with a prison or jail. Of course, considering my feelings about Poor Nicholas Bartalotta, that was a reasonable conclusion.

Clemens was sitting opposite a short, stocky man in a dark, pin-striped suit, Kirk Wallchak, Poor Nic's operations manager. Spence was roaming around Kirk's office pawing every knickknack and photograph like a kid in a toy store.

To my disappointment, I arrived too late to catch the opening salvo of questions. They must have been good ones, too. Wallchak didn't look happy and was letting Clemens have it.

"Look, fellas, no offense, 'cause we want to cooperate," Wallchak said.

"Then cooperate." Spence's voice was testy and he wasn't trying to hide it. "Now."

Wallchak shook his head. "We already gave statements to the other two cops."

"Braddock and Tucker." Clemens wasn't asking. "We know."

Spence tossed an autographed baseball to Wallchak from a collection on a wall rack. "We're just following up. Can we see your boss?"

"He's out. And he said no more information without a warrant."

Wallchak's desk phone rang and he picked it up. The voice was loud, but I couldn't make out any words. Whoever it was, was chewing Wallchak's butt. Wallchak hung up and threw a thumb at the door.

"Sorry, interview's over. No warrant, no cooperation. You gotta go, I have a meeting."

Clemens shot a glance over his shoulder to Spence who was playing with a model airplane he had taken off the bookcase. Spence dropped it back onto the shelf, fumbled with it, and broke off the propeller trying to right it on its stand.

Spence ignored the crash landing. "Okay, Kirk, have it your way. Be seeing you with a warrant." The two detectives didn't wait for a reply and meandered out of Wallchak's office.

I stayed put.

Wallchak waited a minute before escaping to the corner office down the hall. I, of course, was in tow. We entered without knocking past the brass plate that read, "Chief Executive Officer, Nicholas Bartalotta."

Kirk Wallchak was a liar.

Nic was sitting behind a large antique desk, not quite as grandiose as the one at his home, but impressive. He looked up with a stern, unamused tightness in his face. "They gone?"

"Yeah. They wanted to rehash the entire murder."

"Which one?"

Now, that was an odd question. "How many are you involved with, Nic?"

Wallchak paused, then said, "Salazar's of course."

Nic shook his head. "Christ, anything new? What have they come up with?"

"Nothing, I guess. They don't know about Iggi Suarez, though. They never even asked about him."

"Good. But you make sure they don't. "

Wallchak nodded. "The boys won't say nothing."

"Keep it that way. All we need now is for somebody to find out about Salazar's moonlighting."

"They won't from us, Boss. Count on it."

Poor Nic turned in his plush leather chair and gazed out his window for a long time. Without turning back to Wallchak, he said, "Is there anyone else who might talk?"

"Well, I dunno," Wallchak muttered. "Maybe Sarah. But I think she knows better."

"Yes, yes, Sarah. You make sure the other boys are loyal. Leave Sarah to me."

Kirk Wallchak knew when to exit stage left. When he closed the door behind him, I slipped into a cozy chair opposite Poor Nic and put my feet up onto his desk.

"So, Nicky, who's Iggi Suarez and what's this about Salazar moonlighting? You never told me about that when I was alive."

Poor Nic sat staring out the window. He sighed and looked thoughtful, as if he was contemplating Plato or a new bank heist.

"And what are you going to do with Sarah Salazar? I'll be watching, pal. You be nice to her."

He ignored me. "Stupid bastards have no idea what's going on. None at all."

⚭

Downstairs outside in front of the entrance, Spence stopped and retreated two steps. His face went pale and he looked like he was having a heart attack. "Ah, shit."

I stopped beside him and looked out. Yup, he was having a heart attack.

Bear Braddock sat on the hood of his car. He did not look happy. When Bear didn't look happy, the world around him got unhappy.

We made it two steps from the car before Bear lurched forward. He landed a right hook into Spence's face that sent him crashing to the ground. To his credit, he didn't make any overtures to stand up or be a hero. He lay there, stunned and dazed.

Bear stood over him. "You son of a bitch. Carmen Delgado called me. What the hell do you think you're doing going after Angel like that?"

"Easy, Bear." Clemens started forward, but Bear's stare stopped him. "Easy, man. Let him explain."

I said to Bear, "Carmen's hiding something, pal. Even Spence knows that."

"So," Bear hesitated and bit his lip—his eyes seemed unsure of his words. "Carmen said … she said…"

Clemens looked from Bear to Spence and back. "What's with you, Bear? You okay?"

"Yes, shut up." Bear settled his thoughts. The buzzing in his head must have stopped. "You told the captain that Carmen said we were screwin' around?"

"Yeah, so?" Spence was defiant but he stayed down. "She did, Bear. Really. She brought it up."

"Hey, go easy, man," Clemens said. "Let him up. This ain't the place for this."

Spence rose to one knee. "Look, we have to chase every lead. You know that. Affairs are the leading cause of murder. We were asking questions. No harm, no foul."

"Bullshit," Bear said. "That's not the way Carmen sees it."

"I'll fix this," Clemens said, stepping between them. "We got a little overzealous. I'll straighten the captain—promise."

"We're trying to find a murderer." Spence stood up, eyeing Bear for any sign of attack. "We're on the same side, man. Relax."

"Are we?" Bear poked a finger at him. "I'm not so sure what side I'm on."

TWENTY-ONE

NAVIGATING WHEN YOU'RE DEAD is like watching television. If you don't like the show, change the channel. It was, to my annoyance, also like watching without a television guide. I had to switch from place to place until I found what I wanted.

It took me three tries to find Angel—home, the university, and finally Kelly Orchard Farms. That's where I found her.

Kelly's Dig was located a half-mile deep in the farm's original apple orchard. About a third of the orchard was cleared. The remainder of the farm was still lined with rows of overgrown trees that hovered over the hills like ranks of weary soldiers ready for battle; in a few short weeks, many of them would be slain. The actual dig site was in a small clearing made by bulldozed apple trees and brush plowed into a two-story debris pile behind the main site. At the rear of the clearing was a pile of stones and earth that was once an old barn's foundation—this was ground zero.

All this was surrounded by two bulldozers, a backhoe, and two large road graders—the idle reminders of the battle between history and development.

A sleepy security guard lounged in a lawn chair in front of a portable construction trailer that sat at the far end of the site. He sat sipping coffee while he watched Angel at a worktable in front of the trailer. She was examining a pile of stones and dirt, which she photographed with a small digital camera. André Cartier hovered over her taking notes.

"I appreciate you coming today, André," Angel said.

"Of course. Ernie told me about what happened at his house yesterday morning. Perhaps if I'd stayed a little longer, I would have seen something."

"I don't know, André. Yesterday, I was positive about the intruder. Today, I'm not sure it ever happened—no one is. I don't want to talk about it. It's over."

André studied her for a long time. "I understand—completely. You have so much on your plate. Have you made the arrangements?"

The arrangements would be for me.

Her eyes dropped. "Yes, two days from now. Just a small service. The department is upset—they want a full ceremony with the police honor guard and the like."

"Of course they do, Angela." André looked solemn. "But it's your decision. Just family?"

"Yes, just."

"And Detective Braddock?"

Angel stopped taking photographs and looked over the camera at him. "Of course. Why?"

"I don't care for the way he's hovering over you." André was not a historian just now, but a surrogate father. "He was only Tuck's partner, for heaven's sake. He's overstepping himself."

"Nonsense, André. They were more than partners. Bear's been family for years—to both of us."

When André frowned, she changed the subject. "I'm going to finish logging these samples. Then, I want to excavate some more."

"Yes, of course." André took the hint. "I'm sorry, Angela."

"We need to find much more of the skeletons to determine if this were a gravesite or not. So far, with the few skeletal pieces we've found, an argument could be made they are mere fragments from a battle and not an intentional interment at all."

"If there are more bones, we'll find them."

Angel pointed to a stack of books and folded documents on the end of the table. "There's an 1860s land map with property recordings in there. I found it in the town archives. It shows a structure—probably this old barn—on this site. That's the foundation Tyler's equipment dug up."

"What are you thinking?"

She stood up and stretched. "Well, I suppose it could be an unmarked family cemetery, but I doubt it. Both the Confederate and Union armies used the main house as a headquarters at different times."

"Perhaps," André said, picking up the papers, "the old barn was a field hospital."

"Yes, that could explain the remains. The surgeries were very brutal, as you know. They could have discarded amputations or other remains in makeshift graves. When the bulldozers unearthed the stone foundation, they might have uncovered those. Burials could be haphazard and unrecorded after the battles."

André nodded. "We should have a team sift the debris pile. Byrd's men were using a backhoe when they found the bones. They could have plowed up the remaining skeletons into the pile. I'll work the debris pile if you want to keep working the foundation here."

"Good idea." Angel descended into the big pit beneath the old barn's crumbled foundation. There were a few piles of hand-honed timbers on one side and the remnants of the stone foundation on the other. The entire site was only perhaps thirty feet across and about twelve feet deep.

This was the heart of Kelly's Dig.

I stood on the edge and looked around. A breeze blew through the tall grass and nearby trees, rustling what few fall leaves were left. The air smelled of turned earth and that musky, autumn smell I've loved since childhood. The breeze, the scent, and the sound of the trees were magical. Closing my eyes, I took it all in.

I'd been here before.

No, not chasing Civil War skeletons or battlefield historical markers—but watching two dark-skinned men digging in the night. Digging in my foyer. Digging here.

My vision.

If it were here where those men were sweating in the lamp-light, what did it mean? When had it happened? Was it recent? The future? Perhaps years or decades ago? Had it been them who buried soldiers after some horrific battle?

No answers fluttered to me. I sat on the edge of the pit watching André and Angel work.

Thirty minutes later, Angel's excavation stopped.

"André, I've found something."

He joined her in the pit. "What?"

"Here, at the corner of the stones." She chipped away at the base of the foundation ten feet below the lip of the pit. "The foundation goes down deep here. This must have been a root cellar beneath the barn. Byrd's people broke through the corner stones and collapsed the walls. There was definitely something down there."

The foundation stones ended in a crude pattern, covered in clay. There was a two-foot hole dug into the corner of the stones, probably by a backhoe, and a few of the stones were missing. Angel had dug deep into the soil on the fringes of the hole and more of the stones were now falling away. The foundation's corner was fully exposed.

"Look, " she said, pointing her trowel. "Looks like bone."

André knelt down and brushed the loose dirt away from the stones. A dull, dirt-crusted, grayish saucer, perhaps six inches in diameter, protruded out of the ground.

"Well now," he said. "This looks like a partial parietal bone. It's in remarkable shape, too."

"This piece was inside the old foundation, I think." Angel picked up her camera and took several photographs. "I cannot imagine someone being accidentally interred this way."

"The heavy equipment could have moved all this around." André stood up. "We might need ground-radar equipment. That'll show us if there are actually more bone or graves here. It's going to take a lot of time."

"And cost a lot of money." Angel frowned. "A *lot* of money. Tyler won't be very happy."

"No, least of all with us."

TWENTY-TWO

WHILE ANGEL AND ANDRÉ worked Kelly's Dig, I spent the rest of the day mulling Angel's abduction. My premonition in that dark parking lot, somewhere in her future, terrified me. If there was any good news, it was that I had not seen her death, or witnessed worse. Worse, I say, because now that I've experienced the "after" side of death, it's not being dead that is troubling—it's how you get that way. My demise was just a blur of movement, a flash of light. It was over in an instant. What may lay ahead for Angel might be far more horrifying.

If only I could reach her. If only I could warn her or Bear. My faded voice on Bear's cell phone ignited an argument between them that ended in a draw. Angel chose hope, Bear denial. I wasn't even sure which Angel embraced the most. Bear was a lost cause, but there might be a way to reach her.

If only I could find it.

It was nearly dark before Angel drove home and went to shower off the dust and grime from Kelly's Dig. She changed into a business suit and put on some expensive perfume. Twenty minutes later, we were driving toward the far side of town with her briefcase between us. I'd used the "being there" trick that Doc taught me and popped into the passenger's seat for the ride.

"Ah, Angel? Where are we going?"

A smile cracked the corners of her mouth. I asked again and just when I thought she might answer, her cell phone rang. "Hello? Oh, hello, Ernie."

He was giving her an ear full. She interrupted him, saying, "Yes, André and I photographed and documented the skull bone. The judge will have to keep the injunction in place for at least a couple more months. That should please you, Ernie."

More ire from him.

She frowned. "It'll take longer, but yes, we'll do the excavation ourselves. We'll find every skeletal fragment we can. I promise." That seemed to calm the old coot down and Angel's smile confirmed that. "I'm pulling into the parking lot now. See you inside."

Oh, hell no.

As Angel turned into the Northern Shenandoah Valley High School parking lot, a searing ice pick penetrated me. The lot was filling but she was able to park two rows from the front on the far end. It was a large campus with a grand, three-story, brick and stone main collegiate building that joined three other structures around a quad. The campus was rich with oaks and evergreens that enveloped the grounds—particularly the parking areas—and gave the campus ivy-league charm. That charm was gone now, shrouded by a veil of dread and hopelessness.

I couldn't move. I couldn't focus. I couldn't stop her.

Angel climbed from the Explorer and joined a group of people walking toward the quad. In a moment, she disappeared in a gathering of others and was gone.

Dear God, not tonight. Not here. I wasn't ready. I had no plan.

The school's marquee announced the Frederick County Board of Supervisors meeting. A special town meeting to discuss the impact of Kelly's Dig on the new highway bypass. Anyone and everyone with the tiniest bit of interest in the project were expected to be here. Ernie, André Cartier, Tyler Byrd, and of course, Angel.

It was all here. The parking lot. The premonition. Angel. Only one thing was missing and I prayed it stay away. It did not. The darkness turned desperate and the clouds chilled me.

Then, it started to rain.

TWENTY-THREE

ANGEL HAD BEEN INSIDE more than two hours and most of the other people attending the meeting were gone now. Only a few cars remained. While she was inside, I stood vigil over her car and watched, hoping I was wrong. At the front of the quad, I searched the trees and bushes for any sign of danger. Everyone who passed by was a potential stalker—anyone walking instead of running through the rain was him—but none were. Maybe I was wrong.

No.

He was there. I saw him just beyond the rim of wet, tense darkness—waiting. No, that was wrong, too. I felt him. Danger and lethality simmered somewhere ahead, just beyond recognition. Through the dark, there was the tenseness of waiting, ebbing patience, and anxiety.

He was waiting for Angel.

A dark panel van sat in the center of the lot, three rows behind Angel's Explorer. I couldn't see inside but knew a man was there.

I felt the intensity of his focus. How I felt the connection, I don't know—but it was unmistakable. The image of a tall, powerful man filled me. His raw, uninhibited menace stabbed at me like hot, burning pokers. His image fit my premonition. Perhaps he was the same man who shot at Angel. There was no evidence of that, but there could be no other explanation. Who else would do her harm?

A twinge of angst struck me and I felt anticipation. Was it his or mine?

Through the quad's darkness, I heard a door shut. Angel emerged from the main school building and walked alone into the parking lot. I ran to her, staying just a few steps ahead. Fear made me stay between her and the van; reason said I could do nothing to save her.

"Angel, you have to go back inside. Please, go back inside."

I focused all my thoughts on her—trying to will my words into her conscious but couldn't penetrate the veil between our worlds. "He's here, in that van. You have to go back."

She slowed her pace and dug inside her bag. As she moved, her head pivoted around, searching the parking lot. Something startled her. Her pace quickened as her hunt for keys became frantic. I urged her to move faster—prodding her, pleading with her. I didn't know if my words were reaching her, but she was responding, feeling the danger, seeking safety.

"Angel, get into the Explorer. Go. Run!"

She strained to see into the darkness as the van's engine started. It was moving; now two rows away, rolling forward. She groped deeper into her purse and grasped her keys. Her pace was near a run.

"Go. Get out of here."

She kept an eye on the van and she hastened her steps as the danger prodded her on. We reached the Explorer and she triggered the electric lock. "Tuck, why aren't you here?"

"I am. I'll get you out of here. Hurry."

The van was on us. Its lights were on high and bore down on Angel. She sprang into the Explorer and started the engine. I waited outside urging her to safety. The engine roared but before she could pull away, the van stopped perpendicular to her door. He flashed his lights. The high beams blinded her and she froze, staring into them, uncertain of what to do.

The man slid from the van and took two steps, stopping outside the cone of Angel's headlights and behind his own. He wore a long overcoat with its hood drawn over his head. He pointed toward her front wheel and patted the air. The rain and his hood shielded his face.

He pointed at her front tire and motioned for her to cut the engine.

Her tire was flat—flat to the rim.

Angel tried to roll the Explorer back away from his van. It resisted and its sluggish steering fought her until she heeded. She yanked the shift back into park and grabbed her cell phone from the console. With an unsteady finger, she stabbed speed dial 2.

"Please, Bear. Answer ..."

He didn't.

"Angel, stay in the truck. Try to ..."

The man went to her door and pulled his hood tighter around his head. When he stepped closer to the Explorer, I saw his face—or what should have been his face. It was veiled behind the dark material of a balaclava.

"No, you bastard, no."

"Leave me alone." Angel shook her head, her eyes unable to hide the panic. She looked around. There was no one to come to her rescue. She dialed Bear again, cursed, and punched redial. Voice-mail.

Before she could redial, the assault began.

The hooded man's hand lashed out in a vicious arc and smashed her window with the butt of a knife.

Angel jolted. Her cell phone tumbled out the shattered window onto the ground. She tried escaping across the seats, clawing for the passenger door handle to pull herself free. She fumbled for the door lock and handle. Terror blunted her success.

She screamed.

"Jesus, no," I yelled as the hooded man grabbed her hair and hauled her back behind the wheel. He grappled through the window, fought for control, and twisted her head backward. His strength was overpowering.

With little hope, I tried to intervene. I swung at him, tried pulling his hands from her. My fists found no bone, my grip found no flesh. I swung again and again—cursing and yelling at my own impotence. I was watching my wife's death and was helpless to do more than cry.

"No, you bastard, no!"

He wrestled through her flailing arms, twisted her hair, and slammed her backward. His silent, focused assault was deafening. And what was most precarious was his foray, which came not from trepidation or any spontaneous rush, but from an obvious familiarity with violence.

"No." I felt it. The rage began careening inside me. Singeing heat surged into me in a rush of angst and rage. Exhilaration shuttered me as sparks ignited inside and the power flashed.

"No, let me go." Angel thrashed and tried to claw his hands loose. "Please … no …"

He cursed and pulled her into the window. Twice, he struck at her but didn't land a solid blow. He struck her again. This time he connected with her temple. She went limp. He reached inside and tore the ignition keys free.

"No." The energy in me burst into rage. "You bastard."

I grabbed him by his throat and whipped him backward. His body spun and I propelled him to the ground. He crumbled four feet from the Explorer and Angel's ignition keys dropped to the pavement. "Angel, the keys—get the keys."

The hooded man froze. He lay on his back, staring at the Explorer. He looked around, unsure of who attacked him.

The shock didn't last. He recovered faster than I expected. Angel lurched from the Explorer, hunting her keys. He sprang up and grabbed her. He took hold of her arm and stopped her in mid-stride like a marionette on a string. He shoved her backward and pinned her arms to her sides. He kneed her in a violent strike. She coughed and cried out.

She was done.

"No." I kicked hard into the back of his knee but there was little impact. His head spun around, but he was unfazed. I kicked at his knee again. Nothing. Something was wrong.

Jesus, no. I was draining, losing focus...losing the surge of energy...losing.

The hooded man hammered her against the Explorer and she coughed again. He tightened his grip on her hair and shook her. He spun her around and wrapped his knife-hand around her neck.

The blade pressed her cheek. She stiffened. "Please, no..."

I tried to grab him but couldn't find a hold. Then, I saw my chance. Angel's cell phone lay at my feet, open. The screen was bright and alive with power—I grabbed it. My fingers tingled and the energy gushed into me. I grew stronger and stronger as my anger boiled and sought an outlet.

"Angel, drive yourself against him. He'll loosen his grip. Then smash his balls. Now, Angel, now!"

Time froze.

She stared—stared right at me. Her eyes exploded and her mouth went agape. It wasn't her attacker's knife she saw; it was me. "Tuck? Help me."

The hooded man twisted her sideways and pinned her again. She cried out for me again and his head spun around. His eyes found me and he gasped; surprise loosened his grip.

"Angel, now."

She growled a war cry and thrust her body against him. Her legs went limp and she dropped her weight against him. As his grasp loosened, she slipped down, momentarily free. She dropped to one knee, pivoted, and hammered her fist into his groin—once, twice.

He howled and released her.

She twisted free and sprang up. She kicked him hard in the groin.

He exploded with a guttural slur of pain and surprise. He sank to his knees and clutched his crotch. The knife clattered to the pavement. His eyes never left mine—they remained fixed on me—uncertain and terrified.

Angel screamed, "Help me."

I swung as hard as I could and drove the cell phone into the hooded man's face. The phone crushed into pieces and blood erupted through the ski mask from his face and nose. As I reared back for another strike, the surge faltered. The phone's screen dimmed and with it, my strength. The blow struck and I felt flesh, but it was weak and without steel.

"Go, Angel. Drive as fast as you can. Forget the tire—drive."

She leapt into the Explorer, fumbled with the keys, but started the engine. The Explorer lurched forward and she floored the gas. The steering fought back, but she forced the vehicle to obey and lumbered from the lot.

She never looked back.

"Oh my God, was that really you? Tuck, please?"

I sat beside her in the front seat. I was drained and fading. My entire body was numb as my strength ebbed away. There was a hole in my being and the energy was oozing out. A moment ago, I'd struck down her attacker. Now, I was spent—slipping away in a steady, murky stream.

"Drive Angel, drive. Go somewhere safe—a gas station, a store...anywhere with people. Call Bear."

She had a death grip on the steering wheel and her foot hard on the accelerator. Crying and near hysteria, she shot glances at me as she strained to control the injured vehicle. Her face was ashen and she trembled in jerky, uncontrolled spasms.

"Tuck...if you're really here. Stay...I need you."

She wanted desperately to believe.

For a few brief moments, we bonded. It seemed so simple now. Emotions allowed it—love and terror—with some help from Ben Franklin's kite. That's how I reached her. When her heart was breaking or when danger was close, somehow, she found me. Death and life are separated by so many plains and so much unknown. Yes, it was love and terror—the strongest emotions—that bridge the two worlds and somehow let us bond again. Even for just a brief tryst.

This time, though, it had been enough. Just enough.

Darkness was swallowing me and yet there was no darkness. There was nothing. "I love you, Angel. You're safe now."

"Was it really you? I'm not sure—I just don't know. Tuck?" She crushed the brake pedal and the Explorer lurched to a stop. "No, come back, it's all my fault!"

TWENTY-FOUR

"I told you to lighten up, Oliver."

Doc Gilley was somewhere nearby. I couldn't see him—I couldn't see anything. Emptiness enveloped me. I felt suspended in darkness without footing and without frame of reference.

"Focus, dumbass. Focus on me and it'll pass."

I did and it passed. As I concentrated on his voice, the darkness shifted, and the light ebbed toward me like the dawn. When the blackness evaporated, I was back in my den. This time, I was flat on my face in the center of my expensive Persian rug. I felt sick like I had the flu. The room was teetering and disorientation welled inside me.

I sat upright and the greasy ball in my stomach eased. "Doc? Did you call me a dumbass?"

Doc Gilley was standing behind my desk. He smirked and folded his arms in that classic "I told you so" pose. A lecture was coming.

"Stand up, you're embarrassing."

With effort, I rose to my feet and fell back into the leather recliner normally occupied by Hercule—who, I might add, was nowhere around. I felt winded, frail, and if it were possible, starved. My limbs were rubbery as though I'd just risen for the first time after weeks in a sickbed.

"Doc, what happened?"

"You pushed too far, too fast. You weren't ready for that stunt with Angela and it cost you."

It cost me? "What does that mean?" My head ached—well, at least I think it did. If I were alive, this would be the worst hangover in my life and I'd be wishing I were dead. Funny how that works now.

"You never listen." Doc didn't feel much pity for me. "You drained yourself almost dry. Don't ask me what would have happened then. It never happened to me. I'm smarter than that. You've been gone for two days. I just now..."

"Two days?"

"Well, two days for Angel." He frowned. "She's been pining over you. You made a mess of things. You stirred her up and now she's lost and confused—more than before. Dumbass, I told you not to do things like that."

Dumbass? Was it proper spirit etiquette to call me names?

"Come on, Doc. Quit griping. I saved her life."

"I'm not sure." He sighed and looked at me like a teacher scolding a student. "You bonded with her and that's okay. It doesn't work that way every time. Bonding is one thing; contact is different. In

138

fact, it's downright unheard of. You were Angela's love and those emotions allowed you to intercede in the parking lot."

I remembered. "Doc, I hit the guy. I actually hit him. You said ..."

"Dammit, Oliver, putting words in her head is different than appearing—or fighting. You can't do that."

"Can't or shouldn't?"

"Both. You're lucky I got to you when I did. If you don't go a little slower, I can't be responsible. If you go too far, I may not be able to bring you back."

"From where?"

"Hell only knows. No pun intended."

I shrugged. "Two days? What'd I miss?"

"Your funeral. It was quite nice, too."

"What?" I noticed his smug expression. "I missed my own funeral?"

"Yes." He waved in the air. "Just a small affair, mind you. Very tasteful. It's best you missed it. She looked rather ... *content*."

"Content? Oh, sure, because she knows I'm still around."

"If you say so."

I got serious. "Doc, is Angel all right?"

"She's fine—for now. Oliver, you're dead. Your senses are gone. You have to stop fighting that."

"Yeah, yeah. I remember—no concentrating, no thinking. Be there and all that."

"Then do it." He folded his arms and lost clarity. "And stop screwing around."

"Doc, the last thing I heard was Angel say, 'It's all my fault.' What did she mean?"

For a moment, he started to fade, but it wasn't his leaving that unnerved me, it is what he said next.

"I'm so sorry. I really am."

"For what?"

"You made a mistake, Oliver." His voice was hushed and sad. "You misunderstood your premonition. It's already too late."

TWENTY-FIVE

Doc's voice faded and he was gone.

So was I.

I stood up from the recliner and walked toward voices in my foyer. But, once again, it wasn't my foyer anymore. It was a strange dining room with a small, round table in the center. The voices were coming from another room. I walked through a kitchen and an adjacent breakfast nook, then into a large living room. The apartment didn't look familiar, but the eerie déjà vu throbbed in my head.

Bear was standing across the living room with an arm wrapped around Angel. She was flushed and upset. "Oh, my God, not again. When will this stop? Poor Carmen."

Not again? This was Carmen Delgado's home. No, oh no.

Captain Sutter stood beside Bear speaking on her cell phone. Amid hushed comments, she looked up and barked orders at Clemens; his sidekick was nowhere to be seen.

"All right, Bear," she said. "From the top."

"Damn, Cap, again?"

Her frown made the question moot. He began, "Been here a couple times since yesterday and came back an hour ago. No answer again. It's been two days and no one's been home, so I thought I'd better check. The office manager let me in. I found this place like this—torn up. She was in the back room and I called for backup. No signs of forced entry. Just all this."

"All this" was a war zone. The hall closet door was open and its contents strewn on the floor. Bookshelves were emptied onto the living room floor. The contents from end table drawers were littered everywhere. The kitchen was the same. Someone was looking for something they wanted very, very bad.

"And you saw nothing all the times you came by?" Captain Sutter knew the answer. It was obvious she'd gone through Bear's report before. "Think. Anything at all?"

"Nothing."

"Think."

"That's it." Bear waved his hand around the room. "You have all I got from the neighborhood canvass. No one saw shit. Same as always."

"Yeah they did." Spence strode past a uniformed deputy at the front door waving his notepad. He was still writing, and when he looked at Bear, he grinned. "You forget something?"

I hated that grin. It always came with an overdose of irritation.

"What?" Captain Sutter demanded. "Fast."

"Bear's a real celebrity, Captain." Spence flipped his notebook closed. "Two of the neighbors saw him coming in and out—a lot—

over the past few weeks. At least three times in the last two days. Earlier today, around three, he came back. Mrs. Shannon, who lives across the parking lot, got a good look at him. She saw him sitting in his car two nights ago, too. She was about to call 911 when he left."

"So?" Bear stepped toward Spence. "Just what the hell are you saying, Spence? I already went over this."

"You left out the part about visiting so much. Several times, and not just yesterday and today."

Bear reared up. "Go to hell—that was personal. She's missed work and Angel asked me to check on her. I did. What of it?"

Captain Sutter turned to Angel. "How long was Carmen out of work?"

"Two days," she said. "I called her but she never returned my calls. When she didn't come to Tuck's service, I asked Bear to check."

Spence cocked his head. "If you were so worried, why didn't you call the police?"

"I did. I called Bear." Tears welled in Angel's eyes.

"Sure, right, okay." Captain Sutter threw a look at Spence that said, 'shut up.' She nodded to Angel. "We have to check everything. Too many incidents like this lately and they're all centered on you."

Angel flushed. "I know that. That's why I asked Bear to check on her. That's why he was here."

"Sure, sure." Spence sealed his fate. "Unless he already knew she…"

"Bastard." Bear's powerful hand snatched Spence by the shirt, and dragged him close. "I'm getting real tired of your bullshit, Spence."

"Enough," Captain Sutter said, then waited until Bear shoved Spence back two steps. "Spence, take Clemens and finish the canvass. Check for any security cameras in the neighborhood." She turned to Bear. "You need to explain the missing details."

"I can. But later, okay, Cap?"

"My office." She frowned as her cell phone buzzed. "Sutter. Yeah, right. Good—no great … okay. Put a uniform on her door and don't let her out of sight." She flipped her phone closed.

"Is that about her?" Angel asked. "Is she …"

"She's awake—concussion and some broken ribs. She's dehydrated from being tied up for two days. She'll be okay, but she's pretty shaken up and doesn't remember anything."

"Thank God." Bear touched Angel's shoulder. "She's lucky. Whoever did this must have been scared off before he could finish her."

"I'm not sure about that," Captain Sutter said. She threw a chin toward a pile of china and books in the middle of the room. "He had plenty of time to do whatever he wanted—kill her or worse. He knocked her out and tied her up instead of outright killing her. No, I think he came here for something else."

Angel asked, "Do you think she saw him?"

"Fortunately no," Captain Sutter answered, "or she'd be dead. Unfortunate for us, though."

"Leaving her alive was a hell of a chance." Bear walked to the back patio doors and brushed the blinds open. "He had to be sure she didn't see him. Or, maybe I scared him away by banging on the door. I've done that a half-dozen times in the past two days."

"I think he was here," Sutter said, "waiting for her when she got home."

I leaned close and whispered to Angel.

"Oh my God, no," Angel whispered as her face contorted. Her words didn't escape notice. All the eyes fell on her. "I mean, oh my God, maybe she was taken from campus. That would make sense, right? The night it rained?"

"Why do you say that?" Sutter asked. "That's the same night you were attacked."

"I spoke with her that afternoon. That's the last time I heard from her."

Bear glanced at her. When their eyes met, he cocked his head. "Angela, are you okay? I know a lot has happened, but …"

"I'm fine. Really." She held up her hands and closed her eyes. She did that when she was flustered and confused. "I'm just, you know … never mind."

Angel was in denial and I guess I didn't blame her. As much as we'd bonded in the rain that night, she was still unsure and confused. Doc said I'd been gone two days since her attack. During my absence, someone tried to kill Carmen Delgado. I guess now wasn't the time to try to convince Angel I was truly back. As hard as it was, I stayed quiet and listened.

Bear waited while Angel composed herself; when she looked up at him with a forced smile, he said, "It does make sense, Cap. The last time anyone saw her was at work that night, late. Her car is out front here, and no one has seen her around. I'll have someone check the campus security tapes."

"Run everything—and I mean everything." Sutter regarded Angel with a hint of doubt in her eyes before lifting her phone again. "I'll have the uniforms start tracing her movements all week." She nodded to Angel. "And we'll start at the university."

A uniformed deputy emerged from the rear of the apartment. He handed Captain Sutter a large, clear plastic evidence bag. Inside was a folded, tan bundle. "Here you go, Cap. Her raincoat all bagged and tagged. Might have some trace."

I knew the coat on sight—it haunted me from my vision. Doc was right all along. I hadn't witnessed what I thought that night. I didn't understand. I got it wrong—all wrong.

Angel closed her eyes. "Oh, no."

"She was wearing this." The deputy threw a thumb toward the rear bedroom. "Paramedics cut it off to work on her. I bagged it right away."

"Thanks, Don." Captain Sutter handed it back to him. "Get this to the lab ASAP."

"That's my coat," Angel whispered, the words catching in her throat. "She sometimes uses it if she forgets hers. It's always hanging in my office."

"She was wearing your coat?" Bear asked. "From campus?"

Angel nodded.

All eyes fell on her again and she looked away. The same question formed in everyone's mind, but no one dared ask it. No one had to.

Was Carmen Delgado the real target or was Angel?

TWENTY-SIX

THE DRIVE HOME WAS solemn and silent. Angel looked out the window and Bear focused on the road. I stayed quiet in the back seat. Angel was distant, more than I'd seen in a very long time. She was worried about Carmen, of course. When Bear dropped her off at our front door and offered to make dinner, she just shook her head and bolted from the car.

She didn't even wave back to him.

Hercule was watching out my den's bay window and that signaled all was fine inside. No monsters roamed. No killers waited. If Hercule was happy, all was safe.

The uniformed patrol sitting curbside helped, too.

As soon as the front door closed, Angel dropped to her knees in the foyer and burst into tears. Her body quaked as the tension and horror, kept well hidden at Carmen Delgado's home, burst out. Since my murder, she's been shot at, attacked, and nearly abducted, and now Carmen lay broken but alive in a hospital bed. It was too much for her now.

Hercule moaned and leaned into her, offering his strong, warm body as comfort. His head went over her shoulder and she enveloped him in a tight, soothing hug. Her emotions drained over him. He moaned and rubbed his head against her, lapping at her face and erasing the sadness dampening it.

I cried, too. My tears were not fear or sorrow, but anger. So much was swirling around her, so many dangers, and so few answers. I was powerless to comfort her. I sat down on the stairs facing her. There was nothing for me to do. Nothing to say. No way to console her—no way for anything. I felt a nasty brew of rage and sadness starting to boil over, and its scent was revenge.

I wanted to reach out and tell her I was right beside her, but feared making things worse. Her worries might explode out of control if I lumped more onto them. Doubt—doubt about me— might push her over the edge. Just now, I had no idea how close she was to it.

Hercule looked over her shoulder at me. He always saw me, always heard me, and always knew my presence. His tail swayed as his big, dark eyes captured mine. He blinked several times and with each one, sadness ebbed out.

"Hercule, thank God for you. Take good care of her, boy. I can't." Woof.

Angel relaxed her embrace and Hercule lapped her face again. It took a while, but finally her laugh signaled her weeping was over. He ran into my den and retrieved his favorite ball. I'd learned a long time ago that playing ball was not for the dogs, but for us. It was therapeutic. They just let us think it was for them.

"No, boy," she said, rolling it back when he tossed it. "Not now. We'll play later."

He picked up the ball again, this time turning to me where I sat on the bottom stair. He was eye to eye with me as he gyrated. His friendly eyes sent me a message that I just couldn't receive.

"Herc, what on earth?" Angel sat on the hardwood and scratched his ears. "What are you doing, boy? What is it?"

He never broke focus on me and let out a low, even moan. Then he barked and flipped his ball onto the floor and rolled it to my feet. He looked at Angel, back to me, back to her, and moaned again.

I touched the ball, feeling the wet, slimy rubber tingle on my fingertips. Without thinking, I rolled it back to him. He caught it in his powerful mouth, flipped it back at me as he'd done so many times, and I returned it. The game continued.

We played ball.

"Oh, my God." Angel slid back across the floor and rose to her feet, watching the ball traversing between us—three times, four. "Tuck? Are you here? Tuck?"

Oh, crap, Doc was going to be pissed.

"Oh, Tuck." A smile erupted on her face. "God, I miss you."

Hercule picked up his ball and lay down. He tucked the ball between his paws, mission accomplished, and let out another low moan, pointing his nose at me.

"Babe, do you hear me?"

She turned and retreated to the door, grabbed the doorknob, and closed her eyes. Instead of running from the house, she turned back to Hercule. "Damn you, Herc. You had me going again."

I went to her. When I touched her hand, the sparks singed us both. Her eyes closed and her head drifted down against her chest. "Please … That night, in the rain … did I imagine that? Was it you? Did you rescue me? Am I insane?"

"Angel, it was me. Do you feel me? I'm right here—*try*." I kissed her cheek.

She lurched back and choked in air. "Oh, God. Is it real? Are you?"

Okay, so I'm thickheaded in life and in death. Doc Gilley warned me about pushing things, and the last time got me a two-day suspension. Nevertheless, a time-out is a good place to rest, too. So, I was fully charged and ready to rumble. What would happen if I screwed things up again? Would it kill me?

I touched her cheek. "Angel, it's me." I took her in my arms—moving in close. With every emotion, I willed myself into her. Then, from mortal habit more than any spirit wish, I kissed her on her lips. The familiar scents of bath oil and perfume sent a shiver through me, and for a second the lingering taste of tears wet my lips. Then, it happened—something I'd not felt before. Something pulled me, twisted my senses, and drew me out. Angel's eyes closed. She was willing herself to me—me to her—craving the union that we'd shared for years and that now eluded us. I felt her thoughts; felt her strength inside. She was calling me—inside—willing me to come to her. There was no lightning, no sparks; just a warm, simmering passion like our first time. I didn't know what it was, but a week ago, before leaving her grieving over my body, I called it love. Now, that love was seizing and consuming me.

I was no longer in control; she was.

My eyes closed and I felt her release me. The current of passion subsided, replaced by strange slivers of warmth that shimmered around us like the northern lights on a clear winter night.

Hercule jumped to his feet and wagged. He barked first at Angel, then at me. He pointed his muzzle and stared down his nose at me, raising his eyebrows—first the one, then the other. He barked and moaned, moaned and barked.

"Tuck?" Angel's voice shook me from my lethargy. She was staring at me. Right at me. "Tuck? Is that..."

"Angel. It's me."

"I... know." She stepped back and fixed her eyes on me. A hand lifted to touch my face but hovered in midair. "It *was* you the other night."

What? "Angel, can you hear me again?"

"Yes..." Her eyes cascaded tears. "And I see you."

Doc Gilley was going to be pissed for sure.

"Yes, it's me. I've been here all along."

She came to me. Her eyes were soft and alive, but her movements unsure and unsteady. Her hand reached for mine but found nothing. She pulled away. Then she reached for my face and again withdrew.

"Oh no, I've lost it." Her hands flew to her face.

"No." I touched her cheek and then her hand. I felt a spark as our feelings merged—the warmth like a fire's embers on a cold winter night. "It's real. Real as it can be."

Her face flushed and she retreated into the den, found the recliner, and collapsed into it. I followed and Hercule slipped into the chair with her. He licked her face, soothing her.

"Dammit, Tuck. It's all my fault. All of this. That night... what do you remember? Do you know who killed you? Do you know why?"

"No, no. I think that's why I'm here. Why I'm back." I knelt down beside my quivering wife and took her hand. I could feel her warmth but wasn't sure she could feel mine. "Okay, Angel. I hope you're ready for all this..."

"I don't know, Tuck. I'm afraid."

So was I. But who cares, because at that moment, we were together. I was as real to her as she was to me. Nothing else—including murder—mattered.

"I don't understand. Please, tell me what's going on. How are you here? Tell me what you know. Did you see anything? Are you back because of me? Is it my fault you're not... you know... somewhere else?"

Good questions, all.

"Slow down, Angel. It's like this..."

I took a breath and told her everything since taking a bullet in our foyer. I went through some things twice. Well, twenty times if you count the "me being dead" mantra. Angel tried to deny everything and twice left the den to check her sanity. Each time she returned. When I was through, she began sobbing and laughing at the same time.

"Damn you, Tuck. I always said I'd haunt you."

153

"Yeah," I said, swirling slow circles in my desk chair. "But that was to keep me from cheating on you."

"You're right."

"But I got here first."

"Tuck, neither of us ever believed in, in, well, *ghosts*. Why haven't you, like, you know…"

"Gone into the light?"

She nodded.

"There's no light—not yet. I don't know if there is one."

"Then you're staying?"

"I'm not sure. I think I'm here to find my killer."

"Does Bear hear you? See you? Have you been around us all the time?"

"Only you can see me and I have no idea why or for how long."

Hercule barked.

"I mean you and Herc. He was first."

Angel put a bear hug on him. "Just Hercule and me? Because we love you."

Doc was right and I understood. "I guess so. Sometimes, I think Bear can hear me. You know, inside. Not that he ever listened before."

"That night, with his cell phone. You warned me."

"Yes. Bear wasn't around. I knew you were in danger—it hit me right before the shots. Angel, there are some things I have to ask you. Don't get mad at me, but I have to know about…"

"Carmen was attacked. You told me it was at the campus."

"Yes, I did." Carmen was my fault. "I got it all wrong. I found your earrings at the sink. When I touched them, poof, I saw her attacked in the university parking lot. I thought it was you. The earrings—the raincoat..."

"Earrings?" Angel flushed. "Those were hers, not mine. She left them the other day. She borrowed my coat."

I felt foolish. "Yes, I know that now. About..."

"You saved me in the rain that night—saved me again. Damn, you, Tuck. I don't deserve you."

A wave of guilt drifted from her to me. "Angel? I'm here to find..."

She dropped her face into her hands. "Tuck, I'm so sorry this happened. I'm so sorry you're gone. And you came back. Is it all my fault?"

I didn't know how to answer that.

For a long time, we shared silence. Neither of us understood what was happening—this strange connection. Neither of us understood anything. Just then, for the moments we were sharing, it didn't matter.

"If only I could figure this out." I paced the room, stopping after the third tour of the bookshelves. "I have to find the bastard who killed me."

"What will you do if you find out? What happens then?" Her voice trailed off. Then, she looked around the room. Tears welled again. "No, you're gone. Come back."

"No, babe, I'm here."

She brightened. "I can't see you anymore, but I can hear you. Is this how it's going to be? In and out?"

I thought about that. "Maybe—I don't know. It's emotions or something. Like when you were shot at, and then attacked at the school. You reached me—I think it's all emotions."

Angel sat in the recliner again and tucked her legs up to her chin. She seemed distant, distracted; perhaps denial was returning.

It hit me that she was my only hope. "Angel, you have to help me—to get my killer. You can be my partner, now. I know what to do and you can do it."

She lightened a little. "Right. You're dead and I'm a history professor. What a team."

"Hey, you're not just a great pair of legs and … well, you know. Unless you think you can't handle it."

"I've got a PhD, Tuck." She raised one eyebrow. "If you can be a detective, I can."

"Your doctorate is in history, Dear."

"You never graduated college, *Dear*."

Touché. "So, you'll do it?"

"I don't know. The university gave me lots of bereavement time off. And I guess that won't be so tough."

"Oh? A few hugs and kisses and you're okay?"

Angel's half-smile gave way to tears as she glanced around the room searching for me. "You ass, of course not. But dead is one thing and gone is another. You're not gone. Not really."

Hercule moaned and dropped his head onto his paws, ignoring the mushy words that followed. He was still young and it embarrassed him to hear us carry on.

"Doc told me I had to go easy—not to overdo it. But he didn't say I couldn't use a partner."

"Who's Doc?"

"That doesn't matter. When we find my killer, I'm gonna return the favor."

Angel went to Hercule and rubbed his head. She looked sullen and upset. "Can a ghost really kill someone?"

"I don't know, but I just might find out."

Her face flushed. "If you do, will you leave? I mean, if that's why you're here."

"I don't know. I…"

"Damn you." She burst into tears as she ran from the room, crying, "Will you still kill them if it's someone you know?"

TWENTY-SEVEN

"SOMEONE I KNOW?" HER parting words plagued me all night. When I asked her about them, she dismissed it all as stress, confusion, and the insanity of talking to a ghost. I bought that last excuse. Nonetheless, Angel was struggling with something—something simmering just below the surface that slipped out in a word or a look when she wasn't guarded. Whether it was confusion or insanity, she would not talk about it, and when pressed, she retreated.

Even with her occasional withdrawal, we spent the most unusual night we ever spent together. We talked about my side of "life" and all that I had yet to learn. We discussed death and all we once believed it to be. She compared it to movies and books; I tried to find the answers to her millions of questions. Somewhere between "I don't knows" and a therapeutic cocktail of tears and red wine, she slept.

The next morning, she rushed through her rituals and climbed into her car. In the passenger seat beside her, I asked her again.

"Angel, about last night."

She heard me but couldn't see me. How and when I could materialize was sort of a mystery; one we hadn't solved yet.

"Didn't we talk about everything?"

"Well, you asked what I'd do if it were someone I know. Is there something you want to tell me? Do you know who killed me?"

"Tuck, give me some time on this, okay?" She lowered her eyes. "Think about it. It could be someone you know. Someone came into our house—right into our house. No break in; no anything like that. Spence, Captain Sutter, even Bear, thinks it could be someone we know."

I laughed. "Yeah, and Bear has a key to the front door."

"That isn't funny, Tuck—revenge isn't funny. None of this is. Don't push me, please."

She was right, of course; this wasn't very funny. Despite her settling into our "situation" quite well—odd considering we just reconnected—everything that brought us to this point was dark and scary. Even more was unknown. When I found all the missing pieces, I had no idea what I would do with them. Revenge might cure my appetite, but it might also take me from Angel again.

Would it be worth it?

We drove in silence the rest of the way to the campus and parked in the front row facing her office. She climbed out of the car and had just reached the sidewalk when a voice startled us both and turned us around.

"Angela?" André Cartier walked toward us holding two cups of coffee. He handed her one. "I've been waiting for you."

"André," Angel said, surprised as I was to see him. "What brings you?"

"I wanted to ask how Carmen is. They wouldn't let me see her at the hospital. I was worried about both of you."

"She's alive, thankfully, and doing better. She has a minor concussion and some bad bruises. The doctor says she may go home in a day or so."

"Did she see anything? Hear anything at all?"

She shook her head. "No. She doesn't remember a thing after leaving here that night. Bear is handling it. He thinks it's all connected."

André frowned and took a long sip of coffee. "Angela, please—it's obvious."

"André?"

His eyes rose and they were hard and angry. "Things are certainly connected and that's exactly why he should let someone else handle this. He's too involved."

Angel's silence was chilling.

Finally, André changed the subject. "I have some findings from the skull fragment we found the other day that I need to check against the original M.E. report."

"What findings?"

"The M.E report suggested there are two sets of remains from Kelly's Dig."

"Yes, that's right."

"The report is wrong. There may be three, perhaps four."

"Are you sure? If that's the case, we're probably dealing with an unrecorded cemetery."

He nodded. "Well, I'm as sure as I can be for now. There's other discrepancies with the bones, too. And get this—I found an old coin in the soil samples around the barn's foundation. It was caked in clay and I didn't see it until I got to my lab. It was …"

"Am I interrupting?" Bear strode up from the parking lot. "Hello, André. Angel, I need to talk with you."

Angel's face lit up. "André and I are discussing Kelly's Dig."

"No, I'm leaving." André glared at Bear.

"Don't go," Bear said. "Did I hear you say something about a coin from Kelly's Dig?"

André shook his head and turned to leave. "No, nothing I can discuss."

"André, wait," Angel said, but he shook his head and she relented. "All right. Please call me as soon as you know something."

"I will."

"Sorry, pal," Bear said. "I just wanted to check on Angel."

André kissed Angel on the cheek and winked at Bear. "I trust you're looking after Carmen as well?" He didn't wait for a reply and walked off into the parking lot.

Ouch. Professor André Cartier just scored a direct hit.

"I'm sorry about that, Bear," Angel said looking after André. "I don't know what got into him."

I said, "I do. So does Bear."

Bear watched André disappear. "What's his problem?"

"Oh, you know him," Angel said. "He's been like my dad since I was a kid."

I followed Bear and Angel up to her office as they continued their discussion.

"That doesn't make him your keeper," Bear said.

"Funny, that's exactly what he thinks about you."

"Yeah?" Bear's eyes narrowed. "Maybe I should talk to him about it."

I stood behind Angel and said, "Tell Bear what I told you about Salazar moonlighting from his security job with Poor Nic."

She did.

Bear's face tightened. "How do you know that?"

"Kirk Wallchak and Poor Nic were talking about it the other day."

"Oh, shit." Bear sighed. "Listen, I'm not listening to the buzzing in my head and I suggest you do the same."

"Bear listen..."

"No." He changed the subject. "I checked the campus CCTV security tapes and they caught Carmen's attack. None of the security guys were in the office so they completely missed it. Can't make out any face or details, though—rain and bad lighting."

"Oh my God." Angel's voice was a whisper. "She's lucky to be alive."

"And that begs a question." He leaned forward. "How did you know about the campus? How did you know about Salazar and Wallchak? For real, I mean."

"Go easy, Angel," I said. "Real easy."

She didn't. "Tuck told me. He's here. Now."

Oh, crap. "Not what I had in mind."

Bear jumped back. "I knew you'd say that." He started pacing. "Angela, it's all in your head. Hell, it's all in my head, too. I've heard things, and it's driving me nuts. He's gone, dammit. He's gone."

"No, Tuck's here—so you better watch what you say...and do."

"I'm not afraid of ghosts, even his. Tuck didn't tell you anything."

"Then how could I know?"

"You're a witch." Bear tried to smile but frowned instead. "I don't know. You're saying he was at..."

"The warehouse, yes. Clemens and Spence met Wallchak the day you punched Spence and knocked him down."

"Jesus. Anything else?"

"Poor Nic asked about Iggi Suarez."

"Iggi?" Bear started nodding. "I need to find him. He didn't mention where he was, did he?"

"No." Angel smiled and pointed a finger at him. "There's more. Wallchak told Poor Nic that Spence and Clemens were asking about the murder. Poor Nic asked him, 'Which one?'"

"Which one?"

"Isn't that an odd question?"

"Yes it is." Bear's voice trailed off. For a long time, he stood shaking his head. Finally, he said, "So tell me, why is Tuck haunting you?"

"He's not just haunting me." Angel leaned forward on her desk and captured his eyes. "He's here to find his killer."

"Then why isn't he haunting both of us?"

TWENTY-EIGHT

"He meant because you were partners, Tuck."

Did he? We'd been arguing that point Bear left Angel's office two hours ago. "Sure, okay, maybe. I'm just saying it's a strange way to look at this."

"Oh, please," Angel said, sighing. "He doesn't even believe you're here."

"Of course I'm here." I was lying on her office couch watching her work. "Where else…"

Her phone rang.

"Hello, Tyler." It was Tyler Byrd and she put it on speaker at my request. "Yes, I spoke with Dr. Cartier this morning."

Byrd's voice was edgy. "It's disappointing that Cartier is already drawing conclusions. Your analysis isn't finished and he's suggesting Kelly's Dig could be a cemetery. That could cost me a fortune."

"Tyler, we've not reached any conclusion. He's trying to consider other possibilities on the remains' origins. That's the whole point here, right?"

"Well, yes of course, but …"

"And he has a question about the number of remains. And he found a coin in the site that might be helpful dating the remains. He's onto something."

Silence. Then, "Cartier didn't tell me those details."

"Well, he didn't give me any details, either." Tyler grunted something and Angel went on with, "He's following it up himself. I'm sure we'll both know as soon as he has all the analysis completed."

"He should check with Ernie Stuart."

"Ernie?"

"Yes, Ernie." Tyler seemed more relaxed. "Stuart and his historical society pals have gotten their hands on some antiques from Kelly's Dig. I'll deal with that in court, so no matter now. When is Cartier headed back to Kelly's Dig?"

"Tomorrow, I think."

"Good. I'll pay him a visit."

When she hung up, I said, "Swell guy, that Tyler Byrd. I wonder what he meant about Ernie."

"I don't know." Someone knocked on her door. "Come in."

I nearly wet myself when the door opened.

Poor Nic Bartalotta stood in the doorway. Behind him, a beefy bodyguard with no neck and less gray matter blocked all light from the outer room.

"Professor Tucker?"

Angel went pale. "Mr. Bartalotta? What can I do for you?"

"May I come in?" The aging gangster didn't budge from the doorway. Gangsters are like vampires—they can't enter without an invitation.

"Well, yes, I guess so."

"Angel, tell him to leave his goon outside."

Before she could, Poor Nic whispered to the man who then disappeared from view. Then, Poor Nic walked into the room, quietly closed the door behind him, and stopped in front of Angel's desk. He reverently bowed his head.

"Please accept my deepest condolences, Professor Tucker. I was saddened—and shocked—by your husband's death. I should have sent my condolences before. Forgive me for that. His death was so tragic."

Angel's face tightened. "You mean his murder."

"Of course—*murder* is such a ruthless word." He offered a grandfatherly smile. "Professor ... may I call you Angela?"

I said, "Sure, let's all be pals. He probably killed me so we're all family."

"No," she said. "I don't know you that well."

"Ah, of course." He looked down at the two chairs in front of him, waited for Angel to nod, and sat. "Let me get to the point."

"Please do."

I sat beside him. "Easy, Angel. Let him talk. He thinks he's safe here with you. Maybe he'll tell us something."

She nodded.

"Professor Tucker, many believe I was responsible for your husband's death."

Kapow! The words etched across her face and she looked straight at him. Then she glanced around the room, perhaps hoping to see me. Poor Nic noticed and followed her gaze.

"Murder," she repeated, snatching back his attention. "And yes, I've considered that you murdered Tuck."

"Yes, of course—his murder." He didn't flinch. "I am here to tell you in person—I am not responsible. Because of that, you should be concerned."

"Excuse me? I don't understand, Poor…"

He laughed and his smile lingered. "Yes, they call me Poor Nic—policemen and reporters love the drama. Please call me Nicholas."

Angel stayed silent, waiting for his lead.

"You see, Professor Tucker, it's very simple. I did not kill your husband, and the police aren't looking elsewhere very hard. They're so focused on me that they aren't looking anywhere else at all."

Angel thought about that. "You were involved in Tuck's last case—maybe others, too. You're a…"

"Easy Angela," I said. "He doesn't take criticism well."

"Now, now." He raised a hand and patted the air. "I'm retired. Let's leave it at that, shall we? And I don't kill policemen. I never have and never will. Your husband was a good man I'm told. To me, however, he was a pain in the…"

"Often to me, too." Angel caught him off guard and they both chuckled. She added, "Yes, he was a good man—and husband."

Poor Nic's face hardened as he lifted his chin. "Professor Tucker, I am not in the habit of stalking women in parking lots. How stupid could I be to kill your husband and then attack you? Let alone twice. Don't you think the police have had me under surveillance all this time?"

"Perhaps. But, you wouldn't do these things yourself, would you? You have others to do your dirty work."

Sweet mobster-mash, Angel was pushing his buttons hard. "Easy, easy. And you say I have no couth."

"No, very good, Professor. Let me be straightforward. I am concerned for your safety. If anything happens to you, it would be tragic. More to the point, however, I might be blamed."

"I see." Angel let his words settle. "So, you've come to proclaim your innocence. You've done that."

Poor Nic stood up and clasped his hands in front of him. "A crazy person killed your husband. I believe that same person killed Raymundo Salazar. Perhaps he even tried to kill Miss Delgado."

"Perhaps," she said.

"I must ask," he said in a quiet voice, narrowing his eyes on her. "The night your husband was murdered ... what did you see? What did you ..."

"Nothing," Angel said in a sharp tone. "Tuck was shot downstairs while I was in our room. Someone tried to come upstairs and I let Herc go. He saved me."

"Herc?"

"Hercule, our Lab. A bullet grazed him. He's fine, though."

He laughed. "Ah, very Agatha Christie. I adore Labradors. I have three myself. Good for Hercule. Keep him close, Professor."

And with that, Poor Nicholas Bartalotta gave her that warm, grandfatherly smile. He handed her a card that read simply, "Nicholas" with a handwritten phone number.

"Angela," he said in a soft, calming voice, "you are a strong and charming woman. Your loss is my loss. I will check in on you from time to time—if you don't mind. Should you need anything, do not hesitate to call." He turned and disappeared through the office door.

Angel watched him leave. "What just happened, Tuck?"

"Hell if I know, Angel. But I think Poor Nic just became your godfather."

TWENTY-NINE

It was a coin toss whether I stayed with Angel or tagged along with Poor Nic. Since he was my nominee for murderer of the year, he won the toss.

I slipped into his Lexus when Bobby, his driver, opened the door for Poor Nic. Then, Bobby drove us straight back to his estate ten miles out on the west side of the county. When we pulled into the gated, high-walled property, the first thing I noticed were the two men standing guard. They became animated and attentive. I guess everyone likes to look good for the boss.

The house—I'd call it a mansion—was immaculate and as grand as I recalled. It was a two-story Tudor-style that looked like it belonged outside London instead of Winchester. Gardens and trees surrounded the property, and of course, more big goons with guns patrolling all around. Okay, so maybe London was wrong. Maybe San Quentin was a more appropriate venue.

With or without the gun-toting hoods, Poor Nic had style.

He stopped at his front door and turned to Bobby. "Keep the car ready. I may be going out later. Get Tommy and come to the great room."

Inside, Poor Nic helped himself to a five o'clock cocktail and took his customary place behind the huge antique desk. Bobby and Tommy were standing in front of him before his ice got wet.

He looked at his men and took a long swallow of his drink. They neither drank nor sat.

Poor Nic said, "Tommy, what's new from your friends downtown?"

"Braddock is getting close on Salazar. He's made the connection." Tommy was one of Poor Nic's knuckle-draggers—muscle. While I hadn't recognized him on the golf course when Bear met him, his resume was clear now. Tommy was playing both sides of the game. He was snitching for Bear on Poor Nic and reporting Bear's demands back to him.

Tommy was a double agent.

"I see." Poor Nic sipped his drink and contemplated the glass. "And how is he making such progress?"

"Dunno. He called Wallchak with a bunch of questions. He knew just about everythin'. Bear knows a lot more than we thought. All of a sudden-like."

"How is that?"

Bobby spoke up. "Boss, I was with Wallchak the other day. He said he hadn't talked with Braddock about that stuff. In fact, he said he hadn't seen him for a while. I'll go see him."

"Call him—now." Poor Nic gave him a dismissive wave and returned to Tommy. "What else about your friend?"

"He's gettin' to be a pain in the ass. He knows about Salazar moonlightin', but he dunno where yet."

"Can you slow him down?"

Tommy shrugged.

"Try."

I watched Tommy. He was playing his cards like a riverboat gambler. It was obvious Poor Nic knew about his connection to Bear—perhaps it was at his direction. Yet, at the same time, Tommy wasn't giving him many details. Perhaps he'd already filled Poor Nic in on the golf course meeting. Perhaps not. Like his master, Tommy was no doubt a stone-faced thug and capable of the deepest deceit. The lingering question on my mind was, of course, who was he deceiving the most—Poor Nic or Bear? The difference could mean jail or sleeping with the fishes—as they say.

Bobby returned. "Wallchak hasn't spoken with Bear for a week. He showed up the other day but got into it with Spence and left. Wallchak never talked to him."

"Then Braddock has inside information. Someone's helping him. I don't like that."

Both bodyguards shrugged.

"Perhaps he knows about Iggi, too. Bobby, you'd better pay Iggi a visit—and Salazar's widow, too. Make sure they understand things. Take care of Sarah Salazar—good care. If Iggi doesn't feel like cooperating, well, take care of him, too."

Bobby disappeared again.

"Tommy, get the box, won't you?"

"Sure, Boss." Tommy walked to the far corner of the room and pulled on one of the heavy bookshelves. Like an old Hollywood movie scene, the heavy oak bookshelf glided forward and revealed a wall safe. Tommy deftly manipulated the dial and opened the door. Inside, he retrieved a heavy wooden box adorned with brass hinges and a heavy ornate lock. It resembled a pirate's treasure chest, but was no larger than a shoebox. Reverently, he carried it to Poor Nic's desk and laid it before him. Then, he retreated to his post behind the leather armchair and waited.

"Thank you. Recent events force me to consider my actions all those years ago. There were so many questions. I am close to the answers, Tommy. No one is going to keep me from them."

Tommy remained silent.

Poor Nic sat stoically holding the sides of the box. His eyes said he was miles away. The box had a profound spell that seized him when his eyes rested on its lock. When he reached into his pocket and withdrew a skeleton key, I'd swear he held his breath. He manipulated the lock and lifted the lid. Before he looked inside, his right hand signed the cross as his lips proclaimed his faith.

I couldn't see what treasures lay inside. Strange, though, as I felt no compulsion to move closer. There was something about the box. Something powerful that repelled any notion of violating the old man's privacy.

He withdrew several folded newspaper clippings and read them. Then, he withdrew photographs and other papers and laid them down in a neat stack beside the box. There was also a gun—a nickel-plated derringer that he hefted and seemed oddly pleased to hold. Poor Nic was lost in memories. After reliving some long ago secret, he replaced each item inside the box. He locked it and sat back, closing his eyes.

Tommy's voice startled me. "Do you want me to take care of this, boss?"

"No, but thank you," Poor Nic said with a low, sardonic laugh. Then, in a graven tone, he added, "I will handle this myself. Perhaps not today or tomorrow. Perhaps not this year or next. But I will take care of this before I die."

"Okay, Boss. I'll leave you alone."

"Yes, please do. Go make sure Wallchak has everything straight."

"Sure, Boss."

"We can't afford another Salazar situation, can we?"

Whatever that question meant, Tommy knew it didn't require an answer and left.

The desk phone rang. He let it ring three times before lifting the receiver and grunting a shallow greeting. He twice closed his eyes and drummed his fingers against his temple. The tightness of his lips and the telltale shake of his head told me he was not pleased with the call.

"Hold on." He lurched forward. His fingers whitened around the receiver. "I'm aware of our liability. Don't presume to explain that to me. Get your hands on those other pieces or else."

Poor Nic's face twisted as the caller spoke. He cut in. "We share that responsibility. Do you understand? Do your part and I'll do mine. Iggi is for me to handle and Lucca is your problem—I cannot deal with him yet. So do it. Do it soon."

He hung up the phone. As he leaned back in his chair, he sipped his cocktail and contemplated the box once again. His demeanor softened and his face relaxed.

"Lucca, Lucca, Lucca. You've been a bad boy. Very bad indeed."

THIRTY

"Angel, you here?"

"Oh, for heaven's sake." She spun around at our kitchen table and looked around the room. "Tuck, you scared me half to death."

"Well, it could have been all the way," I mused. "Like me."

Her eyes followed my voice to the kitchen chair opposite her. "Herc and I have been looking for you."

I told her about the visit with Poor Nic. "So, if you're up to it, I have an idea."

She listened and when I was through, said, "I'm not sure of this. Let's call Bear."

"What's wrong?"

Her eyes dropped. "You want to find ... can't you be happy the way things are?"

"No, I can't. There are no leads on my case. Maybe if we solve Salazar's it'll help."

"If I help you solve Salazar's murder, we could link it to yours?"

"Sure, maybe."

She thought about that. "Then I'm calling Bear. I don't want to …"

"No, wait until we're done. Sarah never trusted him."

⁓

Ten minutes later, we pulled into a parking space in front of a long block of row houses. The homes were in poor repair with dirty brick exteriors and paint-chipped windows. Boxes of trash piled out front spilled into the street. Many of the houses were dark and most of the streetlamps were, too. The parking lot was eerily dark and forbidden at this nine o'clock hour.

Angel looked around and frowned. "Oh my, Sarah lives here?"

"Nice, isn't it? Raymundo Salazar was working two jobs for this. Sarah has a young baby, too. And, she's not working."

"How do they do it? And with a baby?"

I looked around the neighborhood and saw two men climbing into a large sedan down the block. "There goes Bobby and one of his pals, Angel."

"Terrific, just what we need. Remember, Tuck, we have a deal. I do some detective work and we turn it over to Bear, right?"

"Right." Hercule was sitting in the front passenger seat. I whispered to him and he barked. To Angel, I said, "Leave your window down. Herc will have you covered. You'll like being a detective. Trust me."

"Tuck, I mean it. I'm not doing this after tonight."

A moment later, we were standing on Sarah's stoop as Angel rapped on the door. It opened almost instantly. Perhaps she was expecting Bobby again. The expression on her face said she was not expecting Angel.

"Yeah? Who are you?"

Sarah was a plain girl of about twenty. She was blonde with large blue eyes and a broken, but pretty smile. She was tiny—about five feet tall and slender. The remnants of baby fat showed above her jeans. She bounced and coddled a young infant in her arms.

"Sarah," Angel said in a small voice. Then she gained her confidence. "Sarah, I'm Angela Tucker."

Sarah looked her over and then peered around her into the parking lot. "So? What's that mean to me?"

"Angel Tucker, Sarah," Angel repeated. "Tuck, my husband, was murdered—Detective Tucker."

Sarah's face paled and she stopped bouncing her baby. "Oh, I'm sorry, ma'am. I didn't know. Right, Tuck's wife. Sorry."

"May we come in?"

"We?" Sarah looked around Angel again. "Is someone with you?"

Angel blushed. "No, I'm sorry. I left my dog in the car. Just me. May I come in? I need your help. Please?"

"My help?" Sarah's face transformed from cold and angry to shameful. A couple tears filled her eyes and began the journey down her face. She pushed the screen door further open. "I'm sorry, Mrs. Tucker. I heard about him on the news. I'm real sorry. Come in."

Angel followed Sarah into her tiny kitchen. The room smelled musky and damp. Overhead, a single, bare bulb lighted the room. A baby's bottle was warming on the stove and there was a small plate and spoon ready on the counter.

"Sorry 'bout this." Sarah moved a pile of laundry off a kitchen chair and motioned for Angel to sit. Then, she opened the refrigerator. "Hope you don't mind if I feed Annie. She's hungry—as always."

"Go right ahead." Angel winced when Sarah's refrigerator revealed only a half-empty gallon of milk, two jars of baby food, and some old, browning fruit. "Can I help?"

"No. Annie's funny with strangers."

I said, "I wonder how she took to Bobby and the other hood."

Angel was thinking the same thing. "Sarah, don't Poor Nic's men scare her? Or is she used to them?"

Bullets wouldn't have gotten Sarah's attention any faster. "What does that mean? You tryin' to say somethin'?"

"We—I saw them leave."

Sarah shrugged. "Bobby brought Ray's last paycheck. I couldn't pick it up. My car don't work."

"Of course." Angel nodded. "I'm very sorry about your husband, Sarah. I know what you're going through."

"Thanks. My Ray was a hard worker—he was always workin'—two jobs for me and Annie. And he would'a had three if I'd let him."

"There's your cue, Angel," I said. But when she sat watching Annie and didn't make a move, I pressed her. "Angel, come on. The faster you get what we came for, the faster we're out of here."

Sarah spooned some mushed food into Annie's eager lips. "What you want? You didn't come here to say you're sorry."

"No," Angel began, "I came to ask about Ray and his friend Iggi."

"What about them? I thought you was gonna ask me about Tuck?"

"Yes, but it may be connected."

"Huh?"

Angel used a warm, trusting smile to ease Sarah's angst. Annie liked her smile, too. She cooed and wiggled, and reached out her arms. Angel looked to Sarah, got a nod, and took Annie in her arms.

"Sarah, I think whoever killed Ray may have been involved with Tuck's murder, too. That's why I'm here."

"I dunno." Sarah watched Annie atop Angel's knee. "The cops don't seem to know nothin' about Ray's killin'. Your husband told me that much. I ain't seen his partner for a couple weeks, either. I guess nobody cares about Ray no more—not after your husband got killed."

Angel tensed before her eyes softened, and a painful, almost teary glistening filled them. "I am sorry, and I'm sure that's not true. Bear is trying hard to find Ray's killer. I know he is."

Sarah shook her head. "Don't matter. Ray's dead."

I said, "Ask about his moonlighting job, Angela."

With a reluctant bite of her lip, she did.

"I'm not real sure." Sarah didn't hesitate. "He went out most nights after the warehouse shift. Whenever I asked, he said he got somethin' part-time. Said he had to get us outta this place. He got mad at me a couple times, so I stopped asking. He was like that. But, he brought in good money."

"Good money?" Angel asked. "Doing what?"

"Not what you think. No drugs or nothin'. We were trying to get Annie outta this damn place—outta this neighborhood. He worked odd jobs everywhere he could find 'em. Sometimes he painted houses. Sometimes he mowed grass or somethin'. I dunno where

180

this last one was. His friend got him a few hours a week—you know, just here and there."

Angel asked, "Was that Iggi?"

"Yeah." Sarah retrieved Annie. "Is he in trouble, too?"

"No, no trouble. I think Iggi can help me figure this all out. And if I can, maybe that'll help find Ray's killer, too. Where can I find Iggi?"

Sarah looked at her and sat quiet. If there was something I'd learned about life, it was that a hard one made you distrust everyone. Sarah had a hard life.

"Don't know," she said. "What's the difference how Ray got jobs? What's Iggi got to do with this? Does he know somethin' about the murders, too?"

Too? I said to Angel, "That's what Bobby was doing here, Angel. Finding out what she and Iggi know."

"Is that what Bobby was doing here, Sarah?" Angel asked, touching Annie's hand and made her smile. "Please, I need to know what you told Bobby."

Sarah bit her lip. "Look, I got nothin' to tell you. Poor Nic is being good to us—Annie and me. I don't want to piss him off."

"He came to see me, too, Sarah. He said he wanted to help me. But, he scares me. He scares me a lot." Angel watched Sarah closely, looking for a crack in her armor. "If Iggi knows something and Poor Nic's men find him first, he might not help me."

Sarah looked away and stayed silent.

"Angel, she knows something."

Angel leaned forward. "Sarah, please. Iggi could be in danger. Since Ray's murder, Tuck's been killed, someone's tried to kill me, and a friend of mine was almost killed, too. Please. Help me."

"Okay, okay." Sarah stood up and shifted Annie in her arms. "Ya want some coffee? I wanna help, I do. But I don't know nothin.'"

Angel took over the task of making coffee while Sarah fed Annie. Small talk began and I took the break in tension to snoop around. In a small, rear bedroom, I found what I was looking for on her nightstand—an envelope stuffed with cash. The money was half-out of the envelope and fanned open as if Sarah had been counting it. I counted five thousand dollars. But, it wasn't the cash that had my attention, it was the three old gold coins in the ashtray nearby.

I sat on the bed and when my fingers touched the coins, they ignited the explosion.

THIRTY-ONE

IT WAS DARK AND a steady wind blew, rustling trees and tall grass all around me. I didn't recognize the stand of trees either. There were no landmarks to give me the slightest hint. Night sounds surrounded me and the thick canopy of trees blocked much of the moonlight. Then there were voices—two curt, harsh tones ahead in the darkness. They were getting louder and angrier, though the words escaped me. I moved toward them, conscious of the sudden heaviness of the air around me. As I moved closer, my steps became harder and harder, like trudging through ever-deepening water.

I emerged between several tall, bushy apple trees. Ahead of me were two animated figures—silhouettes of flailing arms and harsh voices. The moonlight broke through the trees and bathed them. The smaller figure was a girl in a long dress that billowed in the breeze. The moonlight suggested she was young and blonde; her movements told me she was frantic. She held her shoes in one hand and the other chopped the air—vigorous and angry. The other person was a tall, broad-shouldered man. His fists were clenching and threatening with every angry word. His appearance didn't match hers—he wore dungarees and a dark shirt, but the darkness hid their details. I was straining to move closer when he lunged forward and grabbed the girl's arm. He shook her with mounting violence. Angry words. Rage. He shook her again and again—her body flailed like a marionette.

She screamed.

Dread seized me, but my body couldn't move to intercede. Just as I had been impotent to stop Carmen's abduction, so was I to stop this violence. "No … oh, no."

Something startled the man and he spun around. Another girl, young and brunette, erupted out of the darkness. She lunged and clawed at him. He swung wildly, striking her in the face, stopping her advance and knocking her down. The blonde kicked him and fought back, trying without success to break free. He swung her around and downed her with a vicious punch. Her attack ended in a sickening, dull crack of bone on rock.

He froze and looked down. He yelled out, but the words never formed in my head.

The brunette crawled to her companion and grasped her. She shook her but her body bobbled lifeless and doll-like. She shook her again and began screaming, thrashing at the ground as life escaped her.

"Leave them alone," I shouted, but they would not hear me—I wasn't there, I wasn't with them. "Damn you, leave them alone."

The end came.

Sorrowful wails lifted the brunette to her feet. She whirled on the man and unleashed a flurry of punches and screams. Arms and feet thrashed in a ravenous foray. The man deflected the assault with mere bats of his hands. Then, in a sudden, silent assault, he grabbed her, first by the hair, and then the throat. His strength overwhelmed her, twisting and bending her backward until she writhed on the ground. He followed.

A cry. Arms flailed. Broken words; gasps—silence.

He stood, looking down at the result of his rage. His hands crushed to his face as a he gagged back words I couldn't understand. At that moment, he knew what I did.

He was a murderer.

THIRTY-TWO

REELING, I SHOOK MYSELF free and backed into the darkness from which I'd emerged. After two steps, I returned to Sarah's bedroom. I looked around, thankful for the unmade bed and disheveled baby clothes. It took me minutes to shake off the ugly vision before returning to her kitchen.

Angel was warming to Sarah. "I know things are hard, Sarah, but there's a killer out there. He might kill again. No one is safe. No one."

"Yeah?" Sarah was wide-eyed and I believed her fear. "Ma'am, I …"

"Call me Angela."

"Angela, I'm real sorry. I don't know anything. Bobby gave me some money. He said it was life insurance from the company. I know it wasn't, but I need it bad. And Poor Nic wants to know everythin' I do about Ray's death."

Poor Nic was doing his own investigation into Ray Salazar's murder. Either he was hunting down all the witnesses and evidence against him—or he was innocent and trying to prove it. If it was the first reason, more people would die. If the latter, well, maybe he'd lead us to the real killer. After all, gangsters don't use search warrants and "good cop-bad cop" games.

Angel asked, "What did you tell Bobby? It's important."

"Nothin', honest."

"Sarah, please?"

"Really, I dunno anything to tell you. Bobby asked about Iggi and I dunno where he is. He also asked about some guy Lucca. I never heard of no Lucca."

I knew that name. "Lucca? What about him?" Angel repeated my words.

Sarah pushed away from the table. "Nothin, Angela. I don't know no Lucca. That's what I told him."

"All right, Sarah," Angel said with slow, drawn words. Even Sarah had to know Angel didn't believe her. "But if you're lying and someone else gets hurt, you could be in bigger trouble than anything Nic will do."

"I doubt that," she grumbled. "But I ain't lying."

"Good." Angel stood and gently stroked Annie's thin hair. "Do you have a job?"

"No, can't with a kid this young. I'm getting' public assistance—it helps some."

Angel reached into her purse and withdrew a business card, laying it on the kitchen table in front of her. "Go out to the university. See our Human Resources people. Ask for Janice and show her my card. We have a daycare program for staff and students. Volunteers run it. I think we can find something to help you out."

"You kiddin'?" Sarah picked up the card and looked over the top of it at Angel. She tried to hide a smile but her crooked teeth broke free. "Why? Why do you want to help me? I don't know anything."

"Because I know how it feels to lose a husband. Maybe I can make it easier—for both of you."

Sarah clutched Annie and tears replaced her distrust. "Thank you, Angela. I liked your husband, I really did."

"Let's go, Angel."

We were out the door and getting in the car when Sarah emerged through her front door and called for Angel. We returned to her stoop.

"Angela, I dunno if it's important, but ..."

"What is it?"

She looked into the darkness, up and down the rows of cars. Perhaps she feared Bobby was looming, waiting for us to leave. Her voice was nervous. "Ray was always worried 'bout money. Then, a few days before he was ... killed, he was talkin' about us getting outta here real soon. He said in a week he'd quit all his jobs."

"He was going to quit?"

"He said we'd be okay for a while 'cause the money would last a long time."

"The money?"

"Yeah. But, Angela," Sarah whispered, half-closing the screen door, "we don't have any money."

188

THIRTY-THREE

As soon as Angel's car door closed, I told her about the murders I'd seen take place in Sarah's bedroom. Well, not in her bedroom, but the murders that I witnessed while in her bedroom. It's a good thing Sarah didn't have a foyer.

"Two young girls?" Angel pulled the car onto the street and headed toward home. "What am I doing? I can't do this anymore. I cannot be responsible for more of this."

"Relax—just listen. I think they've been dead a long time."

"What? How do you know that?"

I told her about the two beautiful young wraiths who visited me the night someone shot the house up. At first, she didn't believe me, but the fact that she was arguing with a dead man played my way.

"And you think they're the same girls?"

"Who else could they be? I mean, how many ghosts are gonna haunt me?"

"Do you know who killed them? Or when?"

"No. It could be last year or a hundred years ago. But they're trying to tell me something. I just don't know what."

"I'm calling Bear." When she started to dial, I asked her to put it on speaker. "No, Tuck. I'll tell you after—please."

"Why can't I listen for myself?"

Angel's forehead wrinkled as she said, "I just need a little privacy sometimes."

From me?

When Bear answered, Angel filled him in on what little we got from Sarah Salazar. She left out the part about the murders in her bedroom. He might not understand that part. The look on Angel's face said he was not happy.

She said, "I decided to go without you. She never liked you. You know that."

Silence, then she said, "Believe me, I'm not planning on doing any more of this. And going there was not my idea, either." Bear's grunting and more silence. "Never mind, you wouldn't believe me."

Bear was ranting something that made her scowl. It was probably best I didn't hear. She flipped on the speaker button and held the phone out for me to hear. Bear was saying, "Okay, Sarah said Iggi got Salazar a moonlighting job—maybe legit, maybe not. Maybe they were planning a big score because money is suddenly no problem for Salazar. Then, he's killed."

"By Iggi?" Angel asked, but then shook her head already sure she was wrong.

Bear said, "I doubt it, but who knows. It bothers me that Poor Nic gave Sarah money."

"Five thousand," Angel said. "And she had some gold coins, too."

"Coins? She said he gave her coins?"

Angel ignored the question.

It hit me. "Angel, the coins might be Poor Nic's. I saw them in his den the morning Bear and I went to see him a couple weeks ago. I can't be sure, but he has a collection of them."

Angel told Bear, "André found an antique coin at Kelly's Dig. This cannot all be coincidence."

"Maybe, maybe not," Bear said. "None of it makes sense. I gotta find Iggi Suarez."

I reminded Angel about the girls. She was reluctant and I gave her a nudge. "Ask him, Angel."

"Bear, someone told me about two young girls being killed one night in the woods. I'm not sure when, maybe a long time ago. I've never heard of anything like that, so, can you ..."

"Oh?" I could hear Bear's sphincter tightening. "'Someone' told you that?"

"Yes—someone did. It could be important. If you need me, I'll be at Ernie's tonight."

He groaned. "Sure, Angela. I'll get right on it. This 'someone' hasn't figured out who killed him yet, has he?"

"No."

"Well, that's a relief."

THIRTY-FOUR

"You're a detective now?" Ernie's tone was dry and contemptuous. He didn't wait for Angel to answer. "However will you find time to be a professor?"

"Oh, Ernie, please understand." Angel picked up her wineglass from his coffee table separating them. "It's something I, well, that I had to do."

"That's the police's job."

We'd arrived a little more than an hour ago. Ernie had been ready with wine and a friendly hug, but his spots changed when Angel turned the conversation to her recent foray as a homicide investigator. Charm turned to irritation.

"My dear, you are too involved in all this. You are not a crime fighter—your first responsibility is to the university."

Angel folded her arms. "Ernie, I have in no way let my duties at the university lapse."

"No, I meant…"

"In fact, you insisted I take some time off. How I spend it is entirely up to me. Isn't it?"

"Yes, of course."

Angel swirled her wine in the glass but kept hold of Ernie's eyes. "I need to help find Tuck's killer, and Raymundo Salazar's, too. It's therapeutic."

"Therapeutic? It's dangerous." The more Ernie fought her, the more willing she became to help find my killer.

"Ernie…"

He bound from his chair and went across the room to the window. "Seriously, Angela. You sound ridiculous. You didn't even have a real funeral. What's got into you?"

"I appreciate your concern." Angel didn't look sure as she gulped some wine. "But I know what I'm doing."

Ernie took a long pull on his wine but refused to look at her. "Perhaps a better subject at the moment is the gold coins you found."

"Yes, Sarah Salazar has several. And André found one in some clay samples he took from Kelly's Dig that day. When I mentioned the coins to Tyler Byrd, he suggested I speak with you."

"Oh, he did, did he?" Ernie was annoyed.

"What is he talking about, Ernie?"

He looked toward the window again but said nothing.

"Ernie, you know more than you're telling me. Where are these coins coming from and why are they important? Poor Nic has a collection, too."

His eyebrows rose. "How do you know Bartalotta has a collection?"

"Tuck told me—ah—before he was killed. He saw them one day when he was in Nicholas's house." She redirected him. "Tyler seemed upset that you have some antiques from Kelly's Dig. What did he mean?"

"Nothing," he snapped. He looked down and then said in a lighter voice, "No, I suppose I should tell you—confide in you I mean."

I wanted to slug the old drama-queen for all the theatrics. Something was up Ernie's skirt and I wanted to know what.

"Confide in me about what?"

"Angela, the truth is I purchased several items on the black market—over my computer. They came from Kelly's Dig." I watched Ernie's face redden and his mouth tighten until his lips were white. "I'm afraid they were stolen from there."

"Holy shit, Angel, Ernie's a crook."

She asked, "What on earth are you talking about?"

"It's simple. Perhaps too simple." Ernie cleared his throat and drained his wineglass. "You see, I trade online and received word from a dealer I know about some rare items for sale. He put me in touch with an anonymous seller offering rare currency and numerous Civil War pieces. I purchased all of them."

Angel cocked her head. "And this person sold you the coins?"

"Yes, about a week before the skeletons were discovered at Kelly's Dig. The pieces I purchased came from there. I suspect that's why he insisted on anonymity."

"Did you recognize the person who sold them to you?"

He shook his head. "No, they were stolen property and all. I never met the person and did everything via the computer and the mail."

Angel contemplated her glass. I knew that look on her face—she was mentally chasing a theory. She found it somewhere in the Merlot. "André is onto something big at Kelly's Dig and he'll need to see those coins. We need to know if your coins, Sarah's, and Poor Nic's all match the one from André's clay sample."

"And if they do?" Ernie looked confused. "What of it?"

"If they do," she said before sipping her wine, "then they could be connected to the murders."

"My dear, please." Ernie gave a dismissive wave. "Buying and selling antique coins doesn't equate to murder."

"I'm not so sure."

He asked, "What has André found?"

"He mentioned a discrepancy in the medical examiner's skeletal findings. He hasn't told me the details except that he feels strongly there are three or four sets of remains—not two."

"Really? That might mean ..." Ernie jumped to his feet. "Angela, stay here. Someone's outside my window."

"Oh, no—not again."

"Someone just walked past." He went behind his bar and returned with a revolver, checked the cylinder, and swung it closed. "Wait here, I'll check outside. Stay away from the windows." He bolted into the hallway and disappeared toward the rear of the house.

"I'll go with him," I said, heading for the hall.

I had not taken two steps when the sound of breaking glass from somewhere in the rear of the house stopped me. There was splintering wood, a heavy crash, and more glass shattering. A shot—Ernie barked "stop" and then another shot.

"Tuck," Angel cried. "Where are you?"

Before I could answer, the room went black.

THIRTY-FIVE

ANGEL WAS STANDING IN the middle of the room fighting panic.

"Easy, Angel, I'm right here. Don't move."

"Ernie?" she called. She got no response "Tuck, he could be hurt. Go see."

Two more loud crashes came from the rear of the house. Ernie called, "It's all right, Angela. I'm trying to get to the electric panel. I've scared him away."

"Hurry," she called. "Are you all right?"

"Yes, stay where you are."

After several long, anxious moments, the lights came on. Ernie limped into the living room holding his head. "It's all right. He's gone."

"Who's gone?" Angel helped him to the sofa. "What happened?"

"I'm not sure. When I reached the back room, someone was at the rear door—a man trying to force it in. He smashed in the door and attacked me."

Angel found napkins and water on the bar. With slow, gingerly care, she began washing a small contusion just above Ernie's left ear. Without thinking, she said, "Tuck, go check."

"Okay—on it."

"Dear, who are you talking to?" Ernie's voice was thick with doubt.

I could not hear her response—but it must have been something.

At the rear of the house, just past the kitchen, was a sitting room. A small antique desk stood against one wall and there was a large round table in the center of the room There were books and work papers strewn everywhere. The rear door was ajar and one of its glass panes was shattered. The doorframe and wall casing were splintered and badly damaged. A broken lamp dangled off the desk by its cord. Another lamp lay on the floor amid the broken door glass, along with Ernie's revolver. Ernie's revolver lay amongst it all in the center of the room.

Not finding any real clues, I went outside.

I searched around the house and the old barn in the rear. There was no sign of anyone lurking around. I made two patrols and found nothing. Next, I searched every room in Ernie's house but came up empty. Once again, the attacker had struck. Once again, he got away.

I returned to Angel, who was still playing nurse. "There's no one around. But the back room is a mess."

"Oh, my." Ernie held a wet cloth to his head and lay back on the sofa. "He hit me harder than I thought."

"Pretty brazen to break in while we're here," Angel said, closing her phone. "Bear's on his way." She touched Ernie's shoulder. "You didn't believe me the morning someone was in your house. Now you have to."

"I do." He blotted his head. "It happened so fast. He crashed through the door and hit me. My gun went off—it was an accident. I don't think I hit anything. The next thing I knew I was on the floor in the dark."

I said, "The desk lamp's broken. So is the one near the table. One of them tripped a breaker."

"Let's check your office." Angel took his arm. "Did you get a look at him?"

Ernie's description sent chills up my spine. "He was tall. Big, you know, broad-shouldered, and he had dark features." I was betting he was the same man who had attacked Angel and Carmen. I was also betting his name was Lucca.

In the rear sitting room Ernie sat at the table and immediately pointed to an empty, felt blotter on his desk. "Oh, no. Angela, they're all gone. The papers, the letters, even the coins I was cleaning. Everything from Kelly's Dig is gone."

I said, "Typical smash and grab. They knew what they were looking for and where to find it."

Angel asked, "Who knew you had these things?"

"Let me think." Ernie dabbed the side of his head and examined the bloodied cloth. "Some of my colleagues at the Historical Society. Of course, Tyler Byrd knows."

"Anyone else?"

His eyes lit up. "Yes. When I was discussing them with Byrd—checking to see if what I'd bought matched anything his work crew found—Bartalotta was in his office. I always suspected Byrd had connections to that sort."

Poor Nic again. What a coincidence. He was the common denominator every time the lights went out.

We heard cars pulling up outside and a moment later, flashlights raced through the backyard. Two sheriff's deputies jogged around the yard and began a search. Then a voice barked from the front door and footsteps entered the hall.

"Angela, honey are you okay?" Bear emerged with a pissed-off expression on his face that he wasn't trying to hide. "Every time I leave you alone, someone gets beat up, shot at, or worse."

By "worse," I assumed he was referring to me.

THIRTY-SIX

"So, do you think he's in there?" Angel asked, sipping her coffee beside Bear in the front seat of his unmarked cruiser. "How long are we waiting?"

We sat fifty yards from the front door of a rundown, doublewide trailer parked in a grove of pines around the bend. There was a green, two-door coupe tucked beneath a fiberglass carport in the front yard. The trailer windows were shaded and there were no signs of life. This was the only home—if that's what you could call it—for a mile, and the dusty road ended abruptly out front. We were fifteen miles south of Winchester in an enclave of trailer parks, decrepit townhouses, and farm country all mixed together like a billboard for community planning. I think all the slumlords in the county chipped in to build this little *community*.

Bear checked his watch. "It's near nine a.m. and his car is out front."

"How'd you find him?"

"Phone trace on Sarah Salazar. She called here two nights ago and again last night. It's a rental and the owner says Iggi's the only tenant."

We'd left Ernie's last night after the crime lab finished—again. The perp, whoever it was, was batting a thousand—no prints, no tracks, and no trace. Later at home, Bear and Angel sat in my living room draining a pot of coffee and discussing Angel's meeting with Sarah Salazar and Ernie's break-in. After three hours, they reached two conclusions. First, Winchester never had a crime wave before, but was having a big one now. Second, Bear was pissed off, and he said so again.

"Angela, you can't play detective alone anymore. You're with me this morning so I can keep an eye on you."

"I did find out about Iggi and Salazar, didn't I? I'm the one who found out about their other job."

"Sure, but…"

"And you said we might be able to link Salazar's murderer to Tuck's, right? And that's good if we do."

Bear threw up his hands. "Okay, okay. Yes."

"And I found the coins…"

"No, I found the coins," I said, but knew I wouldn't get the credit. I didn't, and decided instead to move our morning along. "I'm going inside to find Iggi."

Angel said, "Pull up front, Bear. Iggi's about to wake up."

"Don't start that again." Bear took a precautionary glance into the back seat before he opened the console between the seats and took out a small, compact semi-automatic. He handed it to her. "I'm not expecting trouble, but I don't want you unarmed if there is any."

"All right." Angel took the handgun.

I said, "Angel, give me five minutes, then send Bear in." Then I focused on 'being there' and went in search of Ignacio Suarez.

Iggi lay passed out on a dilapidated sofa amidst a dozen empty beer cans and the remnants of a pizza. The trailer was strewn with trash and broken furniture. But that didn't bother me; it was the 12-gauge pump shotgun nearby. It lay beneath the pizza box on the coffee table in front of him.

Iggi was spooked—and he wasn't taking chances.

The blinds were drawn and the trailer was quiet. A table lamp beside him dimly lighted the room. The only other light was a single, dangling light bulb at the far end of the hall above the rear door. That door was locked and a piece of cardboard covered its window. The other two rooms were stark and empty.

Iggi had locked himself alone in a dark, lifeless hiding place. Either he was terrified of someone or he was a vampire. Both were possible. After all, last month I didn't believe in ghosts.

"Iggi, oh, Iggi … it's time to wake up."

I stood in front of the couch watching the snoring man. Iggi was a short, stout man of about thirty. He had shaggy black hair, and his face showed scars from a war lost to teenage acne. He reeked of beer and dirty clothes. He wore soiled blue jeans and a dark sweatshirt. His cutoff sleeves revealed powerful arms and leathery skin from hard labor in all manner of weather. Those powerful arms also revealed something that startled me. On his left forearm was a tattoo of a cross with a halo above it.

"So, we meet again, Iggi. Been doing any nighttime digging?" He didn't move. "Well, cell phones give me a little pep—let's see what else does."

I grabbed the lamp cord beside Iggi and held tight. A surge bristled through me and exhilarated me. The light flickered and the bulb flashed out. I let go. The tingling continued inside me and I was energized—pardon the pun—and euphoric. It took all my concentration to fight the high trying to get out.

Now I know why some people get hooked on cocaine.

I grabbed the shotgun and hefted it. It felt fully loaded. This wouldn't do.

"Sheriff's Department." Bear was outside pounding on the front door "Iggi Suarez, come out. Frederick County Sheriff."

Iggi's eyes flashed open. When Bear pounded again, he deftly rolled off the couch and grabbed for the shotgun all in one movement.

Fortunately, he didn't find it.

Panic contorted his face. He slid his bare feet into old running shoes beside the couch and glanced around. He saw the shotgun lying in the chair across the room, took it, and crept to the rear of the trailer.

"Iggi, come out."

He flipped open the rear door lock, grabbed the knob, and pulled. The door didn't budge. He tried again. Nothing—I held it tight to keep him from escaping. He double-checked the lock and tugged it again. Panic spread. He jerked the lock back and forth, yanked the knob, and tried over and over. The door didn't budge. He kicked at it. Drove his shoulder into it. Kicked again.

Nothing worked.

He stepped back and readied another kick. I opened the door a foot. When he reached for it, I slammed it closed again. I opened and closed the door twice more.

"*Madre de Dios, fantasmas.*"

I could guess what that meant.

The front door crashed open and Bear charged in. "Police!"

Iggi lifted the shotgun and headed down the hall. When he reached the living room, he flattened himself against the wall and pointed the shotgun toward Bear.

"Get out. I not do nothin'. Get out."

Bear froze. His weapon was out in front of him, but he was looking away from Iggi. "Okay, Iggi, okay. Put the gun down. No one needs to get shot—especially me."

Iggi slid into the living room just as Angel walked in the front door. Her eyes locked onto the shotgun and she stopped half inside the door. She held Bear's .380 down at her side.

No one spoke. No one moved.

I said, "Angel, relax. It's okay."

Bear broke the standoff. "Easy, Iggi. I want to talk." He eased around and faced him, pointing his gun at the ceiling. "Easy, pal. Go easy. You don't want to shoot a cop."

"What you want?"

"Just to talk."

"No, man, no." Iggi shifted the shotgun back and forth between Angel and Bear. His eyes darted between them as sweat glistened on his face. "I did nothin'. Nothin' man."

"Okay," Angel said, trying to appear calm. "I'm Angela. Sarah told you about me."

"Sarah?" Iggi aimed the shotgun at Angel. "How you know that, lady?"

"I…" Angel never finished her sentence.

Bear stepped toward Iggi but the shotgun thrust into his face, stopping him.

"I shoot you, man. Get back."

Enough. "Angel, the shotgun is empty. The shells are in the pizza box."

"The gun's empty, Bear." Angel's shoulders slumped. "The shells are in the pizza."

Bear glanced down at the 12-gauge cartridges lying among two cold slices of pepperoni and mushroom. When his eyes rose and met Iggi's, I saw it coming before Iggi's brain registered the extra pizza toppings.

When Iggi glanced down, Bear grabbed the shotgun barrel and twisted. Iggi flinched, squeezing the trigger. The barely audible "click" sealed his fate. Bear snatched the gun away as his other powerful, ham-sized fist smashed into Iggi's face and set him crashing backward over the table into a heap on the floor. Blood spurted from his nose and his eyes shuttered closed.

"You son of a bitch." Bear descended on him like a vulture on prey. "You have the right to remain silent… but you're not gonna."

Iggi's swelling eyes cracked open and all he could say was, "I talk, I talk. *¡Madre de Dios, fantasmas!* I give back everythin.'"

THIRTY-SEVEN

"Deal first," Iggi said with a mixture of nerves and defiance. "I say nothin' unless you protect me."

"Protect you from who?" Bear stood across the living room. "Help me and I'll help you."

"No, way, man. Deal first."

"Let's see, Iggi. There's resisting arrest, assaulting a police officer—add attempted murder because I heard you pull the trigger."

Iggi bit his lip but never looked up. He sat balanced on the edge of the couch with his hands handcuffed behind him. He stared at the floor, pale and scared. Sweat stained his shirt and he was trying hard not to look around, perhaps fearful he might see me.

"Iggi, please help us." Angel was leaning against the dish-cluttered counter in the adjoining kitchen. "You have information about Raymundo. Help find his killer. That's all we want—Raymundo's killer."

"If I talk," he muttered, "you have to find mine."

"Yours?" she asked. "What did you and Raymundo do?"

"Deal—and you gotta swear."

"Deal, huh?" Bear sneered. "Talk or it's gonna get worse."

"You not scarin' me, Braddock. I know 'bout you. You partner got it and maybe you soon."

Maybe I could help get Iggi talking. I whispered to Angel and a smile etched across her face. "Do you believe in ghosts? '*Madre de Dios, fantasmas.*' Isn't that what you said when Tuck wouldn't let you out the back door?"

He froze and the muscles in his arms flexed. "No."

Angel continued, "Tuck came back, Iggi—he's sitting right beside you. He wouldn't let you out the back door, would he?"

"*Madre.*" Iggi's eyes flashed wide. "You don't scare me."

I touched the lamp for a re-charge and leaned into Iggi, blowing a long, hot breath into his ear. "Start talking, you shit-bird, or I'll ram that shotgun up your ass."

"Ah." Iggi slapped his ear and bolted upright. "*No, Dios.*"

Bear grabbed his arm. "Talk, smart guy."

"Iggi, didn't you load your shotgun last night?" Angel asked. "Wasn't it on the coffee table?"

"*Si, Madre de Dios, fantasmas.*"

Iggi's eyes darted around the room and he trembled, struggling against Bear's grasp. He looked down where I'd been sitting. I was on the other side from him now.

I blew into his other ear. "*Fantasmas.* Talk shithead."

"*Madre. Si, si.* The Diggin' Man pay me and Raymundo do diggin'. Raymundo and me took stuff. We want more money. We had to get away from this place. If the Diggin' Man knew what we done, we be dead. Raymundo—maybe me soon. Please, take me out."

"The Diggin' Man?" Bear shoved Iggi down onto the couch. "Sit. Now, what are you talking about?"

Iggi crawled onto the couch armrest. Sweat pooled beneath his eyes. "Raymundo and me dig up stuff the Diggin' Man didn't know was there. We sold it."

I said, "Angel, it's my vision of the two men. They found those coins and sold them. That's where Ernie's and Sarah's came from— I'd bet on it. Iggi was there."

Angel asked, "From Kelly's Dig? The gold coins?"

"*Madre*, you know. The Diggin' Man find out, 'cause Raymundo got killed. All we was to do was get the bones out. Just bones."

"Get the bones out?" Angel sat down and gently grasped his shoulder. "Iggi, calm down. Tuck won't hurt you unless I tell him to. Tell us about the Digging Man. Who is he?"

I patted Iggi's cheek. He recoiled and almost cried. I said, "Yeah, pal. I'll be good. Tell Angel everything."

Iggi closed his eyes and muttered a prayer.

"Was it Lucca?" Bear asked, and the name sent Iggi rigid.

"Lucca?" He met Bear's eyes and his face said he was more afraid of Lucca than of me. "You know 'bout Lucca?"

Bear nodded, and lying, said, "Yeah, we do. You better decide if you want to talk to me or him."

"*Muy bien.*" Iggi's voice was slow and broken, articulating the words as if they were poison. "Okay, *Señor* Braddock. I never met the Diggin' Man. Raymundo do that."

"Go on, Iggi," Angel said. "Bear will help you."

"Lucca …" Iggi took a long breath. "They say he from New York. He kill for money. He kill me for money."

Tears escaped Angel's eyes. "Did Lucca kill Tuck?"

"I dunno." Iggi's voice was unsteady, apologetic. "Maybe—I dunno."

Bear said, "Cut the bullshit. Start with what you *do* know."

His answer made me shiver.

"*Si, si*. It start when me and Raymundo was workin' for *Señor* Byrd."

THIRTY-EIGHT

"LUCCA TUSCANI," BEAR SAID, peering at Iggi through the observation room's one-way glass. "He's our killer—has to be."

"Can Iggi identify him?" Captain Sutter asked.

"No. Iggi only had the name. He never met Tuscani. I'm heading to the FBI to see what they have."

"Best guess?"

My best guess was that "Homicidal Maniac" was on Lucca Tuscani's business cards.

Bear tapped the glass when Iggi tried to open the interrogation room door. Iggi retreated into his chair. "A New York shooter—mobbed up."

"Smells like Nic Bartalotta. He's the only one I know with that kind of juice around here. But why?"

Bear recapped Iggi's entire story for her, spending most of his time on the mysterious Diggin' Man who hired Salazar and Iggi to move the bones from Kelly's Dig and their treasure hunting exploits that ensued.

He ended with, "And all this started when Iggi and Salazar found those coins and antiques."

"So, I'm thinking Tyler Byrd gains most by getting those bones out of his construction project. How he knew about them, I don't know." Captain Sutter thought a moment before going on. "He sends Iggi and Salazar to move them, but they find some loot and go into business for themselves. And shortly after, Salazar's murdered."

Bear was nodding. "He needs muscle to clean up and maybe gets Poor Nic to bring Tuscani in to clean up."

"We just don't have a connection between Nic and Byrd." Captain Sutter watched Iggi. "Not yet. What's your next move?"

"First, I gotta get what I can on Tuscani. Then, I'm headed to see Liam McCorkle, an antique dealer down south. Ernie Stuart did business with him. McCorkle might know who the Diggin' Man is. It's worth a shot."

"Take it." Sutter was thoughtful. "Spence and Clemens have been running phone and financial records on everyone surrounding Tuck. They said they're onto something."

"Cap, I've been all through those records. There's nothing there."

"Well, for now, I'm giving them some extra rope on this."

Bear grunted. "Great, Cap. I wonder who they're gonna hang with it?"

THIRTY-NINE

BEAR SAT AT HIS desk, focused on Lucca Tuscani. He was shuffling paper and banging on his computer. I was bored watching, so I decided to stroll down to see what my two favorite comedic detectives, Spence and Clemens, were doing. Instead of playing crossword puzzles or video games as I thought, they were rushing out the door like real-life detectives often do.

"You drive," Spence barked. "He'll be leaving soon."

I took the back seat of their unmarked cruiser and expected them to head out chasing some leads. I was wrong. We parked in the visitor's lot where they sat watching the rear entrance of the sheriff's office.

Clemens was looking around, uneasy. "Are you sure about this, Mikey?"

"Hell yes."

"Really sure?"

"There he goes. Wait for him to clear the corner." Spence tapped the dashboard and signaled Clemens to start their car. "The captain says he's heading to the FBI so he'll be gone a while."

A hundred yards away, Bear pulled out of the parking lot and turned right.

I said, "What are you doing, Spence?" They were apparently immune to my ghost-speak. "You're going to tail Bear?"

No, they weren't. I was wrong.

Instead of falling in a safe distance behind Bear, Clemens made a hard U-turn and sped away in the opposite direction. He watched his rearview mirror for several blocks, not relaxing until Spence said, "Clear. Bear's nowhere in sight."

"Ah, boys, what are you up to?" No one answered me.

Fifteen minutes later, I got my answer and I wasn't happy when I did. It would have been better if we'd tailed Bear to the FBI. Anything would have been better.

Clemens rolled up to the curb a half-block from the Hunter's Ridge Garden Apartments. The complex was a cluster of two-story buildings that resembled rows of English Manor houses. Each building housed several condominiums and garden apartments owned predominantly by professionals and academics—many of whom were Angel's university colleagues. Some were close friends; especially one such ground floor, courtyard entrance unit. That was number Three-A West, belonging to one rather unacademic Theodore Braddock.

I leaned forward in the seat and flicked Spence's ear—he recoiled and threw an accusatory glance at Clemens. I said, "You two better not be doing what I think you're doing."

"Okay," Spence said, jumping out his door. "I'll go in. If you see him coming, call fast. That'll give me a good two minutes to get out. Then, meet me around the other side of the courtyard. And Christ, don't let him see you."

"No kidding. Jeez, Mikey. I don't like this. We don't have a warrant. If the captain ..."

"Quit whining."

"But ..."

It was too late. Spence and I were already jogging down the sidewalk toward Bear's backyard. I followed him to the rear patio door where it took him three minutes to pick the lock—about an hour less than I bet. I could have saved him the time and shown him the hide-a-key beneath the patio table, but it was fun watching him sweat.

Inside, Spence zigged and zagged around the five-room flat until he found Bear's computer atop an old wooden table in the spare bedroom. I'd comment on all the junk, stacks of books, and movies piled everywhere, but invading Bear's home was bad enough. Chastising his manly décor would have really been in poor taste.

The computer was in sleep mode. Spence tapped the keyboard, and in a few seconds it came to life. Bear used no password and in a few more seconds, Spence was opening up his files and surfing through his emails. He even came prepared with a USB flash drive.

"Spence, if you plant evidence, I'll haunt you forever."

I watched him peruse months of emails. I was about to chuckle—the knucklehead didn't seem to know what he was doing—when he clicked on a couple buttons, sorted the mail by sender, and clapped his hands in victory.

"Gotcha, Braddock."

Reading over his shoulder, my mouth went dry. Spence was looking at a group of thirty or forty emails. Some went back more than six months and others were as recent as last week. The sender's name bit like a rattlesnake.

Dr. Angela Hill-Tucker—my Angel.

"I'm sure Bear and Angel have a good reason for all these emails. They're pals, remember?" Was I trying to convince him or me?

He was elated. "Oh, my, Detective Braddock. You have some 'splaining to do."

My insides—if I had any—were rockin' and rollin'. As the dozens and dozens of emails scrolled by, Spence's fixation on Bear and Angel didn't seem too stupid anymore. Had I missed something? No. No. They're pals—that's all. It had to be all.

Spence pulled a USB flash drive from his pocket to copy the files just as his cell phone buzzed with a text message from Clemens.

Bear was on his way.

"Shit, I'm not done."

Spence pocketed the USB drive and backtracked out of the apartment. He relocked the door and evaporated through a row of tall ferns. Another two minutes and we were back in the cruiser. I don't think Spence breathed the entire trip.

Clemens was pale. "What'd you find?"

"Emails between the missus and Braddock. I couldn't copy them, but they're there."

"What's that to us?"

"Leads," Spence said. "But, after we get a warrant, we'll be calling them '*evidence.*'"

FORTY

"WHY SO SAD?"

"What?" I looked up, and instead of the bald spot on Clemens's head, I saw the two young girls from my visions watching me. Strange—not that anything was normal anymore—but I was in my den instead of the backseat of Spence's cruiser.

The brunette was kneeling beside my recliner scratching Hercule's ears. He was, of course, all about spirits these days. "Why so sad?"

"Sad? Where'd you come from?"

The blonde seemed to be on the other side of Hercule, standing farther behind the chair. I say "seemed to be" because I couldn't focus on them, and it wasn't my eyes that were blurry—it was them.

"Why are you so sad, Oliver?" The blonde asked, again. "Don't be sad."

They knew my name? "Who are you? What do you want from me?"

"You know." The brunette seemed to be playing coy like school girls sometimes do. "Of course you know."

"Please," the blonde said, "there's no need to be sad. You'll fix everything. You have to."

I stood there looking from one to the other. Hercule woofed and bade the brunette scratch him more. She dutifully obeyed and I continued gawking.

"Please, I have so many questions..."

"You have to hurry." The brunette stood up and reached back, taking the blonde's hand. "You saw what he did. You have to stop him. He will do it again."

A haunting vision of two young girls' murders played in my thoughts. "That was you I saw. Your murders? Who did it—who killed you?"

The brunette said, "That was a long time ago. Very long. Now the soldiers protect us. You can't help us. It's too late for us. Help the others."

"How? Tell me who killed you?" I took two quick steps toward them. "Please. Just tell me who it is."

"Help the others, and hurry." The brunette's eyes flashed wide— my approach startled them. She retreated behind Hercule and joined arms with her companion. "Don't."

"I'm sorry, please..." I stepped back, but it was too late. They faded and were mere dust drifting in the window's sunlight.

As the girls disappeared, someone began unlocking my front door and I went to the den window to check. The instant I did, a brew of jealousy churned inside me. It was Bear. Something startled him and he turned around, visually surprised to see Angel pull up to the curb. He relocked the front door and met her on the sidewalk.

Something strange happened just then. I tried to blink myself outside onto the porch to listen in. I could not budge. Just as I had been twice before, I was stuck in my tracks and unable to spirit myself anywhere. Before, I had been forced to witness the two girl's murders and later, Carmen Delgado's abduction.

What was it that held me now?

Angel and Bear's conversation didn't last long and it was interesting even without benefit of the words. Bear's side was worrisome—I could tell from the way his head shook and his occasional glance skyward. Angel wasn't taking his news well, either. She stepped back from him, glanced toward the house and my den window, and flashed a hand to her face. She looked upset and angry. Their tête-à-tête went back and forth for two or three more minutes until *it* happened.

Angel's hand snapped out and Bear reluctantly removed our house key from his key ring and surrendered it. Afterward, Angel gave him a quick kiss on the cheek, snuck another glance toward the house, and drove off.

Bear watched her go. He looked sad, and if kicking the side of his cruiser meant anything, pissed off.

The newest question on a long list of unanswered ones was—what the hell just happened?

FORTY-ONE

FOR TWO HOURS, I wandered around the house looking for Doc. Even though he rarely gave a straight answer or offered more than ethereal philosophy, talking with him did make me feel better. I could use some of his name-calling and deprecation right now. Of course, I couldn't find him anywhere.

Even Hercule stayed sleeping in the chair and uninterested in either a chat or toss of the ball.

I gave up and dialed into Angel. She was halfway through a Caesar salad at the Old Town Bistro in Winchester. Tyler Byrd and André Cartier were there, debating the pros and cons of protecting historical sites across Virginia. André was an expert on the topic and Byrd was an expert on the free enterprise system—making lots of money.

Considering what Iggi told us, this was one meeting I wished I'd heard from the beginning. Angel was just getting to the good part and the redness on Tyler's face told me he knew it, too.

Tyler was a medium height, stout, balding man. He was in his early sixties and had a muscular, fire-plug build that I found very construction-worker-esque. He looked more like a professional wrestler than a businessman, even in his two-piece suit.

"Suarez and Salazar? Oh, I know where this is going." Tyler folded his powerful hands in front of him and leaned back in his chair. "Let me tell you what I told Braddock—I don't know shit."

André began, "They worked for you ..."

"Listen, I didn't know anything about them hunting for bones or pirate treasure at Kelly's Orchard. I gave them odd jobs here and there. They were supposed to be doing preconstruction site work—clearing trees and helping the surveyors. I had no idea they were prospecting at night. If I had, I would have fired them."

"Some might think you stood to profit from concealing what they found—the bones and such." André was curt. "See the point?"

"Sure, except there's a fatal flaw in your big conspiracy theory," Tyler said, leaning his hulking body forward.

"What's that?"

"It didn't stop anything."

Angel and André exchanged glances that said, "Oops, he's right."

Tyler went on. "Those two knuckleheads dug up their loot a week *before* my crew found those bones—and we reported it to the police. I'm responsible for putting a hold on this project, not those two. Me. I could have plowed it all under, but I didn't."

He had a good point. He had a very good point.

Angel said, "Your survey crews called the police first—before they called you. That's what you told police."

Tyler Byrd was not known as a patient man. Nor for being bullied or intimidated. So, when he lurched to his feet with a steel finger stabbing at Angel, I wasn't surprised.

"Now you listen here, Professor Tucker. I had nothing to do with Salazar's murder—your husband's either. Who do you think you are? You're not the cops. You're supposed to be advising the court on what to do with Kelly's Dig. I suggest you stick to that before…"

"Before what, Tyler?" Angel snapped. "Before something else happens to me? Like getting shot at? Attacked? My best friend attacked again? What else could you possibly do?"

"He could kill you, Angel," I said. "Go easy."

André grabbed her hand and gave it a gentle tug. "Easy, Angela. Please, you don't mean that. Tyler wasn't threatening…"

"No, I wasn't."

The three of them looked around the patio at the tables of people watching. Tyler sat back down. "I'm sorry. I didn't mean what it sounded like. I'm losing hundreds of thousands on this deal and everyone thinks I'm a murderer."

Angel said, "There is more than money at stake here."

"Yes, but a lot of money, too." Tyler wasn't interested in being conciliatory. "My partner was damn careful about the Kelly Orchard historical zone. He negotiated allowances so we could get the excavation through without disrupting the original farmhouse site. He was a fanatic about that, and it set well with everyone at the time. Now, this gravesite business could cost me five million or more."

"Your partner?" André asked. "Who's that?"

The question drew the air from Tyler's bluster. His eyes dropped to the table and he looked irritated he'd spilled the beans.

"Nicholas Bartalotta," he said, and his fingers turned white around his beer.

Angel's mouth dropped. "Poor Nic?"

"Yes, Nic." Tyler went on. "Nicholas's distant family owned Kelly Orchard back in the sixties—at least for a short time. That's why he decided to retire here. He took an interest in the bypass project when it first got started and came to me as an investor."

"I see," André said. "Is that why he wanted the farmhouse saved?"

"Yes. Nic planned the construction through the farm. The original plans brought the main highway ramp closer to the farmhouse. He got it moved. He wanted to save the farmhouse at all cost. Sentimental old fart. He even provides security at the site now."

"Bartalotta runs your security?" André asked. "Isn't that the fox guarding the hen house?"

"No, it's not. He owns a security company, doesn't he?" He pulled a wad of bills from his pocket and dropped several onto the table. When he did, a heavy coin fell out onto the table beside the bills.

Angel scooped it up. "Very nice gold piece, Tyler."

André eyed the coin. "May we ask where you got this?"

"No, you may not."

Angel handed the coin back to him. "Then, does the name Liam McCorkle mean anything to you?"

"No." Tyler strode off and never looked back.

Angel said, "Tyler Byrd and Poor Nic are partners. And Nic's family owned Kelly Orchard forty years ago. Some coincidence."

"I don't believe in them," André said. "And I'd bet those two have many more secrets—much more interesting ones, too. I'd bet my life on it."

FORTY-TWO

"ANGEL, WE NEED TO talk about Bear."

We were standing on the sidewalk outside my office. We'd come straight here after lunch to find Bear.

Angel glanced around to see if anyone was watching. "Tuck, I can't very well have a discussion with you out here, now can I?"

"But…"

"Hold on," she pulled out her cell phone and put it to her ear. "What?"

Wow, neat trick. I got serious. "Is there anything about him I should know? I mean, you know, anything you know about him that I don't?"

"Like what?" Angel scrunched up her face. "What on earth are you talking about?"

Jesus, she was making this difficult. "Angel, it's about our house key and all the emails."

"The key? Emails?"

"Not just a key—our house key. And lots of emails. Is there anything, you know, with you two I need to know? I mean, before I died of course ... no, I mean ..."

"Are you insinuating what I think?"

Yes, I guess I was. "Well, I'm asking."

"No." She stormed into the office and was immediately buzzed into the detective's bullpen. Once inside, she slammed her phone shut. "Really, I cannot believe you."

"Please, just hear me out." I looked over and saw Bear in Captain Sutter's office with a scowl and a bad attitude. His face was drawn and mouth clamped tight, holding back what I knew was a flurry of expletives for the man standing near us watching him. "No, wait a minute. Something's going on."

Mike Spence had a big, evil smile on his face. The little bastard even winked and blew Bear a cute, exaggerated kiss. He wanted Bear to know who clipped him.

The bullpen had a half-dozen cops and detectives milling around, but it was deathly quiet.

"Angel, wait at my desk. I gotta see what's up with Bear."

Angel huffed and headed across the room.

Inside Captain Sutter's office, I said to Bear, "What's going on, partner?" I knew instantly when Captain Sutter held out a clear plastic evidence bag with my .380 Walther backup gun in it. The last time I'd seen it, it was in my den the night of my murder.

"It took us three days, but we fished it out of the sewer drain two blocks from Tuck's house. Ballistics matched it to Tuck's murder."

Bear didn't look at the gun. "And?"

"A neighbor saw you roaming around up the street a few nights ago."

He cursed and said, "No kidding. That's the night someone shot at Angel—it's all in my report. I chased someone up the street. My prints won't be on the gun."

"No, you're right." Sutter set the evidence bag on her desk. "There are no prints at all. Not even Tuck's. Wiped clean."

"The murderer wiped it and tossed it after killing him. I'd expect that."

"Really?" Captain Sutter rubbed her eyes. "Tell me about the emails. I'm told there are tons between you and Angela. More to Carmen Delgado. What the hell is going on?"

"Nothing, Cap."

"Nothing? Bullshit."

Bear folded his arms and set his jaw. "Search my house, read my mail, hell, you don't need a warrant—do whatever. This is bullshit and you know it."

"I hope you're right. The sheriff wants your ass, Bear. But he'll take your badge and gun for now."

"Suspended?" Bear dropped his head and cursed loudly. "For what? Being friends with my partner's wife?"

"How about withholding information?" Captain Sutter went to her office door and looked out. "Tell me again about the night Tuck was killed. Spence pulled your cell records. Angela called you at 10 p.m., right?"

Oh, shit. She did? I said, "Ah, Bear. You never mentioned that before. Neither has Angel."

Bear nodded. "Sure, yeah. Okay, she did. So?"

"So? That's not in your report. First I heard it." Captain Sutter's face was on fire. "She never brought it up, either."

"Now hold on," Bear glanced out the window and saw half the office watching him. "Look, Cap. Angela and Tuck were having a bad time of it. We'd been working night and day on Salazar's case—on top of our other caseload. He hadn't been home at all in almost a week. Jesus, she asked me to cut him loose early. So I did."

"She asked *you* to send him home?"

Bear shrugged.

"And you didn't think that was important to mention?" Captain Sutter dropped down in her desk chair. "You know what this looks like?"

I sure did.

"Listen, Cap," Bear turned his back to the window. "The call is innocent. I swear."

"Christ, Bear, this whole thing looks bad." She dropped her face into her hands and took a few long, deep breaths. When she looked up, any understanding was gone from her eyes. "Anything else I need to know? Put it all on the table now."

I leaned down to his ear. "Well, partner? Something *we* need to know?"

He started to answer when he peered back toward the bullpen and burst from Sutter's office. "Oh, hell no." He charged across the bullpen toward Angel. I followed.

Spence stood over Angel at his desk where she was crying. "Detective, I just explained that."

Bear never slowed and was over Spence's desk before Spence could see him coming. He landed a crushing right into Spence's face that sent him crashing over his desk chair onto the floor. An "oof" of air rushed from Spence's lungs.

"Braddock," Captain Sutter yelled. "Get off him."

Angel grabbed his arm, "Bear, no."

Me, I was enjoying myself. Despite my angst with Bear, I would pay money to see this go on another two rounds. "I dare you to hit him again, Bear. I double-dare you."

"Back off, Bear," Spence snorted, wiping a stream of blood from his mouth. "Back off."

Captain Sutter pulled Bear away, cussing as she did. But, as Spence rose to his feet, Angel stepped in and landed a loud, vicious slap across his face. She followed it with a harsh, head-spinning second.

Spence went down again.

"For Christ's sake," Captain Sutter barked. "Everyone back off."

Holy crap, I wish I'd done that.

"Captain, I was questioning her about that phone call," Spence said as red welts glowed on his face. "She gave me some shit about Tuck working too much. I want charges..."

"Shut up," Captain Sutter yelled. "You asked for that. Facts are facts but you're so far out in left field I could bitch-slap you myself."

"What about the emails and the phone calls? We've got the gun and Delgado said..."

"Bullshit." Sutter bored an iron finger into his chest. "We got a gun with no fingerprints. A bullet matches a bullet—so what? You still don't know who fired the damn thing. And don't bullshit me about Carmen Delgado. I spoke to her myself."

"Angel," I said. "I tried to tell you earlier. When Spence got into Bear's computer—they didn't have a warrant. They broke into his house."

Angel turned to Bear and quoted me word for word. To Spence she said, "You bastard."

"What? You little shit." Bear started toward Spence again but Captain Sutter pushed him away.

Captain Sutter said, "What's this, Spence? You told me that Delgado…"

"I can explain." Spence patted the air. "It's like this…"

"In my office," Sutter said. "Now."

Spence retreated across the room with Captain Sutter behind. Angel stood looking at Bear with half-angry, half-sorrowful eyes. "Bear…"

"Forget it. What's done is done. Besides, I've identified Lucca." He stood over his desk and picked up a large manila file in his inbox. He opened it and took out two photographs. "The FBI sent this over. This is Lucca Tuscani. He's a mobbed-up shooter like we thought. His real name is Lucca Voccelli."

The photographs were old and taken in poor light from bad angles—surveillance shots taken in haste. The man in the photos was in his early fifties and was broad-shouldered and bulky—not fat but muscular and strong. Everything about him was dark—his hair, his Mediterranean complexion, and his angry eyes. He looked ominous and unfriendly. If there was a poster child for a mob assassin, we were looking at him.

Behind us, Captain Sutter's door banged open and Spence emerged, looking a little ass-chewed and whipped. He made eye contact with Bear—unfriendly contact—and trudged out of the office. Captain Sutter headed straight for us.

"Okay, Bear, Spence's screw up bought you a couple days. The sheriff owes me a couple favors and I just called them in. For now, you keep your badge and gun."

"Cap, listen..."

"No, you listen." She stepped into him and rose on her tiptoes to meet his eyes—she still fell short. "If you're lying and make me look bad, you ain't gonna make it to trial."

"I'm not, Cap, I..."

"You have two days, max. Find me a killer, Bear—or Kelly's Dig might be your grave, too."

FORTY-THREE

STAUNTON, VIRGINIA, IS A quaint historic town some ninety-five miles south of Winchester. The town is snuggled into the heart of the Shenandoah Valley and much of it has shown little change since the Civil War. Historians will tell you, as did the Internet welcome site Angel read to me, that Staunton was saved from the ravaging many Virginia towns took during that war. Pronounced "Stanton" as opposed to the phonetic spelling, its history includes Woodrow Wilson, a famous country music quartet, Mary Baldwin College, and a long litany of historical markers.

None of those brought us here.

It was close to six o'clock in the evening when Angel, Bear, and I turned off Route 81 toward the center of town. During the drive, most of the conversation was about finding Iggi Suarez's mysterious "Diggin' Man," and how Salazar's murder might be linked to mine. They were acting odd, both avoiding the lingering questions that hung between them like fog—keys, emails, unspoken secrets. I understood why Angel was avoiding them—she knew I was sitting in the back seat. Why Bear was avoiding them was the real mystery and I didn't like it at all.

Silence hung over the last half-hour.

Angel broke the quiet. "Why did you ask me along? I thought you wanted me to stay out of your investigation."

"I do, but now that everyone thinks we're the new Bonnie and Clyde, you might as well tag along." Bear slowed as we approached the outskirts of town. "And, you're safer with me."

I said, "Maybe, maybe not."

Angel ignored me. "Where's McCorkle's shop?"

"A mile up ahead."

Liam McCorkle could be the key to all the mayhem surrounding Kelly's Dig. He could have information on the Diggin' Man and that might mean on Salazar's murder. If we were lucky, maybe my own, too.

Since we were short on leads and long on murders, McCorkle was our best shot.

"Here we go." Bear made a sharp left into an alley that caught Angel and me by surprise. Above us was a second-story billboard affixed to the alley wall that announced, "McCorkle's Heritage Antiques."

"It's down the alley," he said. "This town has hundreds of antique dealers. But McCorkle is the king of the hill."

The alley led to a large gravel parking lot where only one car remained. At the far end of the lot was a three-story, clapboard building. Bear wheeled in front of the wrought iron fence that surrounded a fieldstone walk and narrow garden. The walk led to McCorkle's shop.

"By appointment only." Angel read the sign on the iron gate as she climbed out of the car. "That's us."

"I hope it'll be worth the drive. Not that the company was bad, mind you." Bear leaned over and threw an arm around Angel. "Dinner on me later."

"Why, Detective," Angel said, batting her eyes. "It's a date."

Ouch.

I leaned into Angel. "Hey, don't forget about me. You know, your recently dead lover and husband?"

"Dinner sounds great," she said, turning away from Bear. "I'm sure Tuck would understand. After all, a girl has to eat."

"Tuck?" Bear's eyebrows rose. "Him again? I suppose that was for his benefit?"

"Yes, me again," I muttered. "You watch him, Angel; close."

Angel started through the gate when Bear stopped her. "Hold it. I know Ernie thinks McCorkle is clean, but I'm going to grill him. Keep your ears open for any history crap that doesn't make sense."

"History crap?" Angel voice was thick with irritation. "History crap?"

"What do I know about that? If he lies, I want to know."

Angel rang the doorbell. "Of course."

No one came to the door. Angel rang again, and then a third time. "Didn't you tell him six sharp?"

"Yeah. It's two minutes 'till."

I peeked in the window beside the double front doors. "Maybe he's snooty like Ernie and wants us to wait. I'll go see."

"No, be quiet," Angel said, and when Bear's eyebrows rose, continued, "I mean, no, maybe he's on his way."

"Yeah, right." Bear headed for the gate. "I'll go around back." He disappeared down the alley.

After five minutes, Angel got bored and began peeking in the windows, pressing her face against the glass like a child at a toy store. "Where the devil is Bear?"

"Angel, watch him," I said. "Something's not right with him lately. And we need to talk, too."

"Oh, Tuck. You're jealous. Bear is ..."

A dull, metallic pop split the air as the window shattered beside Angel's head.

"Angel, get back!"

FORTY-FOUR

"STAY HERE," I YELLED and thrust myself through the front door.

Inside, I was standing in a huge, grand hallway. There were no lights on, no sounds, and no sign of the shooter. Only musty air and the familiar sensation of danger greeted me. It itched inside me like a rash. I listened and waited, hoping for a telltale sign of the shooter's position. None reached me. Just as I realized how silly it was for me to worry about danger, something scuffled outside where Angel waited.

Crash!

Bear kicked in the front door behind me. He burst through, gun first, and flattened himself against the wall. We'd done this a hundred times together. Every other time, however, the risk of the chase was checked by covering each other. He was now alone—no backup, no partner, no me to cover his ass. He began to move deeper into the hall when I stopped him cold.

"Get back, Bear. Stay here and let me go first." I watched his eyes flash surprise. "Listen to me, Bear. Listen."

"Shit." He froze, and before retreating to the front door, whispered, "I hope that's you, Tuck, or I'm going crazy. Shit, shit, shit."

I ran into a large office to the right of the front door. Inside was a battlefield-sized desk cluttered with papers and books but no one was there. Across the hall was a similar room filled with red shrouded display tables and wall-to-wall bookshelves.

Nothing. No one. I moved on.

Down the hall was a set of open, grand doors that reached the twelve-foot ceiling. I went through into a cavernous ballroom on the other side—when I did, I felt the uncontrollable itch creeping into my head again; something, or someone, was ahead. Above me was a three-story-high barrel ceiling and endless rows of shelves, display racks, and cubical-like display areas. Each held a plethora of antiques and wares from every walk of life. A dozen sprawling chandeliers hung from the ceiling, reminiscent of the ballroom's turn-of-the-century grandeur. I froze in a mixture of amazement and trepidation.

Still, I saw no one—heard nothing. The itch spread inside me.

The maze would take a dozen cops to conduct a safe, deliberate search—the shooter could be hiding anywhere, ready to kill without warning. He could be there now, waiting. One wrong step and he could shoot and escape. There was just Bear and me to do it.

I considered our options as Bear slipped inside the ballroom behind me. He knelt down beside a display of old furniture and scanned the ballroom in freeze-frame snapshots. I could tell when his lips tightened that he'd drawn my same conclusion—this was a dangerous, impossible task.

"Slow, Bear," I said. "Let me go first. Listen for my voice. Listen, *listen*."

His breathing was heavy—not from exertion but tension. He surveyed in front of him for danger and readied himself. "Damn."

"Okay, let's move." I started forward, not sure he could hear me or sense what I was saying. "Slow."

He broke from cover and slithered to the first display case ten feet away. From there, he leapfrogged from cover to cover through the ballroom. He took refuge behind furniture and shelves of books and glassware—anywhere to stop a bullet. Each time pausing to listen and waiting for an attack. Each time breathing a sigh when none came.

Shadows haunted us everywhere. Cluttered displays offered refuge. Rows of furniture and tall racks suborned a shooter's escape. Everywhere was a stalker's ally. Nowhere was there any safety from every line of fire. Every step was exposed—the wrong step could bring death—his.

I stayed ten steps ahead of him and used every sense and instinct to find danger. "Hold it, Bear."

He froze.

I moved ahead checking the blind spots that were as plentiful as the dust and cobwebs. Twice, I ordered his retreat but found only old uniformed mannequins and garment racks. Each time, his conscience heard me and obeyed.

If I weren't dead, this place would have given me a heart attack.

On a hasty retreat, Bear crashed into a shelf and sent a cringing sound of shattering bottles and crystal. Then came the cursing and fuming. I jogged farther ahead and cleared a path to the far end or the ballroom.

Nothing. No shooter. No stalker. No Liam McCorkle. No one.

At the rear of the ballroom were tall, hanging draperies that reminded me of a fortuneteller's stage. Behind them, a short hallway disappeared into darkness. I followed it to a door that led outside to the rear of the antique shop. I emerged a block from the front parking lot, just down the alley from where we parked. The door was open and its lock forced.

Bear appeared behind me and glanced around the alley. He didn't waste much time and returned to the ballroom.

"Bear," Angel called out from the front of the ballroom. "Come here. Upstairs, look."

We retraced our path and emerged ten feet from her. She stood just inside the ballroom entrance, pointing above our heads to a balcony overlooking the entire ballroom. "There."

When I first entered the ballroom, my focus was on the thousands of possible dangers ahead of us; neither of us looked up behind us at the balcony. Had a sniper been nested behind its banister moments ago, Bear could be dead.

Instead, someone else was.

Protruding through the balcony banister above our heads was a man's arm.

I knew who it was—*by appointment only.*

"Angel, stay there." Bear found a door obscured behind a stack of old shelves that led to a narrow stairway. He started up, one wary step at a time.

I waited beside Angel, watching the balcony. She was shaking and her face was ashen and drawn. I wanted to comfort her, but the best I could do was whisper that she was safe. The itch was gone, now. Everything would be all right. At least for us.

"He's dead," Bear called over the railing. "I'm going to check up here. Stay put."

He was gone only a minute. "Angel, get outside and call 911 on your cell. And make sure you tell them I'm a cop and armed. I don't want them shooting *me* when they arrive."

She ran for the parking lot and I joined Bear.

"Liam McCorkle, I presume." Bear knelt down and began examining the body. "You won't be telling anyone anything, will you?"

McCorkle was in his seventies. He was well-groomed and dressed in an old suit—not worn or unpressed—just old. His body appeared to have dropped as he walked; his legs were in mid-stride and he lay on his side. His aged body crumpled to the floor when life ceased and death refused to guide his limbs any further. Despite this violent end, death didn't seem too far away. He was painfully thin and tall, with a gangly, disconcerted frame. He face was gaunt, at odds with a heavy mustache hanging over his lip. What hair that was not matted with blood was neatly cut, although age left it gray and thinning. His eyeglasses were smashed beside his outstretched left hand and his right still held a spilled can of cola. He lay on his right side, legs apart and bent.

He died of a gunshot wound. The shot entered through his rear skull and exited the right eye. Blood formed an eerie pool around his head. Death was instantaneous—I doubted Liam McCorkle knew it arrived at all.

Angel and I didn't hear the shot that nearly killed her, and that meant the killer came prepared with a silenced weapon. He took his prey from behind—silent, swift, exact. Either McCorkle was surprised on his balcony, or he knew his killer and had dared turn his back. His skull showed no signs of powder burns or singeing; the killer had not been close. The path of the bullet told me it was fired level at its victim. Blood and brain matter splattered the side balcony wall and indicated McCorkle was facing down the hall, away from the ballroom toward the offices there. Whether his killer had emerged from hiding behind him or had accompanied him up the stairs would require more investigation. The difference could solve his murder.

Either way, Liam McCorkle was just as dead.

FORTY-FIVE

DETECTIVE JACK DOUGHERTY SIGNALED Bear that he was finished with Angel and was satisfied with her statement. It had taken more than three hours to reach that point, and while Jack and Bear were old friends, Jack had a homicide to investigate. His questioning left Angel tired and edgy.

Jack was a short, round man with reading eyeglasses forever perched on his nose. He was the senior man at the Staunton P.D. detective squad and had a good reputation. Years ago, he and Bear roomed at the FBI's National Academy and they'd been friends since. That kinship allowed Angel fewer biting questions now.

He was rereading his notes and didn't look up when he said, "Mrs. Tucker, I am sorry about Tuck. He was a great guy."

"Bullshit, Jack," I snorted from the window where I'd been during her interview. "You didn't like me any more than I liked you."

"Thank you, Jack." Angel sounded sincere. "Call me Angela."

"Angela, then. Yeah, it's been a night, hasn't it?"

"Are we through? I have to get home."

Jack nodded. "Soon, I promise. Bear's digging around upstairs with my men. As soon as he's done, you can go. I have your statement and we know where to find you."

"Is there anything you can tell us? Anything at all?"

"No, you know what we do." He stood up and wandered around the front office as he had a hundred times. Jack was a pacer. "The shot through the front window at you is long gone. The team's looking, but I wouldn't hold my breath. Maybe we'll get lucky and find it in the wall down the alley; needle in a haystack, though."

"What about Mr. McCorkle?"

"What about him?"

Angel looked down. "I feel somewhat responsible."

"Don't." Jack stopped pacing and tucked his notepad into his suit coat. "McCorkle is a well-known antique dealer in Virginia—hell, in the entire country. If it was old and worth a fortune, McCorkle traded in it. He was worth a bundle."

"Robbery?" Angel asked. "You don't think it had anything to do with Bear and me coming to see him?"

"I didn't say that. I don't believe in coincidences. As soon as Mrs. Lexington gets here—that's his assistant—we'll do an inventory to see what's what."

"You should start with the computer problem."

"What computer? I haven't seen one."

"That's my point."

Jack nodded but didn't take out his pad. "Not everyone uses computers, Angela. I can barely turn one on myself."

"What a surprise," I sneered. "He probably still has a typewriter."

"Oh, stop," Angel said, but then added, "stop and think, Jack. With all these antiques, he'd need a computer to keep records, right? And he traded online."

"Hmmm, yeah." Jack walked to the doorway rubbing his chin— all cops did that when they were deep in thought, or wanted to look that way. "You might have something. Let's see what Mrs. Lexington says before we get upset about a missing computer that may not be missing."

There were low whispers in the hall and a uniformed policeman guided an older black woman into the office. Bear was in tow.

Jack said, "Here she is now."

"Detective Dougherty, what happened? The officer said something has happened to Mr. McCorkle."

"Yes, I'm sorry to say it has, Irene." Jack introduced Mrs. Irene Lexington and Angel made her comfortable in a chair beside the desk. Clumsily, Jack explained McCorkle's murder. The seventy-year old bookkeeper was crying into her handkerchief before he got past "found murdered."

Bear waited for her to compose herself. "Mrs. Lexington, do you know if Mr. McCorkle had any appointments this evening? Other than Angela and me?"

"No—and it's Irene." She straightened herself and dabbed the tears from her eyes. "No, but I didn't know you were coming. That is not unusual for Mr. McCorkle. Not lately."

Bear and Jack exchanged sideways glances. Bear asked, "He's been secretive? Do you know why?"

"Mr. McCorkle often handled his own affairs when he was working a special exchange. I wouldn't call him secretive—I think 'private' is more appropriate."

"Uh, huh." Jack was writing. "And when did he become, ah, private?"

"About three, maybe four weeks ago. He was doing an unusual project and asked me to handle all the routine transfers. He was searching for a unique piece of jewelry—paid quite a large retainer as well."

"Retainer?" Angel asked. "Someone paid him a retainer to find a piece of jewelry? Who?"

"Oh, I don't know." Irene looked around the room as though she were searching for something. "You'll find all his notes in his computer. Mr. McCorkle was a fanatic about keeping a business diary. I see you've already taken it."

"Ha," I roared, "She told you so, Jack."

Jack shrugged at Angel. "No, Irene. It's gone. Do you have duplicates of everything?"

"Duplicates?" She raised an eyebrow. "You mean 'backups,' Detective? My, my, you really have to get out from behind your desk more often. Yes, the backups are in the safe upstairs."

"We'll need the combination, Irene." Jack handed her his notepad and she wrote the numbers on it.

Bear asked, "What else can you tell us about McCorkle's new project?"

Irene wiped her eyes and glanced over at the cluttered desk, then out the window, lost in silence for a long time. I didn't blame her—murder was a shocking and horrible thing. After a few more tears, she cleared her throat and straightened in her chair.

"I don't know much. Mr. McCorkle was private about the new business."

"You don't know who the retainer came from?" Angel asked.

"No. That's all in the computer I'm sure. Oh, wait …"

Jack leaned forward. "Yes? What do you remember, Irene?"

"There was a man—a big man as I recall—he scared me. He delivered a package to Mr. McCorkle. It was concerning one of the new accounts. Oh, I can't recall his name. I'm sorry. I'm just so upset. May I go?"

"Irene," Angel said, moving beside her. "Please think. That name is extremely important. Try to remember. The man may have killed Mr. McCorkle. He may also have killed my husband; perhaps others, too."

"What, oh no. Oh my, I didn't know. Oh, oh … I can't … the safe …"

Jack called the uniformed officer from the hall and met him in the doorway. He gave him instructions in a hushed voice. When he turned back to us, he frowned and waited for Irene to calm again.

He said, "We'll take her home now. One of my officers will stay with her for the evening. As soon as she's able, we'll get her to help with the inventory and see what we can do with those computer records from the safe."

"Yes, of course." Angel walked Irene to the waiting policeman. "Irene, I'm so sorry. Thank you for helping us."

Irene stopped in the doorway and brushed Angel's cheek with a shaky hand. "My dear, it's me who is sorry. I don't understand what's happening, but I will do everything I can to help you. Everything. I just need to rest. It's so, so terrible…"

"Yes it is. And it's not over yet."

FORTY-SIX

THE NINETEENTH-CENTURY RAILROAD SAFE sat in the corner of the second floor office. It too was an antique and fit in amongst a wall of old clocks and artwork. It took Jack ten minutes before he was able to combine the numbers Irene gave him with the correct turns left and right. It might have taken another ten if I hadn't whispered in his ear.

"Go ahead, Bear," Jack said, dropping into a tall-back wooden chair against the wall. "Use gloves; evidence is evidence."

Bear withdrew stacks of folders, old cigar boxes, and several jewelry containers of varying sizes. There was even an unlocked, canvas deposit bag still containing several thousand dollars in cash. He stacked everything on the round table in the center of the room and Jack started an evidence inventory.

Angel sat watching the process unfold.

It took thirty minutes to sort through the contents of the safe. When Jack was finished, he allowed Angel to sit at the table and examine it. Angel found what we were looking for in a cigar box buried beneath the first stack of documents.

"Here are the flash drives."

"Flash drive?" Jack made no pretense about his computer skills. "I've heard of them, but never quite understood what they are."

"There're three here." She handed the cigar box to him. "They're small USB storage devices that can hold several gigabits of data."

"Yeah, USB." Jack rolled his eyes and jotted notes. "My computer guys will know what to do with them."

"I wish we'd arrived an hour sooner," Bear said, flipping through several shipping envelopes. "McCorkle may have been killed to keep him from talking to us."

"It just doesn't make sense," Angel said. "None of this."

"Murder doesn't always make sense. Sometimes it just happens," Jack said.

Bear added, "Whoever's behind this isn't short on bullets. Maybe ballistics will match Salazar and McCorkle's killers. Maybe not. But…" Bear's eyebrows raised and he handed Angel a large packaging envelope. The "to" address label was peeled away leaving a large, odd shaped scar on the orange paper. The return address was still intact and read, "Byrd Construction & Development Corporation." It was a Winchester post office box.

"Very interesting." Angel opened the envelope. "Why keep an empty envelope in the safe?"

Bear winked. "So the hired help doesn't know you have it."

Jack stretched and looked at his watch. "Listen, we have no idea what we're looking for. Anything or everything could be important.

I'll get a couple of my squad to go through this in more detail. I'll send you a copy of everything."

"Great, but email it, will you?" Bear asked. "Don't leave any messages at the office."

"Oh?" Jack's eyebrows rose.

"Long story, Jack. Just email me, okay?"

Angel was studying some photographs and drawings stuffed in a folder. There were dozens of sketches and snapshots of rings, necklaces, and other pieces of jewelry. She showed the file to Jack.

"These must be the special projects Irene mentioned. I guess he used the drawings and photographs to find them. I'm no expert, but some of these look pretty valuable."

"I'm going to chat with Tyler Byrd tomorrow," Bear said. "I'm curious about his business with McCorkle. When can I have a copy of his client list?"

"Soon as my boys get into these flash things," Jack said. He turned toward a uniformed officer in the doorway. "I want this room processed by morning."

The officer got on his radio and relayed the command.

Jack's cell phone rang. He took the call and disappeared into the hallway.

"Bear, let's go," Angel said. "I'll call André on the way home. He was at Kelly's Dig tonight. Maybe he's got something new."

"All right."

I was in the doorway listening to Jack's call. I figured out what was happening before he did. "Angel, Captain Sutter is a little pissed. You guys better scram before she shows—she found out

251

about McCorkle and is a half-hour out. Jack's people called her to let her know her detective was involved in another murder."

Angel gestured to the door, "Bear, Sutter's on her way here."

"How do you …" Bear rolled his eyes. "Oh shit, you're doing that Tuck thing again."

Jack came red-faced into the room. "Thanks, pal. Why didn't you tell me you were already on thin ice. You're captain is hot and said to keep you here."

"Sorry, Jack." Bear gave him a dismissive wave. "It's a long story. When she arrives, you don't know when we left."

"Damn right I don't. You owe me *big*. Now, get the hell out of here."

Climbing into Bear's car, Angel's cell rang. "Yes? Oh, hello, Ernie." She listened. "I can't discuss that right now." Ernie was jabbering on and on until Angel interrupted him. "Ernie, listen. I'm afraid he's dead." She explained the details.

In between sighs and "I can't believe its," Ernie asked ten minutes of questions. She ended the call with, "The computer records were stolen, but we may have found the backup files. We also found an empty mailing envelope from Tyler Byrd's company. Bear is following that up."

When she bade him goodnight and closed her phone, her face was tired and drained. "Ernie and McCorkle were close friends. He's devastated."

"There's a lot of that going around," Bear said. "What did he call for, anyway?"

Angel brightened. "André spoke with him. André now has proof the medical examiner made a huge mistake. He wants to meet me tomorrow morning at Kelly's Dig to show us what he's found. Ernie's meeting us there, too."

"I better join you," Bear said, taking the highway on-ramp. "God only knows what'll happen if I don't."

FORTY-SEVEN

IN THE MORNING, WE got a late start to meet André at Kelly's Dig. Angel was tired—I guess "tired" would be the polite word after she and Bear emptied two bottles of merlot. Another attempt on her life and Liam McCorkle's murder weighed heavily on her. I can't blame her for tipping a few.

If given the chance, I'd tip more than a few.

During the night, Angel and Bear took time off from playing Agatha Christie. Instead, they bantered on about almost nothing, seemingly avoiding all discussion of my case or the events surrounding Liam McCorkle. I stayed close but didn't participate for fear of angering Angel or invading her sudden need for "privacy." During the wine and small talk, I studied Bear and paid careful attention to every ounce of body language. My heart ached, fearing that Spence might be right—that Bear had a thing with Angel. Making things worse were Angel's odd comments of late and the way she had been acting, well, guilty. So, I sat petting Hercule and gave them the opportunity to make mistakes.

They didn't and with each passing hour, guilt buried jealousy.

It was before eight when Angel poured another cup of coffee and I took a seat cross from her. I don't recall what time Bear left, but looking at Angel now, it was very late and she hadn't slept.

"Angel, I think you need to be careful around Bear. Don't you?"

"No—just stop." I'm not sure the ire was my question or the wine wearing off.

"But, Angel, last night, someone shot at you—again."

"Tuck, please." She dumped the last of her coffee in the sink. "It certainly wasn't Bear. Besides, you're back and I'm so confused. Don't you get it? As much as I miss you … you shouldn't be here. I don't know if I'm glad or not about that. This whole thing is my fault and I don't know what to do."

Huh? "How's this your fault? You keep saying that."

The answer wasn't coming any time soon. Our conversation was over when she locked the front door and put Hercule in the Explorer. I barely popped into the back seat with him before she was off.

Something I said?

Twenty minutes later, we passed by Kelly Orchard Farm's main house—well, mansion was more the word—on the way to the dig site. It was an enormous early-American antebellum estate. The two-story, white stone house had four tall chimneys that reminded me of a Georgia plantation house, with stone steps leading to the front veranda where heavy columns stood guard. Even the rear servant's cottage, which was a smaller two-story stone house on the north side of a landscaped courtyard, presented a stalwart charm that exuded aristocracy.

It was not difficult to understand why Kelly Orchard Farms was a battle cry for historical preservation.

Angel looked around and checked her watch. "Bear left a message that he'd be late. We might as well go on to the dig site. André and Ernie will be there."

"Do you still have Bear's gun?"

"Of course." She patted her small backpack that was normally full of university books and papers. This morning, it hefted a few extra pounds of steel, brass, and lead. "I don't want anyone getting lucky on the fourth try."

"Then let's go."

We continued down the gravel road through the apple orchards a half mile southeast until we saw the huge debris pile that overlooked Kelly's Dig. But as we approached, it was obvious something had changed. There was a wide, newly worn patch of earth where Byrd's heavy equipment had been parked just days ago. Now, only one bulldozer and backhoe remained. The debris pile blocked the gravel road and we couldn't reach the construction trailer on the opposite side of Kelly's Dig. The trailer now sat obscured behind the pile of trees, brush, and earth.

"Someone's been working again," she said, jumping out of the Explorer. "This debris pile is much larger and now it's blocking the road. No one should have been working."

"Most of Byrd's heavy equipment is gone, too." Something was nagging at me again. "Stay here. Let Herc and me check around."

A green, late model BMW bounced up the road behind us and the driver waved out the window.

Hercule growled low and bounded out onto the ground.

"Hercule, it's only Ernie," Angel said, kneeling to pet him as Ernie rolled to a stop. "It's okay, boy, it's safe."

"Good morning," he called. "Where's André and Bear?"

Angel shrugged. "I haven't found André yet. Bear had a meeting with Captain Sutter. He'll be along later."

"How are you holding up? Last night must have been terrible. Liam McCorkle was a good man and a good friend. Frankly, I can't believe what's happened. None of it."

"I know, Ernie. I feel the same way." When we rounded the far side of the debris pile, Ernie pointed to a sleek, blue Mercedes convertible parked with its top down near the road coming from the highway. "That's André's car. Now where is he?"

I added, "Let's check around. I don't like this at all."

"I'll check the orchard," Angel said, walking toward the far end of the debris pile. "Can you check the trailer, Ernie? Maybe he's inside."

"Of course."

Ernie first went to André's convertible and looked inside. Then he walked to the trailer and tried the trailer door several times but the door didn't open. He took out his cell phone and dialed. After several seconds, he redialed, and waited longer before closing it. He returned to the Explorer and met Angel.

"The trailer's locked and there's no sign of André. I called his cell, but he's not answering. Byrd's security guard is gone, too. They're supposed to be here."

"I wonder what's going on." Angel scanned the orchard in all directions. "This isn't like him."

"Shouldn't security still be here?"

"Yes. Tyler told me yesterday he'd let them know we were still working." Angel's voice was curt and irritated. "I don't like this, Ernie. We better call Bear."

"Wait," Ernie said, walking to the edge of the pit. "The site's been compromised. Someone's been digging—far too much—and they've been reckless about it."

The damage to the dig site was obvious. The pit, like the debris pile, had changed from last week. The barn's timbers from inside the pit were now broken and strewn far behind it. The rear foundation wall was smashed through and a large swath of earth removed. Fresh backhoe tracks marred the area surrounding the pit. The pile of foundation stones where André and Angel had last been working were now scattered haphazardly. A fresh cavity of missing earth remained where the foundation had been there last.

"Ernie, call Bear—now."

"Yes, yes. I'll do that. This is terrible. Any chance of properly excavating more remains has been destroyed."

As I was about to go search for André, something caught my eye from the corner of the pit.

A flicker of light glinted in the morning sun. The twinkle came from beneath one of the remaining foundation stones overturned by the backhoe. A faint, eerie glimmer sparkled and bade my attention. I slid into the pit and knelt down. There, I found a tiny, half-inch stone caked in earth. It was no larger than a dime and only a sliver of its face was free of clay. That sliver caught the sunlight and simmered with a glint of green light.

"Angel, look at this ..." I said and touched it ...

The sun disappeared but left a strange aura surrounding the dig site. My fingers tingled and a foggy haze engulfed me. I couldn't see the orchard trees or the debris pile any longer. In fact, I couldn't distinguish anything but the crumbled stones and timbers lying above the pit.

Angel and Ernie were gone, too.

The haze was growing and someone was walking toward me—a faint image emerging just yards away.

It was the young brunette who had visited me twice before. But unlike her previous visits, I saw her with clarity and distinction. She stood above me at the pile of foundation stones and gazed down at me. A faint smile crept across her lips. I was seeing her clearly for the first time and I understood why. She was pretty and young, and most importantly, she belonged here—right here at Kelly's Dig.

"Hello," she said in a calm, whispered voice. "We've been waiting for you to visit us here again."

Crap, that can't be good. "Really? Why here?"

"It's all right. You'll understand." The girl turned and waved behind her. "It's all right. He's here. He finally came. He's going to help us."

Her blonde friend appeared. She stood next to the brunette beaming at me as though some surprise was looming. "Yes, you can help us. But first, help them. Help the others. You can stop this."

"Stop what?" I asked, trying not to frighten them as I had before. "Who are you? Will you tell me your names so I can help you?"

"It was all here." The brunette's face darkened and she took her friend's hand. "He killed us."

"Who? Who killed you?"

"He's not going to stop until you make him. We can't—it's too late for us. It's too late for you, too. But you give us hope. You have friends. Get them to help you; get them to help us all. Hurry."

I started to climb up out of the pit, but they withdrew. I smiled again, trying not to scare them as I had before. "Do you know who killed me? Can you tell me that?"

The brunette shook her head. "Oliver, it's not about you."

"No, not about you." The blonde gripped the brunette's hand tighter as they backed away. "We want to go—to leave here. We can't until he does. And we can't leave the others behind, they protected us for so long. Oh, no, it's happening again. Save him!"

"Again?"

The sky lit up and the explosion rocked me.

FORTY-EIGHT

WHEN I RECOVERED, THE girls were gone. Smoke churned in the air and I could hear Angel crying out. I scrambled up the pit to find her and Ernie running toward the pillar of smoke behind the debris pile. I ran after them and we rounded the debris pile just yards from the front of the construction office trailer.

The trailer was on fire.

Hercule charged ahead, barking, and leaping into the air. He ran toward us, stopped, howled, and ran back toward the trailer. He continued this frenzy as the flames crackled behind him.

"Angel, stay back. Stay back."

"Let me try," Ernie yelled and darted toward the trailer. "Hercule, come boy."

Hercule became more frantic and animated. He barked and dodged back and forth, churning the earth with his paws each time he got close to the trailer; each time the flames drove him back. He wouldn't stop. His retreat got shorter, his daring got too close.

"Angel, watch out," I yelled as she reached Hercule and tried dragging him from the fire. He fought her and pulled free, barking and bolting back again.

"No, Angela." Ernie grabbed her and pulled her to safety. "Stay clear. It might explode again. Hercule, come. Come, Hercule!"

I watched Herc and knew what he knew—someone was inside the trailer. André Cartier was inside. "He's trying to warn us. André's inside."

"What?" Angel looked at the convertible. "Oh my God, André!"

Ernie charged the trailer, protecting his face with his arms. Two steps before the door, smoke forced his retreat. More flames rose from the far end of the trailer but the side nearest us had yet to be engulfed. Ernie made three attempts before surrendering and retreating to Angel's side. "I can't make it, Angela. It's too much for me."

A car roared down the gravel road and skidded to a stop behind the convertible. Bear leapt out and ran to us. "Are you all right? What the hell happened?"

"It's André," Angel cried. "I think he's inside."

Bear's mouth dropped. He turned and saw Hercule's frantic dance back toward the flames. "Jesus, no."

Without hesitating—that's what I remembered about Bear— he ran to his cruiser, pulled out a large, hand-held fire extinguisher from the trunk, and dashed to the rear trailer door.

Fighting the smoke and heat, he made his move.

He sprayed the trailer handle with a long, heavy burst and gave the door a violent kick. The flames engulfing the roof were unmerciful and twice he withdrew. On the third assault, he drew his handgun and shot the door lock off. Spraying the remaining handle with the extinguisher again, he cursed, yanked the door open, and dove inside.

I followed.

Smoke made it impossible for him to see. The searing heat was already blistering Bear's face and hands. Only seconds remained before he would have to withdraw or die. Unfazed, I ran deeper into the smoke and searched around until I found a body. It was lying face down on the carpet against the far office wall.

André.

I tried to reach inside him and pull his being—his thoughts—to me. There was nothing returning my probes. There were no thoughts, no emotions, nothing I could take hold of. Death was seeping in; André was slipping away.

"Bear, follow my voice—like last night—listen. Stay down; stay low. Come to me. Here, Bear, here."

He threw himself to his knees and crawled forward, groping inch by inch, hand over hand. He choked smoke and cursed loudly as the heat blistered his skin. "Dammit, André. Can you hear me? André?"

"Another foot, Bear. Come on. You're here."

Bear fell upon André's lifeless body. He grabbed his arms and pulled him backward to the door. There, the heat overtook him and he collapsed. I tried to move him but all I found was emptiness in my grasp. I screamed into his head, commanded he listen and obey.

"You son-of-a-bitch, get up. Get up. Three more feet. You can't give up, not yet. You're there. Dammit, fight. Fight, Bear."

He did.

In slow, beleaguered moves, Bear's powerful arms grabbed André's shoulders and he stood. With the last of his strength, he propelled himself out the door and onto the ground. Their clothes were smoldering and Bear's shoes were blackened and scorched; their faces red and blistering.

Neither moved.

Bear gasped for air but couldn't rise. André was still.

Through the smoke, Spence and Clemens charged in spraying fire extinguishers over the two men, then fought back the flames. Spence grabbed Bear and Clemens grabbed André. They dragged them back to safety, rolling them onto their backs and instantly triaging their wounds. Clemens took the lead, first checking their pulse, then their breathing. He barked at Spence who instantly tore at André's shirt.

Ernie and Angel clung together and watched.

Bear coughed and gasped for air. After a second, he stirred and got to his knees. He pushed Clemens off André's body and descended upon it. He checked his pulse—once, twice, three times. Clemens began chest compressions—Bear tried breathing life into his dying body. Spence pulled Bear free and took up the cause.

Feverishly, the three detectives fought André's failing body. Seconds. Minutes. Breath after breath. One more compression, five more, fifteen … twenty-five …

"Stop." Clemens sat back and slid his fingers from André's neck. "You can stop."

"No," Angel cried. "Please, he can't be dead."

Spence pressed his fingers to André's throat. He looked up, closing his eyes as his chin dropped to his chest.

"No, he's alive."

FORTY-NINE

BEAR SAT WIPING THE soot and smoke from his face as the ambulance pulled away. Angel was helping him. Leaning on their own cruiser, Clemens and Spence talked with the fire chief—they looked grim. Ernie Stuart looked the worst. He was sitting in the fire chief's Suburban taking breaths from an oxygen mask. Every word the chief spoke seemed to make his breathing all the harder.

I was standing beside Angel. She knelt down and rubbed Hercule's face with a damp cloth. There was an acrid scent of burnt hair around him, but he looked okay. Once again, Hercule saved the day.

"Herc, you're a hero—again. If it weren't for you, we wouldn't have found André in time. Good boy, another steak tonight."

Hercule, not wanting to display any false modesty, wagged up a storm and barked at Bear to make sure he knew who the real hero was—and who would *not* be sharing a T-bone.

"Angel," I said, "you know this was no accident, right?"

"Yes, I know."

Bear looked around. "You know what?"

"Someone just tried to kill André." She stood up and faced him. "My God, I don't know how you found him in all that smoke. We're lucky you arrived in time."

Bear turned away for a long, silent moment. Finally, he said, "Angel, it's the weirdest thing. Inside the trailer … damnedest thing … I swear I heard someone yelling at me. The voice brought me right to André. Like last night at McCorkle's place. I swear I heard someone telling me what to do. I'm going nuts."

"No," Angel said, taking Bear's arm and turning him toward her. "We both know who it was. You weren't imagining it, Bear. You know it was Tuck."

His jaw locked tight and he shook his head.

"Yes you do," I said. "You are just too stubborn to admit it."

Bear changed the subject and his face shot an angry, distrustful look at Spence and Clemens. I've seen that look a thousand times directed at lying suspects. "I'm very curious why those two happened to show up."

"And the timing," Ernie added as he walked up beside Angel. "How absolutely convenient. One has to wonder."

"Well, then I guess you should wonder about me, Ernie," Bear said. "After all, I got here in the nick of time, too."

"Yes, you did, Detective. You're always close by." Ernie didn't wait for Bear's response and returned to the Suburban for more oxygen.

Spence walked up, jotting something in his notebook, and when he stopped beside Bear, he flipped the notebook closed.

Bear asked, "What do you have, Spence?"

"Chief thinks it's arson. The construction crews left some gas cans beside the trailer. It looks like someone rigged them to explode. He's just speculating for now. He'll have more later. Cartier could have done this by himself and got caught in his own fire—he smelled like gas."

"No," Angel said, snapping her hands to her hips. "I think someone trapped him in there and tried to kill him."

"Why him?" Spence shriveled up his face and looked more like a rodent smelling a trap than a homicide detective asking questions. "Why murder Cartier? There's no proof."

I said, "Even he has to know André was already out on the floor when the explosion happened."

"Spence, think about it." Bear looked sheepish and I could tell that buzzing was back in his ears. "André was unconscious when the fire started."

"And how would you know that?"

Bear took it from there. "Because the clothes on his back were scorched and his hair blackened with soot—the front of his body wasn't. He was face down on the floor when the fire started. His head also has a nice knot on it."

"Sure, right." Spence made a note. "But, there are other reasons Cartier could look like that."

Angel said, "Well, when André recovers, he'll tell us."

"Yeah, right." Spence shook his head as Clemens joined us. "Medics aren't sure if his lungs are burnt. The hospital's waiting on them to arrive. We won't know for a while."

Angel started to cry and Bear threw an arm around her. "Easy, now. He'll be okay."

"By the way, Braddock, the captain is looking for you." Spence aimed his pen at Bear's face. "You missed your meeting this morning."

"Screw you." Bear slapped the pen out of Spence's hand and closed the distance between them to a few uncomfortable inches. "What are you and Clemens doing out here?"

"The Captain sent us."

"Bullshit."

Clemens stepped between them. "Listen, Bear, you weren't answering your cell or radio. The captain got worried—everywhere you go someone gets killed. She sent us looking for you."

"Bullshit." Bear turned around, climbed into his car, and threw a wave out his window for everyone to move. When we did, he sped off in a hail of gravel and dirt.

I leaned over to Angel. "Angel, I want to show you something. Go to the dig with me."

She excused herself and walked off toward the pit, leaving Spence and Clemens scoffing and muttering about Bear. Ernie followed us but waited until we were out of earshot from the others before speaking.

"Angela, I'm curious about Detective Braddock." Ernie glanced over her shoulder. "Detective Spence said he missed his meeting this morning with Captain Sutter. You told me that's why he was late earlier."

"Ernie, I don't like what you're insinuating."

I was about to suggest how stupid Ernie's questions were when I realized they weren't stupid at all. Was this another question spilling goo all over Bear? I swallowed my answer hard.

Ernie continued, "You told me that he wasn't right there with you last night when someone shot at you."

"Well, not right with me." Angel tried to hide the conflict in her eyes by looking away. "Bear would never hurt me. And why would he hurt André? I trust him."

Did she? But did I?

"My dear..."

"Bear would never do such a thing." Angel pointed a scolding finger at him. "I won't hear that from you again—ever."

"I, I...I'm sorry, Angela. Forgive me." Ernie's face reddened and he turned back toward Spence and Clemens. They were watching now. "I should go. Be careful." He headed for his car.

"Damn him." Angel wiped a few tears away. When she turned back away from the watching eyes, she said, "What do you want, Tuck? I'm not sure how much more I can take."

I stood above the pit and told her about the two wraiths visiting me again. I connected the dots for her between Kelly's Dig and their murders I saw in my vision. It didn't take a lot of dots.

"Angel, it all starts and ends here. We just have to figure out who and why."

"Tuck, I cannot do this. I just can't. Not now..."

"Just look at this." I showed her the emerald stone I'd found and she dug it out of the clay and rock. Her face softened and she turned toward the orchard. She glanced off into the trees, perhaps expecting the girls to appear to her.

"An emerald? How did this get here?" Angel wiped it clean and held it up to the light. Her demeanor changed with every dim sparkle of green light.

I reached out and touched the stone. No sparks. No lightning. No eerie fog bringing pretty girls imploring my help. There was nothing.

Then it hit me.

"Angel," I said, looking at the emerald in her hand. "I understand now. The girls—they're dead like me, but they know who killed them. They just can't do anything about it. They hope to stop their killer so they can move on."

"Is this all about you? Your murder?"

I thought about that. "They said it wasn't about me. But I think it's that I've made contact with you. I've done what they couldn't. They tried to warn me about André, too."

"André?" she whispered. "They knew someone was trying to kill him?"

"I think so. They can't reach out for help and they know I can."

"What are you saying?" Angel's brow furrowed. "They want you to help them because you're dead?"

"No, because you're not."

FIFTY

THE OMINOUS BANK OF monitors and life-support apparatus encircling André's bed made it difficult to see him. Tubes and a spaghetti-like array of wires protruded everywhere and covered him with an aura of desperation. His face was pale but his breathing regular. The machine's constant beeping explained everything of importance—André Cartier was alive.

A uniformed deputy sat beside André's room door. Bear wasn't taking any chances with the only potential witness in Winchester's crime wave. Someone tried to kill André once. Perhaps they would try again.

Angel was crying and I said, "Hey, he'll be okay."

"He has to be. I cannot believe someone would hurt him. We have to stop them."

"We will, Angel. We will."

She folded her arms. "How do you know that? You can't know that. Tuck, you just don't understand."

Oh really? "Actually, Angel, I think I do. I'm a little worse off, don't you think?"

She started to debate me when André's doctor, Dr. Pandreas, walked up behind us. The nurse came out of the room, handed him André's chart, and walked down the hall. The doctor studied it before coming to Angel's side.

"Dr. Tucker," he said in a heavy Greek accent, "he's going to be fine. It's a miracle considering what happened. His lungs were not affected as we feared and I'm amazed he didn't sustain more serious burns. You got to him in time. You should go now—we'll call should anything change."

"I'll wait a while longer." She looked through the observation window again. "Just a little while."

He reached out and took her arm, guiding her toward a couch in the nearby waiting area. "Dr. Tucker, you have to trust me. He has a concussion and we'll run more tests when he wakes up. But he *will* wake up and he'll be fine."

Angel thanked him and he excused himself.

Instead of sitting in the sparse waiting room, we went to visit Carmen Delgado two floors up. We arrived as she was leaving her room. She was checked out and heading to stay with family in Pennsylvania. After some happy conversation and hugs, Carmen was wheeled away under escort by another sheriff's deputy. As she left, Angel wondered aloud if Carmen would ever return to town.

Neither of us would blame her if she didn't.

We took the elevator to the basement cafeteria where Angel purchased a large black coffee. We found a table and sat.

"Tuck, I don't know what to do next."

"Let's wait for André to wake up," I said. "Maybe he'll have some answers. Oh, shit …"

She nodded, "What?"

Tyler Byrd was heading straight for us. He was smiling, though it looked like an effort. He stopped behind the chair I was sitting in and without asking, dropped down into it facing Angel. I barely made it clear before the behemoth smothered me.

"I'm glad I found you, Angela. I'm very sorry about Professor Cartier." If I didn't know better, I'd swear the bastard was being honest. "As soon as I heard, I came here to check on him."

"Really?" Angel's eyes flared. "How nice of you, Tyler. What happened out there?"

"Excuse me?" He sat back in his chair. "You think I had something to do with this?"

"Shouldn't I?"

"Why should you? I've got more to lose than anyone. Every incident around that site costs me money and more of my reputation. Cartier's accident is gonna make things worse."

"Accident? It wasn't an accident."

"Listen, Angela." Both Tyler's hands landed on the table and nearly spilled Angel's coffee. "Do you think I'm stupid enough to try to kill Professor Cartier the day after you call me a mobster? On my own site with my own equipment?"

Damn if he didn't have a point. "Angel, ask him about the package at McCorkle's."

She did. "I'm curious what business you have with him—considering he's dead, too."

"For Christ's sake." Tyler thrust himself back in his chair. "I don't recall doing business with any antique dealer in Staunton. If I needed one, I'd find someone right here—hell, there are hundreds of them."

Another good point.

"Then explain it," Angel demanded.

"I can't."

"How convenient."

"Now, you listen. That envelope could have come from one of my clients. Anyone working for me could have taken one home. Jesus, we don't lock them up."

Angel said, "Maybe they'll find your fingerprints on it."

"Fingerprints?" He laughed. "You think it odd my fingerprints *might* be on my own business stationary? You can do better than that."

Okay, so Tyler Byrd was batting a thousand. I asked, "Why did he pull his security guard from Kelly's Dig after talking with you and André yesterday?"

She asked him and he dismissed her with a wave of his hand. "Nicholas did that."

"Nicholas? Why?"

"I told you yesterday he handles security. We use some from his warehouse. When I told him you needed more time at Kelly's Dig, he raised a big issue."

"What issue—that a witness would get in the way of killing André?" I asked.

"What issue?" Angel asked.

"Money." His voice was flat, void of any apology. "Why should we foot the bill for security there? The county stopped the work on us—it's their contract and their land. The state historical people have writs and court orders out the... Why should I pay for security?"

Angel shrugged. "Yes, I suppose."

"I pulled my equipment out around dinnertime yesterday. All that's left are a couple big cats and our trailer. If the State wants to guard a hole in the ground, let them."

Angel took a long sip of her coffee, watching Tyler over the cup. He had all the right answers. Maybe he was being straight or maybe he was a damn good liar. Right then, I couldn't decide.

She said, "All right, Tyler. It's all very convenient. But it's reasonable."

"The truth sometimes is, Angela."

For a history professor, she was tough, and wasn't taking his guff. "Tyler, I'm sorry, but a lot of people have been hurt. All of them are somehow connected to Kelly's Dig and..."

"And what—me?" His mouth tightened as veins emerged on his forehead. "This is bullshit. The Historic Society is screaming. The county is screaming. The cops are breathing down on me. It ain't my fault. Do you think I wanted to find skeletons buried there?"

Angel shook her head. "No, I guess not."

"Do you think killing people helps me? I got judges slapping me with court orders, history nuts picketing my office, and now you're accusing me of attempted murder. I build things, Angela, and it's costing me millions to sit on my ass."

Angel stayed cool. "We're talking about murder, not money."

"I know that. I had nothing to do with any of them. How stupid do you think I am? Every murder is connected to Kelly's Dig and me."

Wow, when he put it that way, he was either very, very stupid—or very, very innocent.

"Okay, Tyler. I'm sorry. Truly, I'm sorry."

"Angela, forgive me, too." His tone softened. "Of all the people who don't deserve any of this, it's you. You've been very helpful to me and I appreciate it. I'm feeling like a deer wearing a bright-red vest on the opening day of hunting season."

They sat silent for several minutes, letting the anger cool. Tyler took a call from his office and Angel looked on.

When he hung up, she asked, "Do you know anything about two missing girls over the years?"

"What are you suggesting now?" Tyler's temporary calm vanished. "That I..."

"No, no, don't take it that way." She held her hand up. "I was doing research about the site and came across references to two missing girls from the area—several years ago."

"Who were they?"

Oops, she was caught. "I don't know—I don't have any details yet. I wondered if they might be connected to this."

"Why? What are you getting at, Angela? What's this got to do with Civil War skeletons?"

She shook her head. "Never mind. You're right, it's probably nothing."

"Perhaps you should stick to history and leave the detective work to the cops."

"I agree," a voice said from behind us. Bear was standing behind Angel and touched her shoulder. "We need to talk—now."

Angel looked up. "Oh, all right. Excuse me, Tyler."

"Yeah, sure." He stood. To Bear, he said, "Braddock, I want to talk to you anyway."

"Later. I don't have time right now. I'll call you."

Tyler started to argue, but Bear wasn't having it. "Later."

"Fine." Tyler nodded to Angel and walked off with a brisk, if not angry pace.

Bear took Tyler's seat and leaned close to Angel. "Jack Dougherty called. He has some good news."

"What is it?"

"They pulled all McCorkle's computer records and Irene Lexington put some information together for us. But Byrd's name isn't anywhere in McCorkle's files. Neither is Salazar's or Iggi's."

"Then how did Byrd's shipping envelope get there? And who has been making those deliveries Irene told us about?"

"My guess is it's all the same person—Irene remembered the big, mysterious delivery boy's name. She pulled the account file for us."

"Who is it?"

"There's just one name on the file." Bear looked around and spit the name out like something bitter in his mouth. "*Tommy.*"

FIFTY-ONE

CACAPON STATE PARK IS a beautiful park resting along, what a surprise, the Cacapon Mountains in the eastern panhandle of West Virginia. Cacapon—pronounced "kah-KAY-pon" for those who might bastardize the word as I have—comes from the Shawnee Indian word for medicine waters, or something of that sort. The park is located about twenty-eight miles north of Winchester and among its many popular features is a scenic overlook of the valley below. The overlook also features a dramatic and rocky drop of several hundred feet to the base of the park—the express lane to the park entrance.

Why is this all so very important?

First, Bear Braddock was entertaining a guest at the overlook—his wayward informant, Tommy—doer of deeds for Poor Nicholas Bartalotta. Second, Tommy was dangling backwards off the overlook as Bear raged about the perils of keeping secrets. Lastly, if the Cacapon's Shawnee medicine waters couldn't fix Tommy up when

Bear was through, then the Winchester Hospital was a short drive away. It all makes sense when you think about it.

"You son-of-a-bitch." Bear pressed the large, bulky bodyguard over the waist-high railing that barred him from a five-hundred-foot drop. "You're holding out on me, Tommy. I want to hear about Nic's antique collection."

"Jesus, Bear. Relax. Get me off this wall—I don't like heights."

"I don't like liars."

"You never asked about none of that, Bear. You never asked anything about stuff like that. Dammit, let go." Tommy's face was normally round and dark, a product of pasta and Sicilian heritage. Now, it was round and white, like a giant snow cone about to hit the sidewalk.

"Really?" Bear nudged him closer to the wall's edge. "I hear the probation department calling, Tommy. Should I let go and take the call?"

"No. Jesus, Bear, pull me back. *Please.*"

Bear hauled him back and relaxed his grip.

Tommy dropped on his haunches onto the rock wall. He scrambled back and peered over the edge. His brow beaded with sweat.

I was enjoying myself. I hadn't seen Bear this upset since setting him up with an Internet date last year. His date, as much of a surprise to me as him, turned out to be a fifty-year-old transvestite from Baltimore. I wasn't good at computers, so how was a guy to know?

"All right, Tommy, give."

Tommy wiped perspiration from his face and sized Bear up, perhaps contemplating some retaliation. I'm sure somewhere in the back of his mind he was considering snapping Bear into fire-wood and tossing *him* off the overlook. Tommy could probably do it, mind you—he was a very experienced, very capable man. He made a wise choice and cooperation reigned. He slinked away from Bear and caught his breath resting on his Buick.

"I dunno what you want. How can I tell you if I dunno what you want?"

Bear closed in on him, leaned forward, and eyed him. "What's Nic got to do with Liam McCorkle's death?"

"Who?"

"You heard me."

Tommy's mouth gaped open. "Nothin', Bear. I'm sure of that. Nothin'. I didn't even know he died."

"He was murdered."

"Shit, no." Tommy looked down at his feet—not that he could see his feet. "Okay, look. When I first started workin' for the Man, I delivered packages back and forth to McCorkle. I guess it's been a few years. I don't know what's in 'em, and I don't wanna know. It's a private thing. *Capisce?*"

"Keep going. I'll tell you when to stop talking."

"Jesus, Bear. This is all innocent, I swear."

"If you don't know what's in the packages, how do you know that?"

"Ah, I dunno." Tommy frowned. He was a terrible liar. "Bear, there are some things that ain't *that* kind of business, you know? This is one of them. Mr. Bartalotta has a real life, too, you know. This is part of that. Goes back years and it ain't for me to ask about."

"What does that mean?"

Tommy's lips pursed and his one, thick eyebrow wrinkled low across his eyes. He had reached his end. "This is a no-go. The Man is entitled to some privacy when it ain't nothing bad. I deliver stuff between him and McCorkle. The Man keeps the packages in his vault and I never see what's in 'em. I don't wanna see."

"Bullshit." Bear thrust a gun-finger into Tommy's chest. "You're lying, Tommy. You're a phone call from violating parole."

"Then do it. I got nothin' to say this time. The Man is clean on this, Bear. I swear. Whatever's in them packages, he never lets me or Bobby see. He's private—weird private—about it. He gets mad as hell sometimes, and like, you know, sad other times."

"Find out."

"No." Tommy's voice was flat and defiant. It surprised me as much as Bear—maybe Bear more. There was something odd about it, too. Tommy was drawing a line in the sand. He was facing jail and he wasn't budging. Whatever he was protecting, it scared him more than anything Bear could do to him.

"What did you say, Tommy?"

"No. Not this time."

The two stood nose to nose glaring at each other. Tommy's defiance sent an unnerving message. The only things worth guarding this much were treasure and secrets. Both were dangerous. Both might get you killed.

"Tommy, I'm not screwing around..."

"No." Tommy's defiance was clear. "Bust my parole if you want—the answer is still no. You got my word that the Man's clean on McCorkle's killin'. He ain't involved in nothin' bad with him either. It's a family thing. And I know not to step into that. So, no."

Bear wasn't used to hearing "no" from snitches, in particular those who danced with the probation department so often. Nonetheless, he knew wasn't budging.

"Okay, Tommy. Okay."

"Thanks, Bear."

Bear pulled an envelope out of his pocket and tossed it on the car hood. "This month's benefit plan. But listen, *paesano*, you so much as hear him say 'McCorkle' and you better be ringing my phone, *capisce*?"

Tommy hesitated, then picked up the envelope and handed it back. "No, not this time. I ain't givin' on this one. I can't. Anythin' else, okay. Not this. Keep your money. But hey…"

Bear just looked at him.

"Maybe tell your lady pal to stop poking around about stuff. She ain't no cop."

"What?" Bear's face gave away his confusion. "What's that mean —exactly?"

"Just tell her. I'm just sayin', ya know, as a favor. She ain't makin' no friends."

Bear grabbed the envelope of money off the car. "Get the hell out of here before I bust you for being out of state without permission."

Tommy left in a torrent of gravel and dust.

Bear watched him disappear down the mountain road. "Angela, what the hell have you done now?"

FIFTY-TWO

"CHURNING UP TROUBLE? Do you hear yourself?" Angel's face was red. She sat at her university desk opposite Ernie and slapped her hand down on the desktop, killing pencils and paperclips in the eruption. "André is lying in a hospital bed. He could have died, Ernie—*died*. Bear and I didn't do that. And you're only worried about your historical society and Kelly's Dig?"

"No, of course not, Angela. Please, I'm sorry. It's just that it's casting a bad light on the site."

"The site?" Angel jumped up. "I could not care less about your historical preservations right now. But it certainly is about your site. Someone is killing people. All of this—and I mean all of it—is somehow about that site."

"You don't know that," Ernie said. "Not really."

I said, "Yes we do, Ernie. Two dead girls convinced me."

"There have been killings there before," Angel began. "Two missing girls may have been killed there. It's all connected to that damn site."

"Two girls? Murdered?" Ernie squinted at her and his face wrinkled up as though she was speaking in tongues. "Have there been more murders? I haven't heard anything about that and I'm sure I would have."

She was caught.

"Now you've done it." How was she gonna explain the girls?

"Listen, Ernie." She dug into her purse, retrieving the small emerald we'd found. She handed it to him. "I found this at Kelly's Dig this morning. I think there's more going on that we don't know. I did some research into old, unsolved cases and found some information on two missing girls. I asked Tyler about them and he got angry—very angry."

Damn, she lied well, and was fast on her feet, too. I wonder how many times she'd done that to me?

"Really?" Ernie looked up from the emerald and his eyes went dark. The mention of Byrd's name seemed to grab his manhood and squeeze. "Tell me what you've found."

She did. Well, I should say, she told a *story*. She didn't say that I told her about the two dead girls—that would make her a little crazy. She referred to me as a "source." For many years, I'd been a cop. Now I was a "source"—a snitch.

"I see." Ernie returned the emerald. "Angela, I realize you're still distraught over Tuck. Now André's been injured. Nevertheless, my dear, you're seeing shadows. I've lived here my entire life and don't recall anything about unsolved murders or missing girls."

I said, "Angel, let it go. We need names and details. You can't very well tell people, 'oh, my dead husband told me that two dead girls told him' … blah, blah, blah. Leave it alone."

She knew I was right. "Okay, Ernie, maybe you're right. I still have to check it out some more, though. I'm going deeper into the Kelly's Dig history. If I get nothing more, I'll drop it."

His face grew darker. "You mean the Bartalotta family?"

"Yes, you knew his family owned the farm?"

"Of course I did."

"You've never mentioned it."

He looked amused. "Well, neither have you."

"Tell me, Ernie. Anything you can."

What he said changed everything. "Nicholas's family owned the farm many years back. I should say, his cousin did—his namesake cousin. They bought it in the late fifties or early sixties, I think. Just after his family came over from Italy. Nicholas lived in New York back then, and he vacationed at the farm during his summers. I don't think many people know that."

I asked, "Then how does he know this?"

Angel asked him, and his answer added to the swelling ache in my head.

"Very simple, Angela," he said, looking far too pleased with himself. "I've known Nicholas for years. In fact, we knew each other rather well in those days. André knows him well, too."

"André? He never mentioned that." Angel was surprised.

Ernie went on. "Our families—André's and mine—were very friendly as you know. We're all from academic backgrounds, mind you. Nicholas's family and ours did not get on; nor did they with

286

André's. After all, our families were respectable and Nicholas's were rather, shall we say, *notorious.* Whispers followed them everywhere."

Notorious? Whispers? My, my, Ernie sure had a flare for cheap drama. If I didn't know better, I would say Ernie Stuart was enjoying his fifteen minutes of fame as an old pal of the retired mobster. I wonder what Poor Nic would say about him?

"Ernie," Angel asked, "you said Nicholas' namesake owned the farm. I don't recall seeing 'Bartalotta' in the land records."

He grinned as his fifteen minutes headed for twenty. "You wouldn't. His distant cousin, Nicholas, owned it, on his mother's side—*Nicholas Voccelli.*"

FIFTY-THREE

WHEN ERNIE LEFT, HE was gloating. Having a big secret in the game puffed him up like a peacock. Odd, though, that he never whispered that secret before—especially considering his involvement with Kelly's Dig. Then again, there wasn't much I didn't find a little odd about him from time to time. I never knew about André growing up around Poor Nic either.

I wonder what other secrets were out there waiting.

Angel promised to call Ernie the moment something more happened. He left angry, unhappy with her to be still chasing murderers. He meant well, but the old fart was getting a little too protective for me. But, like all good dead husbands, I kept my mouth shut and stretched out on her office couch.

"Angel, do you think old Ernie ..."

There was a knock on the door and Angel called out, "Come in."

"Sorry to interrupt you, Angela. May I come in?" The voice was familiar but the woman who walked through the door was not. "It's me, Sarah Salazar."

If not for her name, I would not have recognized her. As the country folk say, "she sure does clean up good." Sarah was dressed in a white cotton top and a tan skirt. Her blonde hair was pulled back and she was wearing round glasses that made her appear more sophisticated than I knew she was. Sarah had transformed herself into a lovely co-ed who was going to turn a few heads around campus.

"My, my, will you look at her."

"Stop it and be quiet." Angel said under her breath. "Privacy, remember?"

I looked at her and her ire bothered me. She was more and more testy with me, and while all the mayhem may be to blame, I didn't deserve it. Maybe it was never knowing when I was around or not, or, perhaps, not having me really around. Maybe I was wearing out my welcome and being just a voice in the room was no match for flesh and blood and real companionship. Maybe.

She said, "Sarah, come in. What a nice surprise."

Sarah walked in and gave Angel a long, tight hug. When she let go, she blushed and retreated behind a chair facing the desk. "I'm sorry to drop by like this."

"Don't be."

"You've been so kind to me." Angel gestured for her to sit. Sarah went on, "The daycare is perfect, and I start a reception job tomorrow. I'm gonna take some classes if student aid works out."

"That's wonderful, Sarah. I'm happy for you. You'll be back on your feet in no time. Can I do anything else?"

"No, no. I had to say 'thanks.'" She hesitated for a second and I thought she was going to leave. Instead, she fidgeted in her chair. "Well, I wanna to give you some things. You'll know what to do with them—I sure don't."

"Some things? What?"

Sarah opened her shoulder bag and took out a rolled-up brown paper bag. She handed it to Angel. "Ray left this stuff—you know, from the diggin'."

Angel emptied the bag out on her desk and gold coins, a ragged leather pouch, and tarnished pieces of metal spilled out. I recognized the coins from Sarah's bedroom. The pieces of tarnished metal were an old, broken belt buckle and several buttons—pieces of a soldier's uniform. She started to open the leather pouch but decided to wait.

When I looked at the coins, I knew we were closer to a murderer. "Angel, those are 1881 twenty-dollar gold pieces. They look like Poor Nic's."

Angel picked up one of the coins and examined it, holding it to the light to read the engravings. "You got all this from Ray, Sarah? The coins, too? They came from Kelly's Dig?"

Sarah nodded but didn't speak. Angel sorted through the items piled on her desk. Sarah twitched each time Angel picked one up.

"Angela, I lied to you the other night." She rubbed her wrist and refused to look at her. Then, without warning, she began to cry. "I knew Ray and Iggi worked for Mr. Byrd. Ray was so happy about that job. He was makin' more money there than as a guard. Mr.

Byrd and Poor Nic have been real good to me. I lied because Nic's men came by and …"

"It's okay, Sarah. I understand." Angel put a hand on her shoulder. "Really. It's okay."

"No, I should have told you." Sarah continued sobbing. "Mr. Byrd paid Ray under the table so we didn't tell nobody. It was only for a couple weeks."

"I know."

"Then, Iggi got a call from some guy about that farm they was working on—the one that's been in all the papers."

"Kelly's Dig?" Angel asked.

Sarah nodded. "Yup. Ray was real nervous. There was something scary about the deal—but it was lots of money. Anyway, they were supposed to move these bones—"

Angel interrupted her. "I know all that, Sarah. Iggi told us."

"They never even touched those old bones—Ray said they were too scary. But they found all this stuff—more even—and they sold a lot of it."

I couldn't stay quiet any longer. "She's hiding something."

"Hiding?" Angel repeated. "Sarah?"

Sarah paled and her eyes grew rounder. She started rubbing her wrist again and that's when I saw it. She was wearing an ornate silver bracelet that was badly tarnished and bent. Its band was inlaid with green gemstones and it looked as though some were missing.

Angel looked at her wrist and gently touched her hand. Sarah tried to cover the bracelet.

"Sarah, did Ray give you that?"

She nodded and cried harder. "Yeah."

"It's all right, Sarah. May I see it?"

With slow, hesitant movements, she slid the bracelet off and held it out. Her crying made her stutter. "Ray found it with the other stuff. He cleaned it up himself. He said he wouldn't sell it 'cause he couldn't afford anything like it for a long time."

Angel held it up to inspect. The band was heavy, tarnished silver that bore the scars of years buried in earth. The band was decorated with the shapes of musical notes connected by two G-clefs—one on each side. There were mounts for four emeralds. Two were still affixed in the silver; two were missing. Each of the G-clefs had a ruby mounted in its center. The piece was old, but how old I didn't know. I doubted, though, that it came from any Civil War soldier.

"Angel," I said. "Remember those two nice, dead young girls? I think this belongs to one of them."

She held up the bracelet. "Did Ray say anything about finding more pieces like this? Any other jewelry?"

"No, I don't think so. Just those coins and stuff—I brought what's left. "

Angel retrieved her purse from behind her desk. She took out a folded white mailing envelope and dumped out the emerald we'd found at Kelly's Dig. The stone fit into one of the empty G-cleft settings and matched the other emeralds perfectly.

"Sarah, may I keep this for a couple days?"

"Umm, sure," she said, staring at the floor. "Do you think Ray was killed because of it?"

"That's what I want to find out."

"Take it. I don't want it anymore."

Angel smiled knowingly and scooped up the coins and other items from her desk. She carefully replaced them in the bag Sarah brought, keeping the bracelet out in front of her. "I'll try to return it to you. But Sarah, I may not be able to."

She shrugged. "That's okay. I don't want it now. If that's why Ray was killed—even if it's just part of it—I never want to see it again."

"I understand." Angel stood up. "Does anyone else know about this—the bracelet, I mean?"

"Just Iggi."

Angel gently squeezed her arm, making her point crystal clear. "You cannot tell anyone about this. No one. It could be dangerous."

"Yeah, okay." Sarah lowered her head, rubbed her empty wrist, and began to cry again. "Poor Ray. Why did this happen? Just 'cause some old bones got in the way of that highway? 'Cause of some road?"

We both knew the answer to that question, but Angel answered her. "I don't think so, Sarah. I don't think it has anything to do with the highway."

FIFTY-FOUR

As soon as Sarah Salazar left, Angel called Bear. I tried to get her to put the phone on speaker but she waited until after she told him about Sarah, and Bear's mumbled update about my case.

"Nothing new," she said to me, covering the phone. Then she clicked on the speaker. "Bear, I think I saw this bracelet in one of the sketches from Liam McCorkle's safe."

"Are you sure? I mean, just from a sketch?"

"Trust me. Can you get Jack to email copies of them?"

"Yeah, I'm supposed to call him anyway. What are you thinking?"

"If this bracelet is in those sketches, then someone was looking for it. Maybe that's McCorkle's secret project. Maybe that's why Salazar died—because he found it."

I said to her, "Angel, the word is 'murdered' not 'died.' There's an important difference."

"Angela," Bear's voice seemed strained, almost irritated. "The captain is pretty pissed at me. You better be right about this."

Angel took the phone off speaker. "What's wrong with you? No, what? I do understand. Do you? Just hurry."

Bear grumbled for a long while and I couldn't make it out. She hung up.

I asked, "What's he got, Angel?"

"Nothing, really. Captain Sutter thinks the sheriff is bringing in the BCI, too. We're running out of time."

"Some of us already have."

She looked toward me—truth be told she was looking at the couch where she heard me speaking from—and her face was ashen. "I know that, Tuck. Don't you think I know? What do you want me to do? I'm trying to help you—to help Bear, too. It's hard, though. It's very hard on me. You just don't understand."

"Then explain it to me."

She stood up. "I can't. You just wouldn't understand. And it might make things worse."

Worse? Worse than being dead?

For the next hour, Angel and I stayed silent. I laid on her couch, trying to figure her out. When I had first reappeared to her, she seemed ecstatic—confused but happy. She called for me to save her that night in the rain, and later, she cried when she realized I was back. Lately, however, she seemed at odds with that; frustrated and distant.

Was it stress? Or was it something else?

My headache took flight with the famous "you've got mail" ding on Angel's computer. It was from Bear. She clicked on his email attachment and sent the entire file to the printer. It took several minutes—five after Angel put paper in the printer. Finally, the thirty or more sketches began spitting out. Angel sorted through them. Her face brightened.

"It's here, Tuck. I knew I'd seen this."

It was there—a hand-drawn sketch of a bracelet with musical notes and two G-clefs around the band. The G-clefs were set with gemstones in their center and several more around the band. Even in this stark, black and white artist's sketch, it was beautiful and distinctive. At the bottom of the sketch were hand-printed notes explaining the position of the rubies and emeralds. There was another handwritten notation, too—*"Paul Livingston—May 1966."*

Angel asked, "Paul Livingston? Could he own the bracelet?'

"Hell no." The name, and the man, were very familiar to me. "Paul Livingston is retired—the hard way. He used to be a jeweler in Old Town."

"The hard way?"

I laughed—which was rude under the circumstances. "Yeah, when Bear and I were rookies, we put him away for fifteen years. Livingston Senior was more than just a good jeweler; he was a great fence. He handled stuff all the way from Washington to Philadelphia. Who would ever suspect a small town goldsmith would be moving hot goods—other than Bear and me that is. He died a couple years ago."

"We're at a dead end." Angel dropped the sketch atop the bracelet on her desk. "Again."

"No, not yet. Livingston Senior died in prison—Paul Junior runs the family business. He has a shop down in Strasburg."

"And what if Livingston doesn't know anything? What then?"

I thought about that. "If these sketches are the path to our killer, you can bet Livingston knows the way, too."

FIFTY-FIVE

"ALL RIGHT, I'LL GO see Paul Livingston for you." Angel's voice was flat and without emotion. "But that's that. Anything I get, I give to Bear."

She sat on the couch sipping a glass of wine and I was in the chair adjacent to her. She couldn't see me of course, but she knew where I was by my voice. I knew, by her voice, that she was growing disenchanted with being my deputy.

"Okay, Angel, okay. I really don't understand."

She took a long pull on her wine. "Why can't you let this go? Let Bear handle it—just leave it alone, please. Why can't you be content the way things are?"

The way things are? "Because, Professor, I'm dead. I don't particularly like the way things *are*."

She jumped to her feet and headed for the living room door. "Neither do I. But finding your killer isn't going to change anything. Anything for you, that is." And she was gone out of the room.

A moment later, I heard her on her cell phone in the kitchen. She was talking with Ernie and venting about everything she'd learned from Sarah. She even invited him along to Paul Livingston's the next morning. Just what I needed.

Ernie might be her boss and longtime family friend, but sometimes he was just a plain pain in the ass. His commiserating about her chasing my killer wasn't going to help my cause. I needed Angel to do my bidding and help find whoever was responsible for all the pandemonium. Good old Ernie was going to pour cold water on any spark I had lighted in her.

That wouldn't do.

Listening to Angel debating with Ernie, I began feeling jittery, as if the house was sitting over the San Andreas Fault and it was becoming unhappy. The room shifted from side to side and Hercule faded from my sight. That strange, tingling invaded me as it always did when it sent me elsewhere.

And it did again.

❧

When the electricity subsided, I was standing in the familiar haze of nowhere. Through the emptiness, Doc Gilley seized my arm and shook me. He looked perturbed. There was intensity in him—his face agitated and his eyes grave.

What did I do now?

"Hey, Doc, where you been? Boy do I have questions..."

"There's no time." Doc kept looking over his shoulder as if he was expecting someone to appear. "Get back to the hospital—*now.*"

"What's wrong?"

"Oliver, focus." He pointed off into the haze. "I can't do this for you. I'm not connected to them—just you. I can't intervene."

"Doc, you're freaking me out. What is it?"

He pointed into the haze again, but now it was starting to take form. "Don't you feel it? Don't you feel the danger? Focus, Oliver."

Just once, I wish he'd call me Tuck. "Come on, Doc. I want to ask you about…"

The lights flashed on and the haze evaporated. The beeps and hums of electronic monitors and André's respirator startled me. I was standing in the ICU hall, outside André's observation window into his room. The inside curtain was drawn and only a shadow shown through. There was no one nearby except a duty nurse at the far end of the hall, and she was busy banging away on a computer behind a chest-high counter.

Something was wrong.

There was no cop outside André's room. Even the chair was gone. Inside the room, a shadow began moving and I felt a pang of danger. *Oh, shit.*

In a blink, I was standing beside André's bed. He was still unconscious and unable to summon help—he didn't even know he needed it. Across from me was the one man every cop in the county was looking for—Lucca Voccelli—*Lucca Tuscani*. He was fiddling with the medical control panels surrounding André. He read the switches while his fingers flipped from one to the other—he was trying to find the fastest way to finish André Cartier.

"You bastard." He didn't hear me. "Stop."

Tuscani's efforts sent out a warning beep and realizing his error, he grabbed the cords and began ripping them from the wall sockets, flipping buttons to silence their alarms. After the third plug, the monitors went dark and I knew we were minutes from André's last breath.

"You son-of-a-bitch." I tried everything—shouts, the ghost-mind meld, and I even returned to the hallway to seek help. The nurse at her station was oblivious to me. There was a doctor with her now, but neither saw nor heard me, and they were too far down the hall to see the danger in André's room. No one knew. No one knew he was being murdered.

Tuscani leaned over André's motionless body to check his breathing. André grimaced and I knew he was fighting back. Something was awakening in him and his body was trying to defend itself. His eyes fluttered but didn't open. His muscles twitched, but no arm rose to defend himself.

"Leave him alone, you bastard."

I tried grabbing the power cords for some juice and energy—they were unplugged and no power brought me to the rescue.

Panic surged.

Tuscani snatched a pillow from behind André's head and covered his face. He leaned his weight forward and began to kill right in front of me.

No.

Flailing everywhere, I found the nurse call buzzer and grabbed hold of it. Desperately, I tried to suck in the power—command enough strength to stop Tuscani before André succumbed. The buzzer above the door flashed and I held on, draining all I could from the mere trickle of electricity flowing through it.

I felt it.

An almost unnoticeable tingle of strength spread from my fingertips and moved upward. It wasn't much, but it was building, ebbing up my arm and deeper into me. André coughed and tensed beneath the pillow stealing his life. I couldn't wait any longer and lurched forward, grabbing Tuscani's hands. I squeezed them hard and funneled the power in me into him. Rage clamped my fingertips deep into his flesh and I twisted hard and violent.

It worked.

His eyes bulged and he jumped back from the bed in panic—the pillow fell to the floor. He went pale and he looked right at me. His mouth opened for a scream, but no sound erupted.

The bastard saw me.

"Boo." I lunged at him.

"What in the hell?" He tripped backwards, collided with the medical cart, and stumbled again. "Get away from me. It's you. Damn, it's you again."

It was nice to be remembered.

Weakness ebbed in and that damning lethargy started to ooze into me. The power that had just saved André was waning and bleeding me out. In a second, he would be alone and vulnerable.

No. I had to fight. I had to keep André safe … alive. I had to. I focused all I had left on Lucca Tuscani as he stood frozen facing me. I had to fight him.

No, it would be okay.

The door burst open and Mike Spence charged in. He lunged forward and grabbed Tuscani's arms. He spun him around and away from André's bed. Spence yanked Tuscani forward, drove a knee into his abdomen, and landed a crushing left into his face. Another knee. Another left.

Tuscani belched air and staggered, trying to free himself. Spence slammed him face-first into the observation windows. The curtain fell away as Spence hammered several more blows into his kidneys.

Tuscani whirled, twisted free, and landed a powerful punch into Spence's face. He followed with a groin kick and a two-fisted hammer drive into the side of his head. Spence faltered and fell back down to one knee, fighting for breath—pain exploding on his face.

Tuscani pounced.

I tried to intervene but my energy was spent. There was nothing left. Surprisingly, I didn't disappear from the room as I had before whenever my energy was drained too thin. Yet, all I could do was watch as Tuscani pummeled Spence with punch after punch—kick after kick. I was helpless.

We were in trouble. Spence was down, and once out, André was next. Spence tried to rise and draw his handgun but Tuscani anticipated him. He lunged and kicked the gun from Spence's grasp just as it cleared his holster. He kicked Spence in the midsection. Spence staggered and fell. Tuscani grabbed one of the medical carts and smashed it atop him, stomping it down into his body with crushing force.

There was no fight left—Spence was done.

"Freeze, Sheriff's Department." Detective Calvin Clemens ran up the hall with a uniformed deputy two steps behind. Clemens's gun was out, determination raging. "Freeze."

Tuscani groped beneath the cart and returned with Spence's nine-millimeter. Instead of finishing him or André, he fired two shots out the door to clear his path and made his escape in the wake.

More fractious orders—two more shots—three. Running feet. Shouts. Crashes. Nothing.

It was over. Tuscani was gone—for now.

Had I not witnessed it, no one could have convinced me— Detective Mikey Spence had saved the day. Was anyone who I thought they were?

FIFTY-SIX

By eight the next morning, Angel had finished her breakfast and I the third rendition of Tuscani's attempt to kill André. We were waiting for Ernie to arrive for our trip to Strasburg and he was late. Angel called Bear for an update on André, and I could tell he was not thrilled that she learned of the attack before anyone—including the media—got wind of it.

"And how in the hell did you know all that?" he groaned. "Never mind, you'll just tell me..."

"Tuck was there. Spence saved André."

He didn't answer.

"Bear?"

"Angela, listen. Spence pulled the guard off André's door. He was waiting down the hall. I've already complained to the captain."

"He set a trap?" Angel's face turned fiery red. "Using André?"

"You know Spence. He figured someone might try to get to André a second time. And while I hate to say it, it almost worked."

"Please check on André again," she said, and then sent Bear into a fit. "I'm going to Strasburg to see Paul Livingston."

"Livingston?" Bear shouted through the speaker. "What about Livingston?"

She explained about the clues from McCorkle's sketches and Sarah's bracelet. He wasn't amused he was just hearing about it all. In fact, he wasn't amused at anything she'd said this morning.

"Jeez, Angela. You gotta tell me when things happen. Not the next day. You stay away from Livingston. And that bracelet is evidence—so I want it. No, you're not going."

"Ernie's going with me."

"No, Angela. I'll check him out myself. You stay away from him."

Silence. Then, Angel said, "Fine. But let me know what happens."

"Good. I'll call later. I'll come by for the bracelet later this morning."

When Bear hung up, she retrieved her purse and picked up her keys. "If he thinks he can tell me what to do, he's wrong."

Bear touched a very sensitive nerve in my Angel—she never liked being bossed around. A few minutes ago, she wanted no part in my investigation. Now, thanks to him, she was all about crime fighting.

"Okay, Angel, I guess you're going anyway."

"I can handle myself just fine. We'll see what I can find out without him."

There was a knock on the front door and Ernie walked in. He looked like a wreck. His hair was disheveled, his face pale, and he was out of breath. When he trudged into the kitchen and plopped down in a chair in front of the coffee pot, he let out a heavy sigh and dropped his head into his hands. I'd never seen him as disjointed as he was now and it was unnerving.

"Angela, did you hear about André? Incredible."

"I just spoke with Bear," Angel said. "Spence set a trap for Tuscani. They nearly caught him."

"Oh? They're sure it was this Tuscani fellow? This is out of control and getting worse. I hope they know what they're doing."

"They'll figure this all out, Ernie. They have to."

"Yes, yes, you're right." Ernie changed the subject. "Show me what that girl, Sarah, gave you."

Angel went into the den and returned with the folded paper bag Sarah had given her. She emptied it on the kitchen table and handed the silver bracelet to Ernie.

"It was very beautiful once," he said, toying with it in his palm. "Handmade, too."

"Sarah gave us these gold coins, too. They're very rare, 1881 twenty-dollar pieces. Are they similar to those you had?"

"I think, perhaps, they are." He held one and studied it. "I'm certain of it."

"Poor Nic has a collection of these in his den. And he's missing several of them, too. I think…"

"No. Take them away." Ernie closed his eyes and dropped the bracelet onto the table. "Please, I don't want anything to do with them if they've caused all this misery."

Angel sat down beside him and moved the coins around the table like chess pieces on a board. "Ernie, you probably can tell me more about these than anyone. I'd like to know what you can tell me before we go see Livingston."

He frowned. "Well, I cannot go with you this morning. Tyler Byrd called. He wants to discuss Kelly's Dig and he's adamant I see him at ten this morning. He says all the tragedies are ruining him. He wants my help, of all people."

"That's all right, Ernie. I'll be fine." She put the coins and bracelet back into the bag.

"Perhaps you should wait for Braddock." When Angel shook her head, he smiled and stood up to go. "Then be careful, Angela. You shouldn't be going to see this Livingston fellow alone. But I know you; I'll never talk you out of it. If that bracelet is the cause of these murders, you could be in danger."

"I've thought of that," Angel said, shaking her head. "I'm not bringing it with me—I'll show him the sketches first. I'll bring Hercule for a drive. He'll protect me."

"All right, my dear. Be careful."

Angel hesitated before saying, "Will you call me later and let me know about Tyler?"

"Of course, he's definitely very suspect in all this. Nicholas Bartalotta, too," Ernie said with a wink. "And you keep Detective Braddock under your eye, too."

"Listen to yourself. Is everyone a suspect?"

"Yes, everyone is."

FIFTY-SEVEN

Paul Livingston Jr.'s quaint, nineteenth-century shop was a block off Main Street in Strasburg. The brick and colonial-windowed façade had a simple, wooden sign hanging over the door that read, "Strasburg Fine Jewelry and Goldsmith, Est. 1949." That was a misnomer of course; Paul Junior moved to Strasburg ten years ago after dear old dad went up the river. Junior had his father's propensity to be a little on the loose side of the truth.

The shop was small with glass jewelry cabinets surrounding the entrance. There was barely enough room for both of us to enter and move around without a collision. Well, if I were actually occupying space, that is. Beyond the showroom was an office area, and beside that, a door leading deeper into the building.

There was no one in sight, and Angel looked for a bell or buzzer. Before she found it beneath a newspaper on the counter, a voice from the backroom yelled, "I'll be right there. Please look around."

"All right, thank you," Angel called back.

I pointed out the closed-circuit television camera in the far corner of the ceiling. The red light glowing on its face told me it was on. Livingston was watching our every move. "Imagine this guy worrying about crooks."

"Behave. I don't want to be here long."

"Good morning." A somewhat rotund, bald man appeared through the doorway in the rear. He had heavy, frosted eyebrows and squinty, piggish eyes. His reading glasses were perched on his nose with a second pair—probably magnifying glasses—propped on his forehead. He was wiping his hands on a heavy jeweler's apron and ogling Angel.

Livingston wheezed as he approached us, his heavy girth making the floorboards groan and the glass displays rattle. He was sweaty—hopefully not from the ten feet he just walked—and his face was red. Without subtlety, he continued ogling Angel and dropped himself on a padded wooden stool across the center display counter from us.

"Well now, what can I do for you, sweetie?"

Did I mention that Livingston Senior was an incorrigible worm with the charm of a lizard? Obviously, these traits were deeply rooted in the genes.

"Good morning." Angel laid Liam McCorkle's sketches down on the counter but kept her hand resting on top. "Mr. Livingston?"

"Yes. Please call me Paul." Paul couldn't keep his eyes off her—not that his were on hers. He reached into his pocket and took out several business cards. He sorted through them and handed one to her from the center of the stack. "My card, sweetie—with my very private number."

"Ah, yes, thank you." Angel glanced at it but pressed on. "Paul, you were referred by an antique dealer in Staunton. I want to know if you or your father made a piece of jewelry I've found."

"Well, let's see." With one glance, Livingston's face went from sweaty-red to pasty-white. He pulled the reading glasses from his nose. "Staunton? Who?"

"Liam McCorkle."

Someone call nine-one-one.

Livingston tensed. His wheezing stopped in mid-breath. He leaned back on the stool and folded his arms, eyeing Angel with enough contempt to sear his words. "Bullshit. McCorkle's dead."

"Yes, I know. I was there."

"Oh you were?" Livingston sneered. He tugged one of the sketches from beneath Angel's hand and held his reading glasses above it like a magnifying glass. Without looking up, he said, "Where did you get these?"

"From McCorkle."

I added, "You've got his attention, Angel. Play him some line and see where this takes us."

"Lady…"

"Angela, please."

"Okay, Angela. McCorkle gave you these?"

Angel played it cool. "Before he was killed. You see, I have a bracelet that resembles these sketches. I'm trying to find the jeweler who made it—it's an original piece and I'd like some information."

"Show me the bracelet."

"Are these sketches your father's? Or did you do the artwork?"

"It's not mine," he waved a hand. "I never did anything like this. I'm not even sure Dad did. I'd have to see the piece to know if he made it."

"Why?" Angel rolled up the sketches and extended her hand for the one Livingston was holding. "Don't you have records?"

"Sure, some." His tone turned ugly. "What is this really about? And don't give me any shit about McCorkle, either."

I leaned close to Angela. "Tell him there's a reward if he can help identify the bracelet's owner."

She did and Livingston's eyebrows rose. "Well, now. You want to know who had the piece made? Didn't McCorkle tell you?"

"No, he said you could," Angel lied—damn she was good at that. "He said your father made the piece before he was sent to prison. He thought your records would tell me who the original owner was."

The word "prison" put Livingston on his feet and started him sweating again. "That was a long time ago. But sure, I have some of Dad's records from back then. I computerized them for the insurance people. I'll see what I can find. Come back later."

I didn't trust Livingston and the more cooperative he became, the less I liked. I also didn't want Angel coming back. We needed to get what we could and scram. "No, Angel. Tell him he gets five hundred if he IDs the owner and an extra five hundred if he does it right now."

"A thousand?" Angel's voice was higher than she planned; that gave Livingston an unsettled twitch in his face.

"For a thousand, I'll do this quick." He took the sketches from her and headed toward the rear office. "Come with me. I've got some coffee in the back and you can relax while I check the files."

We followed him through the rear door and down a short hallway to a corner room on the left. "That's the kitchen. Coffee is on the hotplate. Help yourself. Give me some time, though. There are a lot of files."

We went in and Angel waited until he disappeared back into the hallway before she let me have it. "A thousand dollars? Are you insane? I don't have that kind of cash with me."

"Relax," I said. "Tell him Bear has the reward. If he balks, call Bear right in front of him. That'll bunch his knickers up."

"It better."

"You can always take it out of my life insurance."

"I will."

After forty-five minutes, Angel was getting antsy. She pulled out Livingston's business card and looked it over. When she read me the card, bells and whistles went off.

"Hey, read me that number again."

She did.

"We gotta get out of here. Now."

"What's wrong, Tuck? What is it?" She glanced at the card again. "Is the phone number important?"

Holy shit it was. "Angel, when we were at Bear's office the other day, I saw him pocket some evidence. He didn't log it into the records like he should have."

"Okay, so he shouldn't have done that. What does that have to do with ..."

"He took a business card out of the file and it had Livingston's phone number. He…"

"Just stop it, Tuck." She glanced at the card again and then toward the kitchen doorway. "You're too suspicious of Bear and I'm tired of it."

"No, you don't understand…" I felt a tingle run through me. "Forget it, let's go. Now. I got a bad feeling."

When we emerged in the main office, I knew my tingle was right. The closed-circuit camera watching the store entrance wasn't watching any longer; its red power light was off. Livingston had turned off his surveillance cameras.

"Angel, get the hell out of here. Something's wrong. Go."

It was already too late.

Livingston's deceit walked in the front door and blocked our escape.

"Good morning, my dear," Poor Nic said with a wide, wolf-like grin. He extended his hand to her, palm up. "And I understand you found my missing bracelet."

FIFTY-EIGHT

"THAT BRACELET BELONGS TO me." Poor Nic blocked the doorway and still held out his hand. His eyes were cold and had lost the grandfather twinkle; the gangster side of him filled its place. "I want it. Now."

I said, "Stay cool. Even this bozo won't do anything stupid in public."

"Nicholas, I don't have it with me. I brought the sketches for Livingston to look at."

"Then you do have it." He motioned to Tommy and Bobby who squeezed into the room behind him. "I'm afraid we'll have to make sure. But use some couth, won't you, boys?"

Tommy hesitated. "Ah, Mr. Bartalotta, are you sure?"

"That's up to her," Poor Nic said, eyeing Angel. "She can turn out her pockets and empty her bag—or you can."

"If they touch me, I'll have you all arrested."

Poor Nic waved at Livingston. "Get lost, Paul."

Livingston laughed and clomped into his office.

"Nicholas," Angel said. "The last time we met, you seemed genuinely pleasant—even innocent. Was I wrong and everyone else right about you?"

He blinked a couple times as she stared daggers at him. I knew that look—she was going to fight it out and it would take both his men to do his bidding. It was going to get ugly.

"No, my dear, you were not wrong. But then, you didn't have my bracelet and I wasn't out millions. So much has happened these past few days—no? Everything has changed, Professor Tucker. Everything."

Angel's chin rose in a defiant arc.

"Now…" Poor Nic took a step forward. "Give me the bracelet and you may go. No one will bother you again. You have my word."

"Who does it belong to—you don't look like the musical type."

Bobby took a step forward, but a sharp hand from Nicholas stopped him. "No, of course not. It was a gift; a very special gift."

"For whom?"

I said, "Don't push this guy, Angel. You were right and I was wrong—we shouldn't have come."

"Who?" She demanded again. "One of the dead girls at the farm?"

Wham-o. She couldn't have shocked him more with a sharp slap. His face contorted as if the life was being squeezed from him. His fists shook at his sides and for a second, only guttural Italian slurs cut the rawness in the air.

Even Tommy winced.

Finally, Nic caught his breath. He thrust an angry, lethal finger toward her. "You be very careful, Professor Tucker. You speak to me without respect—and of things you should not. The past—my past—is not for you or *anyone* to intrude into. What happened is for me to reconcile. Not for you. Not for the police. Me."

What the hell was he talking about?

Angel started to speak when Bobby stepped forward and grasped one of her arms. This time, Poor Nic did not intervene. She tried to pull free, but Bobby's grip was too strong. She and Poor Nic locked eyes and their wills collided. Angel was not going to give in and that was dangerous. She swung her free fist, but Bobby deftly blocked it.

"The bracelet, Angela. Now."

Burglar alarms are designed to stop a robbery or a break-in. They are not designed for an escape. Either way, though, they summon the police. I don't think that fat, lying toad Paul Livingston considered that when he installed his and put the panic button under the counter. Another important fact is that they run on electricity and as I've learned, electricity is my pal. So, when I found the panic button and connected with the juice, the alarm went off. It went off very, very loud.

I can be a mischievous little bastard, can't I?

The deafening, high-pitched siren pierced everyone to the bone—even me. The bazillion-decibel wailing is designed to send would-be holdup men running and the police responding from five blocks away. I had no doubt it worked. Livingston emerged from his office and ran for the backroom. His face was on fire and sweat poured from his brow. Tommy slapped his hands over his ears and Bobby followed suit.

Angel was free.

Only Poor Nic stood unfazed by the ear-splitting cacophony. Red-faced and gritting his teeth, he looked around the room for the source of the siren. "Livingston, for Christ's sake, turn it off."

"I can't," he yelled from the backroom. "It's the panic alarm— the alarm company has to reset it. The police will be here soon."

Just when I thought I understood him, Poor Nic began to laugh. "Why Professor, somehow you have summoned rescue. How on earth did you arrange that?"

"You wouldn't believe me if I told you, Nicholas." Angel brushed past Bobby and Tommy. "Tuck sends his regards."

Poor Nic signaled them to let her pass. "Professor, this isn't over. Your luck is. It has been for a while. The bracelet is mine. I've paid for it a thousand times over the years. It's mine and I must have it."

As the door shut behind us, the last thing he said chilled me.

"Please, Angela, don't let it cost you more than it already has."

FIFTY-NINE

"Dammit, Bear, answer the phone." After the third unanswered call, Angel's frustration was mounting, but mine was days ahead of her.

"So, the bracelet is Poor Nic's. He's behind all of this, Angel."

"I can't believe it. He was so convincing the other day in my office."

"Yeah he was." A lot of people were fooling me. "Like Bear."

"Tuck, please—Hercule?"

Hercule had slept in the backseat the entire trip back from Livingston's shop. Now, he was awake and agitated. As we pulled into our driveway, he jumped to his feet and jammed his head out the partially opened rear window. He growled and barked, pawing at the door to get out. When Angel stopped the car and opened his door, he made a dash for the front porch and jumped up to peer into the front window, barking a warning.

"Angel, stay here. I'll check the house. Keep Herc with you—let him go if anyone comes out." You can't argue with a ghost, so off I went. Hercule begrudgingly obeyed Angel's summons and he stayed beside her on the porch, hair ridging up on his back.

Inside, Hercule's angst became clear before I left the foyer. The entire house was trashed. My den took the brunt of someone's anger. My books were off their shelves and thrown throughout the room. Desk drawers hung open and some were smashed on the floor with their contents littered everywhere. My filing cabinet lay on its side and someone took their temper out on it; all that was left was a pile of crushed wood and metal. The entire room was destroyed.

The rest of the house received the same razing, although our bedroom was perhaps worst. Someone took the time to gut our king-sized mattress into shreds. The contents of our dressers and closets were in debris piles in the middle of the room. The carnage continued through the entire upstairs. Years of our memories lay in piles on the floor. If they found what they were looking for, I couldn't tell. Nothing was left untouched by their search.

The bastards.

When Angel came into the house, I warned her to stay back. The warning fell on deaf ears—two sets. She and Hercule went room to room—she to view the destruction and Hercule to hunt our guest. Neither was happy with the result. Angel returned to the kitchen and tried the light switch. No power. Next she tried the phone—it too was not working.

"Tuck, there's no electricity and the phone's out."

"They probably tripped a breaker trashing the place. The phone's another problem."

Angel righted one of the kitchen chairs to sit on. She dropped her keys and cell phone on the table amidst broken crystal and china. "Tuck, who did this? Why?"

"It's that damned bracelet. Poor Nic's boys, no doubt. You told them you didn't have the piece with you—they came to find it."

"I should have just given it to him." She dug into her jeans pocket and pulled it out. "I had it all the time. Maybe I could have stopped this."

"No," I touched her cheek and for a moment, her hand touched mine. I wasn't sure if she felt me or not, but comfort warmed her face. "I'm sure it was already too late."

Angel's eyes widened and panic whitened her face. "Tuck, what if they come back?"

She was right.

"Do you still have Bear's spare gun he gave you at Iggi's?"

She looked at the open kitchen cabinets and went to inspect the drawers. "It's gone. I left it in this drawer—they took it. I'll try Bear again." She did, but held up her phone. "Battery's dead. I forgot to charge it in the car."

"My police gear bag is in the garage. I have a spare weapon in it. Get my keys."

"Where are they?"

"In the big cup on the shelf." The shelf, of course, was among the destruction on the floor and the oversized coffee mug was shattered. She dug around in the debris on the floor and found my keys.

"Tuck, I have them."

"Get the gun, Angel. Then, use your car phone charger and call Bear. Wait in the car until he gets here. But get the gun first."

I followed her to the back door. Hercule braced himself in front of her legs, refusing to allow her to go outside. He moaned and tried pushing her back into the kitchen.

"No boy, you stay here. Don't let anyone in the house. I'll be right back." Hercule didn't look happy, but he relented and let her through the door.

I followed her to the garage and we slipped inside and shut the door behind us. It was dark, but with the little ambient light from the window, the garage appeared unscathed from the razing the house received.

Angel tried the light switch. "No lights in here, either. I'm scared."

"I'll keep watch. You get the gun."

Angel unlocked the rear hatch of my SUV and grabbed the black nylon gear bag. When she pulled the bag forward, she noticed something else tucked behind it in the rear cargo.

"Tuck, what's this?" She held up a large, manila shipping envelope two inches thick.

"I don't know."

"It's from the local medical examiner. When did this arrive?"

I thought back, but nothing surfaced. "I'm not sure."

"Think, Tuck."

I looked at the package. A memory started to form in my dead brain cells—a memory I didn't know I had. The package was delivered the day I was killed. It was for Angel and I'd signed for it that morning.

"Yeah, I remember now—a special courier."

The courier's recipient copy was still taped to the front of the envelope. Angel read it. "It came the day…"

"Right—I got it when I was leaving for work. You were already gone so I tossed it in the back."

"André and Ernie have been asking me about this—the M.E. sent several items from Kelly's Dig to me. After they cleared the site as a crime scene, he didn't want to keep this stuff. He assumed it would be part of my court research."

"Okay, but we can worry about that later."

Angel ignored me and ripped open the end of the package, dumping the contents onto the SUV's cargo bed.

A thin, white report folder and a clear plastic evidence bag fell out. The report folder was titled, "Office of the Chief Medical Examiner, Northern Virginia District Office" and the citation referenced Kelly Orchard Farms. The bag was still intact and the evidence seal unbroken. Inside was a tarnished, well-worn silver necklace.

"Tuck, why didn't you tell me about this before?"

"I didn't remember it until now." I barely remembered the skinny college kid standing on the front porch that morning. I thought he was selling scout cookies or something. "I'm dead—my memory was the second thing to go."

Angel ripped open the evidence bag and took out the necklace. When she turned it over and held it up in the dim light, we both knew exactly how important it was. Grimy and tarnished, a three-inch G-cleft hung on the end of a silver chain. In the center of the "G" was a dull, clay-crusted emerald.

"Tuck, do you know what this means?" Angel wiped some of the grit from the necklace. "This matches Nicholas's bracelet. It means..."

"Yes," I said, watching the emerald begin to glitter in the window light. "It means whoever killed me came here that night to get this back."

SIXTY

"I'll be taking that," a man's voice—strangely familiar—said from the garage door. "Now."

Angel and I had forgotten why we came to the garage—to retrieve my spare handgun. Hercule didn't want us leaving the house. He knew. He knew that someone was still close by. That someone was now standing with a gun waist high, pointing at Angel.

When she turned toward the garage door, we came face to face with Lucca Tuscani.

"Put the necklace down and step back." Tuscani took two steps into the garage and prodded her backward with his gun. "Don't try anything or, well, I'm sure you know how this goes."

"Please don't hurt me," she said in a low voice, laying the necklace on top of the evidence bag. "Take the necklace and go."

"Where's the bracelet?" Tuscani asked. "And who's in here with you?"

"No one."

"You're lying. I heard you talking to someone." He stepped sideways and worked his way around the rear of the SUV, peeking inside the vehicle. When he came around the other side, his eyes narrowed on Angel. "Where'd they go?"

"There's no one. I was talking to myself. Ever since you killed Tuck—you bastard—I talk to him. That's all."

"Me? You have it all wrong, lady." Tuscani forced a laugh. "Now, where's the bracelet? I came for the set."

"In the house."

"You're lying. Don't make me take it."

I moved beside Tuscani and said, "Give it to him."

"No."

"No?" Tuscani scanned the garage again. "What do you mean, no? Give it to me."

I lunged for the killer but grabbed emptiness. I swung at the gun but hit nothing. Dammit. I couldn't find the strength—couldn't make any connection—I couldn't reach the bastard. My bond to this world needed energy—power—and it was off. Even Angel's cell phone was dead. I was helpless to save her. He could do what he wished and all I could do was watch.

"Angel, I can't help you right now. You have to get him out of here and get me a chance to find a way to help."

Her eyes darted toward my voice. She nodded, and the move startled Tuscani.

He stepped toward her, thrusting the gun into her chest. "Knock it off, lady. Where's the bracelet?"

"Give it to him, Angel—just do it."

She dug the G-cleft bracelet from her jeans pocket and dropped it on the cargo bed beside the necklace. The pieces lay side by side, and I looked at them. This was all about the tarnished silver and earth-caked gems—the killings, the attacks, dead girls, bones, and premonitions. Lying there, they seemed too innocent to have caused all they had. Yet, these two pieces of silver and gems had reigned terror since they were unearthed. Raymundo Salazar and Iggi Suarez found them by lamplight, and that started their killing spree.

"Ah, very good." Tuscani stepped forward and scooped up the pieces. He never took his eyes off Angel. "Now it's time to go for a little ride."

"What? Where?"

"To my aunt, of course."

"Aunt?" Angel's voice was thick with confusion. "I don't understand."

"No?" Tuscani forced another laugh. "You don't understand what you've found, do you?"

"Why don't you tell me."

"No. Better yet, we'll show you."

"We?"

He laughed again. He dangled the necklace and bracelet through his fingers, taunting her with it. "These belong to her—to Amy."

"Who is Amy?"

Tuscani's face darkened and he stepped toward her, lifting the gun up, and touching it to her chin. "It's time we went to see her—her bones anyway. As soon as we get those, I'm going to set this right. I'm going to set everyone right."

"And me?"

"Yes, Professor Tucker, *especially* you."

SIXTY-ONE

"He's taking you to Kelly's Dig," I said. Everything began there. Everything would end there, too. "Try to stay calm."

"Kelly's Dig?" Angel was driving and fighting back the terror. "Right?"

Tuscani grinned. "Yes, good guess."

"I'll find a way out of this." I touched her cheek from the backseat and she peeked at the rearview mirror. "I promise."

Everything surrounded Kelly's Dig, and yet, obviously now, it was more than gold coins and Civil War bones. There were so many unanswered questions. But the "who" part of the equation suddenly seemed too obvious; especially when he continued to poke Angel with his gun.

"What do you want with me?" Angel asked. "I don't know you. What have I done to deserve this?"

"Relax, lady." He traced her arm with the barrel of his gun, laughing in a sadistic, harsh way. She recoiled and sent the car veering toward the median. "Easy. No point getting killed yet. There is so much we have to talk about first."

"Don't touch me again."

"Oh, you can bet I will."

"Lucca, Lucca…" Anger welled inside me and I slid behind him, blowing into his left ear. "Touch her again and you'll be joining me in the dead lane, pal."

"Huh?" His head whipped around and he looked into the back seat. When he turned back, he retracted his arm from Angel's side and rested the gun on his thigh, staring straight ahead.

I do believe Mr. Tuscani is afraid of ghosts.

We entered Kelly Orchard Farm through the construction entrance not far from Kelly's Dig. As we passed the site, the yellow crime scene tape flapped in the breeze and the smell of burnt wire and plastic still hung in the air. She slowed but he motioned for her to continue up the dirt road. Several minutes later, Angel rolled the SUV to a stop in front of the main farmhouse.

"Now listen, no silly shit, okay?" Tuscani tapped her leg with his gun. "There's no one around. And that means no one will hear a loud bang."

"Please, let me go." His answer was a wave of his gun. Angel opened her door and slid out onto wobbly legs. "Save me" was etched across her face—but I was helpless. I needed time and luck, and both were running very short.

"Inside. You brought this on yourself."

"I still don't understand."

"You will. Move."

Angel folded her arms in defiance. "I'm not going anywhere until you tell me …"

Tuscani lashed out and struck her across the face, sending her crashing into the SUV's fender and onto the ground. As she started to rise, he descended on her. He grabbed her hair and dragged her to her feet—shaking her in a vicious and violent display of control.

"Move."

"Leave her alone." I swung at him but struck nothing. "Doc, help me—please, Doc!"

Nothing.

"Okay, I'm going." A trickle of blood blossomed on her lip and her voice was stronger than I could have imagined. "You're a bastard."

He laughed and propelled her forward.

Inside the house, Tuscani navigated as though he knew every inch of the six thousand square feet of hardwood and stone. Even with the covered windows shedding little light, he moved confidently through the house. He prodded Angel through a high-ceilinged dining room and into a great room where another hall opened off the rear. He pushed her toward the southern wing of the house—twice she fell onto the dusty hardwood—both times he yanked her to her feet and shoved her on.

"Through here." He opened a door beneath the stairwell I hadn't noticed from the hall. There were crude wooden stairs leading down into darkness. "After you."

Angel balked and peered into the darkness. "What's down there?"

"Amy."

SIXTY-TWO

THERE WAS NOWHERE TO go. Nowhere to hide. No way out.

We descended the creaky plank stairs down into total darkness. A dozen steps down, Tuscani shoved Angel forward and she fell to her knees at the bottom. Behind us, I heard him flip a switch and two bare-wire lights hanging from the ceiling glowed. Their light was barely enough to illuminate the room, and when they did, my hopes of escape dwindled.

The nineteenth-century cellar was cold and damp. The floor and walls were stone and the ceiling was made of hand-hewn timbers that were easily four feet over my head. There was a rear cellar room ahead of us, but it was dark and uninviting. We stood in a cleared area between empty wine racks and wooden shelves lining one side of the room, and wooden boxes and packing crates stacked on the other side. The room smelled of damp earth and musty air.

It smelled of a dungeon—dismal, hopeless, and lifeless.

Angel stood up and Tuscani shoved her forward into a pile of broken crates. She almost fell but caught herself. She turned toward him as anger and fear fought for control of her voice.

"Don't touch me again."

"Shut up and move back."

"Angel, I need more time." I searched around the room for a plan—any plan—that might get her to safety. "But be ready to run. The second I see an opening, go. Don't hesitate. Don't think. Just run like hell when I say."

"Okay, Tuck." Her head dipped in a slight, terrified nod.

"What? Shut up, lady." Tuscani stood blocking the stairs and pointed toward the dark room off the rear of the cellar. "In there— that room. Go on. Go in there."

That's when I felt them.

They were there, beyond the light, wrapped in burlap and secreted behind old wood planks of a broken wine rack. There was loneliness and sorrow simmering just inside the darkness, and as Angel stepped forward, anticipation waited for her. I went ahead of her and stopped in the doorway. I could feel them reaching out to me. They were there—unsure of their surroundings—disturbed from their rest at Kelly's Dig. Now, they were here, waiting.

And they wanted to end it all.

"Angel, Amy and Caroline are the two young girls appearing to me. I didn't understand before. I think I do now."

"Caroline?" Angel stopped, listened, and turned to Tuscani. "Amy and Caroline are with Tuck. They're all here, Lucca. And they've come back to stop you. Don't make them hurt you, Lucca. Let me go. Let me go and they'll let you go."

"What?" Tuscani peered past her into the room. He prodded her with his gun, but his voice was unsteady. "Your husband's dead, lady. So are Amy and Caroline. They can't hurt me and they can't help you. So move."

"No, Lucca. You're wrong. They're here, right…"

"Stop. You know it was Nicholas." Tuscani shoved her aside and went to the doorway. He still didn't venture in. "Stop your shit and get in there."

"Nicholas?" Angel didn't hide her confusion. "Poor Nic?"

"He killed them. You know that. The bastard killed them both."

"Angel, keep him talking." Time was precious.

She did. "Why did he kill them? Why did you kill Tuck?"

"Shut up." Tuscani whirled around in the doorway. "Just shut up. Get in there."

"What happened to them?" Angel's voice was soft, flavored with understanding—trying to calm and draw him in. "Tell me, please. I want to understand. I want to help."

"No." He shifted his weight and stepped back from the doorway, but still stared inside, wavering as though he wanted to go in, but couldn't make his feet obey. When he turned to Angel, his face lightened and his eyes were not as dark—not as dangerous. Perhaps he was having second thoughts about killing her. Perhaps he was beyond that and choosing how to.

"You loved Amy," Angel said. "Didn't you?"

Then, as though he and Angel were chatting over tea, he said, "Yes, of course, she was wonderful. She took care of me when I was young—right here at this house. She was beautiful—and so good to me. No one else cared. She did."

She said, "And she loved you, too."

"Yes, Amy was my aunt." Tuscani took a deep breath that seemed to cool him. "He found out. Only Caroline and I knew. He found out about her boyfriend. But I didn't tell."

"He was jealous?"

"Yes."

Angel tried soothing him. "I understand. I do. Nicholas is a hard man. Did you see him?"

Mr. Hyde returned. "You don't understand shit." He slid the G-cleft bracelet out of his pocket and held it out in the dim light. "He gave it to her and no one knew that—just him."

I saw it all in my vision. It was late at night in the orchard—right at Kelly's Dig. A young, pretty Amy was arguing with some-one—a man. He struck her down and Caroline tried to intervene. They tried to tell me, to warn me about him. *Stop him. You have to stop him.*

"Lucca, maybe I can help you."

"Shut up." Tuscani stuffed the bracelet back into his pants pocket. Then, a sickening feeling ebbed into me when Lucca's face hardened. His eyes seemed lifeless and he smiled at Angel. I knew that others had seen that smile—none ever lived to tell about its meaning. "Let's go."

"Please, tell me …"

Tuscani leapt across the room, grabbed Angel's arm, and shoved her through the doorway. "Get them." He followed her to the door-way, propelling her deeper inside. He fumbled with a switch on the wall and turned on the light at the far end of the room.

I could feel them stronger now. They were here, confused and scared—just like Angel and me. The difference was the girls and I could not be hurt any more. Angel could.

The room was littered with old boxes and broken, wooden shelving—a scary and lonely place for the girls. Hidden among the debris was the bulky burlap bag, and I told Angel where to find it. She freed the sack, carried it to the outer cellar, and stood beneath the hanging light. There, she stood holding it, her face showing the conflict between sorrow and fear.

We both knew what was in the burlap—bones.

A shudder ran through me. Whispering, fleeting voices jingled in my head and I heard Amy's voice. I understood.

"Angel, it's going to be okay."

She carefully hefted the bag. "Tuck, I'm scared."

"Tuck again? Stop that." Tuscani pointed his gun at her and then gestured at the ground. "Lay it there, on the ground. Get back—step away."

"Lucca," she said, easing toward the stairs with the sack clutched toward him. "Why did you kill Tuck—why my husband?"

"Put them down and back away. Do it." When she hesitated, he lunged and grabbed the burlap bag from her grasp. He raised the gun to strike her, but when she withdrew, he stopped and set the bag on the floor at his feet. "I had nothing to do with your husband. It's Nicholas I came for."

Angel inched toward the stairs. "All right, Lucca. You have Amy now."

He knelt down beside the burlap bag of bones. He was lost in memories, back in another time—a time when Amy and Caroline were alive and caring for him. His face softened. His arm dropped to his side, the gun resting on his knee. He started to smile.

Now.

I reached up and grabbed the overhead light's bare wire dangling above my head. The surge was instant. Current filled me—invigorated me—burned through me like fire chasing a gunpowder fuse. It burst up my fingers into my entire being. It raged and built, spreading through me like a wildfire. Its power exploded in my head and I knew it was time to end this.

"Now, Angel!"

Angel crashed into Tuscani, shoving him off balance. She struck a violent kick at his groin. She missed, but the blow smashed his thigh and sent him backward with a sharp cry. As he tumbled back, she grabbed the burlap bag at her feet. With every ounce of strength, she swung it in a wide arc and smashed it into his head. He faltered sideways and crumbled onto the ground.

"Go," I yelled and she bolted for the stairs. "Run!"

Tuscani recovered too quickly and raised his gun, leveling it the instant she hit the first stair. His finger descended on the trigger.

"No, no." I grabbed the electric wire again. The lightning surged. "Come on, tough guy, shoot me."

He was on one knee. His gun arm was outstretched, tracing Angel's path. His head turned toward the light swinging overhead, but his eyes were riveted on me. Lucca Tuscani was staring right at me and he remembered. Terror exploded in his eyes. The familiar face of a man who struck him—a dead man—from a high school parking lot fighting him in the rain.

"What the hell..." his voice cracked but his eyes were steady and staring. "You... Jesus Christ..."

"No, just me—boo."

Angel's feet echoed off the hardwood above us and I knew she was widening her escape. "Go, baby, go."

Tuscani turned the gun on me now. With uncertain, shaky movements, he stood and backed away until he was flat against the cellar wall. As the lightning faded inside me, I saw him straining to find me in the dim cellar light. I hadn't moved, but he could no longer see me. He searched the cellar, one squinting eyeful at a time—trying to convince himself that I was there; praying, no doubt, that I wasn't.

He never fired a shot.

SIXTY-THREE

"Tuck?" Angel's voice was a whisper, but that's all it took for me to find her. "Please, come to me."

"I'm here, babe."

She was crouched behind an antique armoire in a second floor room that overlooked the rear courtyard. While making herself the smallest target she could, she scanned the courtyard through the window in short, seconds-long glances from concealment. On her third snapshot, she recoiled.

"He's back there."

Tuscani had done as she hoped—run from the basement and out of the house. He'd assumed she was making her escape, trying to get as far from the house as possible. She hadn't, and instead took refuge on the second floor.

"Stay hidden. I'll watch him and when he's a safe distance away, you run. "

The courtyard separated the farmhouse's rear veranda from the servant's cottage and Tuscani was weaving and bobbing through it, searching for Angel. His gun was out and ready for the kill. He stopped beside the stone wall that encircled the courtyard and crouched low, listening and watching the servant's cottage for any sign Angel was inside. He moved like a well-seasoned assassin— methodical, confident, and focused.

I watched him. "If he goes inside the cottage, get out the front. He won't hear you and you'll have a couple minutes. Try for the car."

"I don't know …" Angel was pale and her eyes big and panicked. She clutched herself in a death-like hug. "Tuck, I can't make it. He'll kill me. Can't you …"

"No, I overdid it in the cellar. I'm spent. If I try again, I'm afraid of what'll happen and you might be on your own. You have to do this."

She closed her eyes and nodded, fighting back tears and terror. "Okay."

"Get ready." I watched out the window. "You can do this."

Tuscani was in front of the cottage. He crouched low amidst overgrown shrubs and weeds and peeked into a window. Twice he called out her name, quieted to listen, and called her again. In a sudden assault, he charged into the house and disappeared.

"He's inside." I said. "Go, Angel."

She jumped up but didn't run. "Look."

A vehicle rolled into view behind the house and surprised us both. A long, black Suburban stopped beside the courtyard wall. The vehicle sat just below us, parked partially obscured around the side of the house. We could only see part of the vehicle, but it was enough. The driver got out and stood in the open, facing the cottage. He was a big, powerful man of considerable girth. His back was toward us and we couldn't see his face. He gestured to someone still in the vehicle to stay put.

I didn't need to see the passenger. I knew who was inside.

"Angel, here's your chance."

No, it was too late.

Tuscani erupted in a dead run through the cottage's side door. He fired three rapid shots, screaming a war cry as he charged the Suburban. "Bastard. Bastard ... you bastard."

The driver staggered and tried to raise a weapon as Tuscani fired again.

The driver went down—hit by three of four shots. The fourth cracked the Suburban's side window and splayed a macramé of fractures across it. The passenger's door flung open and a shot rang out—two, three.

Tuscani staggered. His charge slowed to lethargic steps. He fired a fifth time.

Another shot from the Suburban.

A surprised, maniacal grimace spread across the assassin's face. His legs couldn't carry him and he stopped, unable to steady himself. Tuscani faltered, wavered for balance. Defiance made his gun rise again.

A final shot toppled him backward onto the courtyard stone.

"Tuck, oh, my God. We're safe ..."

"No, Angel, wait."

I wanted to go to the courtyard alone. I wanted to see Tuscani dead and know it was safe. Angel wouldn't have it. Instead, I led her downstairs, staying close as she picked her steps and eased across creaky hardwood. At the rear veranda, she took a long, heavy breath and slipped behind an aged oak tree that obscured her from the Suburban's view.

"Wait. Let's see what he does."

I knew who killed Lucca Tuscani. He was kneeling over the body now, staring down at his cousin with troubled, old eyes. One hand clutched his gun. His other hand lay on the assassin's shoulder, giving it a familiar, reminiscent squeeze. Anger. Pain. Anguish—resolve.

Poor Nicholas Bartalotta stood up. Reverently, he touched his forehead, chest, and each shoulder. As he stood, he whispered contrition over the dead man. Then he turned and looked back at the Suburban.

Tommy lay face down and unmoving.

Poor Nic turned back and cursed the man he'd just prayed for.

SIXTY-FOUR

WHAT MADE HIM LOOK for us behind the big oak I don't know.

Poor Nic took two careful, slow steps away from Tuscani as though afraid to wake him. He raised his gun, staring straight at the oak. Then he moved sideways to see around the tree. He smiled, lowering his weapon, and walked toward us—a half-frown, half-smile on his face. I didn't know which was for Angel.

"My dear, Angela. I pray you're unhurt."

"Tuck," she whispered. "What do I do?"

"I think you're okay."

"Yes, Nicholas. I'm fine. What are you going to do now?"

The old gangster stopped twenty feet from us. He motioned for her to come closer and gave a convincing nod. There was something about him—something I hadn't seen before—something very … sad. Poor Nic was a man who knew violence, had inflicted pain. Now, he seemed to have no taste for it.

"Do now? Why, nothing, Angel, don't be afraid. Please, come here."

She stepped from behind the oak and eased toward him. She picked her steps as though she might choose wrong and fall through the stone walk into some unseen abyss. I don't think she breathed until she stopped ten feet from him.

"What about me?" Her voice trembled. "You know I saw you kill him."

"Yes, of course you did." Poor Nic cocked his head and his face broke out in a tentative smile. "He shot Tommy and then came at me. You saw that, too. I defended myself, Angela. Certainly you know that."

"Man's got a point," I said, standing beside him where I tried a ghost mindreading trick. I got nothing. "It was self-defense."

"Maybe." Angel was trying to appear unafraid and confident. She failed miserably. "Tuscani told me you killed Amy and Caroline. Am I…"

"My Amy? That lying bastard. It's been …"

"More than forty years."

Poor Nic lowered his head and turned again toward Tuscani. He raised his gun and for a moment, I thought he'd shoot the dead man once more. He didn't. Instead, he turned back to Angel and held the weapon out, butt first. Tears welled in his eyes.

Angel stayed silent, looking at his offering.

"Freeze," a voice barked from behind us. "Bartalotta, drop the gun and step back. Angel, move away. Come here."

Bear was crouching beside the farmhouse, just behind the court-yard wall. He had his gun extended in a two-handed shooter's grip. His sights rested on Poor Nic; his finger already on the trigger.

"Now, Nic." Bear's voice was calm and determined. He was ready to kill. There was something there, too—he wanted to kill. "Drop the gun, Nic, and step away."

"Stop, Bear." Angel snatched Nic's pistol from his outstretched hand. "I'm okay. Tuscani tried to kill me. Nicholas stopped him. He saved my life."

Something tugged on my brain—something warm and vibrant like a first lover's kiss. I looked at Poor Nic and knew his innocence. There was pain and anger in him. Pain for Amy's loss, for Caroline, and now for Tommy. Poor Nic loved Amy. He didn't kill her. He didn't kill Caroline, either. There was violence in the man, for cer-tain, but none of it had ever touched them.

I knew, but I didn't understand.

"Angel," I said. "Nic didn't kill the girls. He's aching inside. He's innocent." Someone's words tugged at me again and I added, "He didn't murder any of us."

Poor Nic's eyes stayed fixed on Bear. Self-defense or not, there were two dead men, one a killer and the other a gangster's body-guard. It wouldn't take much to cause Bear to shoot. The old gangster knew, too, that Bear was simmering, ready for it.

"Detective, I saved Angela's life." He stayed emotionless, his face unrevealing. "Lucca was hunting her. My men were watching An-gela's home when he abducted her earlier. Tommy and I came here to intervene. He killed Tommy—I killed him. It is that simple."

Bear came closer and stood beside Angel. He lowered his gun but didn't holster it. "I'm listening, Nic. What's Tuscani got to do with you?"

"He was my cousin. And his family sent him to kill me."

SIXTY-FIVE

POOR NIC'S REVELATION SPLIT the air like lightning on a dark night.

"Your cousin came to kill you?" Bear glanced at Tuscani's body as though expecting a rebuttal. "Why?"

"Yes, Detective, he came to assassinate me. All over a forty-year-old vendetta that was ill-conceived."

"Get to the facts. All I have are bodies and unsolved murders. And Nic, your name's on them."

"Ah, then I'd better explain, Detective." Poor Nic drew a long, heavy breath. With an approving nod from Bear, he went to the courtyard wall and sat down. "Back in the sixties, I spent summers at this farm. My Uncle Nicholas Voccelli owned it; well, he was not really my uncle, mind you, but I gave him the respect of one. Our families were, shall I say, business partners."

"That means mob, Angel."

"Our families arranged for me to marry Nicholas's daughter, Amy. That is why I spent time here."

Bear held up a hand. "Arranged? Like you were promised to each other?"

"Of course." Poor Nic laughed. "Ours was a very, very strict Italian family. My father was from the old country. Her father and mine were cousins and they chose me before I was even a teenager. She was younger than me and we had to wait for her to finish high school before we married."

"Get to the point, Nic." Bear never had patience. "Fast."

Poor Nic wasn't going to be hurried. "It was nineteen sixty-eight, and like many, I was headed to Vietnam. Before I went off to war, there was trouble."

Angel asked, "With the law? Your family?"

"No, Angela. It was Amy." Poor Nic looked down. He seemed sad again, perhaps recalling the pain that was now causing his voice to soften and falter. "While I was away at boot camp, Amy had a secret affair. In the old country, her lover would have been killed."

"Nice custom," Bear snipped. "But I'm not seeing the point."

Poor Nic's voice was ice. "No, that's the problem. You haven't seen the point from the beginning." He cleared his throat. "Lucca knew she'd become involved while I was away, but wouldn't tell me who it was. He was young and adored Amy. Despite the situation, I wanted to take her to New York when I returned from the war. It took days, and many arguments, but we reconciled one night."

"You got engaged?" Angel asked.

Poor Nic shook his head. "No, we never did. At the end-of-summer dance, I gave her a bracelet and matching necklace—the one you have, Angela. I planned on giving her my grandmother's engagement ring when I returned, if she would have me."

"Would she?" Angel's voice was soft, sorrowful.

He was silent a long time and the answer glistened in his eyes. "Yes. She left the dance to tell her father. She never arrived. I always hoped she'd changed her mind and ran away with her lover."

Bear asked, "You hoped she ran away?"

"The alternative was unthinkable."

Yes, murder was unthinkable. "Angel, I believe him."

"Get to Tuscani, Nic. And get to Salazar and the rest. Get there fast." Bear's patience was gone. "I don't care about arranged marriages or vendettas."

"Detective, it's all one and the same." Poor Nic walked over and leaned on the Suburban's fender. "Caroline was a sweet, beautiful girl. But Caroline's father was a violent man. He beat her—even raped her once. My uncle took her in and protected her from the monster. She had been Amy's best friend and confidant since childhood. They were inseparable."

Angel asked, "What happened to her?"

"Amy and she never arrived home that evening. They just disappeared. Uncle Nicholas believed I killed them both—jealousy. I hoped they simply ran away. My heart knew better."

"And the police?" Bear asked.

Poor Nic laughed. "Police? No, Detective. This was a family matter. Our families, well, our families would receive no assistance from the police."

"So Amy and Caroline were gone. Her family thought you killed them," Angel said. "Then how did you know…"

"The coins," Poor Nic said. "You see, the night Amy disappeared, so did Uncle Nicholas's coin collection. Several Civil War and Crimean War coins. They were very valuable. I have some of my own pieces at home. I hoped Amy took the collection to make a fresh start—that is, if she truly ran away."

Angel asked, "What changed your mind?" She already knew the answer.

"The truth was dug up, here, at Kelly's Dig." Poor Nic walked over to Tuscani's body, bent down, and took something from his pants pocket. He wiped his eyes and returned to us, holding up the bracelet and necklace that had nearly killed Angel. "When her jewelry and the coins were found, I knew Amy and Caroline had been killed as well."

Angel reached out and touched Poor Nic's arm, resting her hand there to comfort an old man aching from a lifetime of regret.

"Nicholas, do you know who did kill them? Was it Lucca?"

He shook his head. "Lucca was far too young. He adored them. No, it had to be her lover."

"Okay, Nic. Amy and Caroline were buried here somewhere?" Bear's voice was skeptical. "And you're sure because of the jewelry and coins?"

"Yes, of course." Poor Nic's face was stone. "A few weeks ago, those coins were sold on the Internet. Liam McCorkle traced them to young Raymundo Salazar and later showed him the sketches. He acknowledged he had the bracelet but declined to sell it. I knew then that Amy and Caroline's resting place was Kelly's Dig."

Angel's voice was solemn. "There's a burlap bag of bones in the cellar that came from Kelly's Dig. The Diggin' Man paid Salazar and Iggi Suarez to move them before the construction project started. He knew about the bones so he had to have killed the girls."

Bear said, "But the bones were from the Civil War."

"Yes, some. The killer must have inadvertently buried the girls near their grave—Tyler's construction equipment dug them all up together."

"Then, it wasn't about the highway project," Bear said with a slow, unsure nod. "It was about concealing the girls' murders." He looked from Tuscani's body to Angel. "André realized all the bones you found weren't old enough to be from the Civil War—that's what he meant about the medical examiner making a mistake."

Angel was nodding, too. "And the Diggin' Man tried to kill him to cover that up, too."

"I believe that is so." Poor Nic stood up and walked to her, touching her cheek. "And despite Detective Braddock's skepticism, I killed no one." He smiled. "Including your husband."

"Then Tuscani killed McCorkle," Bear said. "Trying to find out who had the coins and the jewelry."

"No." Poor Nic was defiant. "My men have been following him for days. Lucca was here, digging for any of Amy and Caroline's remains still here. And he didn't kill Dr. Cartier, either, but he did go to the hospital later. I understand he attempted to finish him there."

"You're telling me what didn't happen." Bear's voice was dry and he watched Poor Nic with narrow, distrustful eyes. "But you're not telling me what *did*. Like, how's Tuck connected to all this?"

Poor Nic shrugged. "Ah, and you've been blaming me for his murder, too, Detective."

"Yes, and I haven't heard anything to change my mind," Bear said. He caught Poor Nic's eyes and the two men locked like rams in the spring. "Are you telling me you weren't involved with Tuck's murder?"

"Yes, Detective," Poor Nic said, folding his arms and staring back at him. "The question is, were you?"

SIXTY-SIX

"What does that mean, Nic?"

"I think you know, Detective."

Bear's lips tightened and his face turned red—he was mad as hell. He reached out and took Poor Nic's gun from Angel, tossing it down on the ground. "Okay, Nic, you know so much. Who's behind all these killings?"

Poor Nic turned and went over to Tommy's body. His face saddened again. He repeated the sign of the cross as he had over Tuscani, closed his eyes, and said a prayer. When he looked up, he wiped away his emotions without apology.

"Detective, if I were sure who killed my Amy back then," Poor Nic said, giving Angel his grandfather smile, "Tuck and the others would not have died."

Angel asked, "How do we find the killer?"

"Only Amy's lover and I knew what the discovery of the coins and jewelry meant. He must have told Amy's family they were on the farm at Kelly's Dig. After all, the entire county knew I was involved in this development. It would be easy to convince them I sent Salazar and Suarez to move the remains and cover up their murders. So, Amy's family sent Lucca."

"To kill you," Bear said. "The vendetta over Amy and Caroline."

Poor Nic nodded.

"Nicholas, there's something else." Angel explained about receiving the bracelet from the local medical examiner the morning before I was killed. "I think whoever killed Salazar knew the M.E. sent it to me. They came to get it back that night."

"That's quite possible." Poor Nic looked down again. "Tommy was looking into it for me. He spoke with the medical examiner and learned that several people inquired about that package sent to you—the day before your husband was killed."

"Who?" Bear threw his chin toward Tommy. "Besides me, that is."

"Yes, you were on the list." His eyes flashed. "And Tommy learned more about you, too—much more."

"What are you saying?" Bear demanded.

A shiver came over me. I said, "Angel, step away from Bear. Ask him about …"

She was way ahead of me. "Bear?"

He looked first at her, then at Poor Nic. His fingers turned white around the butt of his gun. "You, too, Angela?"

She didn't answer, but her move away from him did.

Poor Nic reached over and took Angel's arm, guiding her a step behind him. "In fact, Tommy was suspicious of you—emails, house keys. Detective Spence seems to share that suspicion. After all, how did the killer get into your house that night, Angela?"

"Quiet." Bear whirled around and threw a hand up demanding silence. His eyes darted across the farmhouse windows, searching for something no one else heard or saw. "Stay here. Someone's inside."

"I didn't hear anything, Detective. Unless you …"

"Stay put." Bear sprinted to the side of the house, slipped around the corner, and disappeared.

"Tuck?" Angel looked at Poor Nicholas's gun on the ground, bent down, and retrieved it. "I didn't hear anything. Did you?"

"No. Nothing."

"Tuck?" Nic asked with a curious tip of his head. Then, he gestured to the gun in her hand. "You don't need that, my dear. I won't hurt you. But keep it if you must."

Angel ignored him. "Nicholas, you know who is doing all this, don't you?"

"Yes." His face softened. "It is …"

The first shot struck Poor Nic's right shoulder and staggered him backward. His eyes exploded in surprise as his body shuddered, dropping the bracelet and necklace. The second shot struck him before the jewelry hit the ground. He crumbled—life gasping from him.

"Angel, get down," I yelled. "Down!"

She dove sideways and rolled behind the courtyard wall. She raised the gun and jerked two shots off toward the farmhouse windows. No one was there to receive them.

The killer—my killer—was already gone.

SIXTY-SEVEN

"Nicholas." Angel looked over at him lying on the ground. "Nic?"

Nothing.

I was torn. Go after the shooter—learn who killed me—or stay with Angel. No, there was no choice. I stayed. Kneeling beside Poor Nic, I touched his shoulder and felt his life still inside.

"Get something to put pressure on his shoulder. Stop the bleeding and he'll make it for a while."

Poor Nic lay on his back. Blood oozed through the hole in his shirt. His lips hissed and his chest barely rose with each labored breath. The first shot passed through his shoulder, perhaps breaking bones, but it shouldn't take his life. The second shot grazed his other arm, just above the elbow—a flesh wound.

His life was saved by the killer firing in haste.

Angel worked fast, grabbing a handkerchief from her pocket, and stuffing it against the shoulder wound. She ripped Nic's shirt and used it around his other arm, tightening the makeshift bandage to stop the escaping blood. She checked his pulse, then his breathing.

"I think he's stable."

"Raise his head. The bleeding has stopped." I looked up at the sound of police sirens in the distance. I was about to run around the house when Amy's voice exploded into my head—*It's him, stop him, stop him ... hurry.*

The shots came in rapid succession. One, two, three.

Screams—unrecognizable rants. A pause. Another shot. Another pause—more shots. The mayhem was not directed at us. The shots were distant, from somewhere out in the orchard closer to the highway.

"Angel, it's him. Come on. Leave Nic—he'll make it."

Angel stood and sprinted to the veranda, holding the gun out in front of her. She hesitated at the door, peeked in, and cleared the opening with the gun. There was no target. She slipped inside. I followed her down the long hall, emerging in the front of the house and out into the driveway. She stopped and listened; there was no more violence in the air. "Which way, Tuck? Where are they?"

"Listen." The sirens were silent now. No gunshots erupted. A voice called me from inside my head. "Kelly's Dig—they're all there. Come on."

"All there?" Angel ran down the gravel road toward the sirens. We weaved down the orchard path and emerged a dozen yards from the debris pile aside Kelly's Dig. At its edge, Calvin Clemens stood alongside the remains of the old foundation staring down into the pit. Angel lowered her gun and stood watching Clemens. "Tuck?"

"Be strong, Angel—promise me." We walked to the pit and stopped beside Clemens. I knew what we would find there—she did not. "I never saw this coming. I'm so very sorry. After all these years."

Clemens gently took her arm, looked down at her gun, and slipped it from her grasp. "You okay, Angela? It's all over now. It's all over."

"Is it?" She shrugged. "Nicholas Bartalotta needs an ambulance—at the farmhouse. He's been shot."

"Already on the way." He turned to go, but stopped, and looked back at her. "I'm sorry, Angela. Really, really sorry." He took off at a dead run back the way we came.

"Oh, God, Tuck?" She looked into the pit. Mike Spence was inside, near the bottom. He was kneeling beside a body whose right arm extended out, still clutching a heavy pistol in a death grip. When Spence looked up, he saw Angel watching. Their eyes met, he patted the air for her to stay away.

"Damnedest thing I ever saw," he said, rising to his feet. His face was ashen and tight. "The son-of-a-bitch was just standing on the edge—right where you are—shooting and screaming into the pit. Just shooting and screaming…"

"Who is it?" Angel strained to see, but the body was turned away and facedown in the dirt. "Who is it—please, tell me."

"Angel," I said. "Babe …"

"Damnedest thing." Spence repeated. He leaned over and pried the .45 out of the body's hand. "He just kept screaming, 'you're dead. You're dead. I killed you.' We drew down on him but he kept shooting into the pit—at nothing—no one was there. Just shooting at the dirt and screaming."

Angel's face tightened when Spence tugged on the body's arm, leveraging it over onto its back. "You shot him?"

"Hell, no. Son-of-a-bitch was nuts—he reloaded, fired a few more rounds, and then grabbed his chest. The fool had a heart attack or something. He just dropped dead, right here. Damnedest thing I ever saw."

I slid my arm around Angel's shoulder and watched her as she recognized the Diggin' Man staring up from Kelly's Dig. "It's over now, Angela. I'm so sorry. He fooled us all."

SIXTY-EIGHT

PROFESSOR ERNIE STUART LOOKED at us with eyes wide open—his mouth frozen in a scream that never took voice—terror seared death across his face.

Angel saw it. Spence saw it. Only I knew why it was there.

The whispers reached my thoughts again and I looked up to the far edge of the pit. Amy and Caroline, still dressed in their pretty summer dance dresses, stood there. They waved at me and I waved back. Amy pointed at Stuart.

"I told him I was marrying Nicky. He followed Caroline and me here—to where we'd meet sometimes. He went crazy when I showed him the necklace and bracelet Nicky gave me. Caroline tried to stop him. He killed her—then me. He went crazy. He didn't understand. I didn't love him. I loved Nicky. Ernie hurt us—killed us. He killed everyone."

"But we weren't alone here," Caroline continued, "not alone. Help our friends, Oliver. They kept us safe all this time. If not for them, you never would have found us. Please."

Amy turned and I followed her gaze. Just beside them, two hazy images began forming. Two men—boys, really—dressed in rag-tag pieces of Confederate uniforms, stepped from nothing into view. The shorter soldier put his arm around Caroline. The other just stood there, watching me. Even now, they were on guard, protecting the girls.

A sad, sullen chill bathed me as I realized who they were. These two spirits, their bones at least, started everything in motion. Had they never died and been buried under this old barn more than a century ago, Amy and Caroline's murders might never have been discovered. Raymundo and Iggi would have secreted away the girls' bones undetected. Raymundo and Liam McCorkle would have been spared. If the soldiers had not been buried here, Tyler Byrd's crew would never have found their skeletons. No medical examiner's report would have been needed or written. Without that report, Ernie wouldn't have killed me. In the beginning of it all, these young soldiers lost their own lives. And in the end, they helped stop Ernie Stuart's treachery. Perhaps—just perhaps—that is some consolation for their many restless years.

The taller one's voice stirred me. "Yassir—took so long to find us."

"What happened to you?" I asked.

The shorter soldier shook his head. "We was down in the ole' root cellar under this 'ere barn gittin' supplies. There was a flash— big 'plosion. Guess Yanks dun it."

"You were hit by Union cannon?" I felt odd talking to them—dead soldiers from so long ago. "And they just left you?"

"Um, yassir. Barn and them walls just came down. Can ya help us?"

"I can't, but Angel can. Who are you—Angel will properly bury you."

The taller one smiled. "I'm Tom Harper and this 'ere's Jimmy Morgan. We was with Gen'ral Ramseur. Yassir, be nice to move on. Thank ya."

They began fading. One gave a wave; the other tipped his hand in salute.

Amy said, "He hurt you, too, Oliver. Because of us."

"It's not your fault."

Amy whispered to Caroline, who nodded and said something I couldn't hear. Then they turned, waved to their soldiers, and stepped into nothing. All four were gone.

Bear stumbled out of the orchard and onto the side of the pit where they had been standing. He was holding his head and blood oozed between his fingers. He walked around the pit, stumbling as he approached us. He stopped beside Angel and looked down at Stuart's body.

"That bastard hit me as I came around the house. Damn near took my head off with a shovel."

"Thank God you're okay." Angel burst into tears and clung onto him. "For a second I thought it was…"

"Me too," I said, and repeated what Caroline and Amy told me. She told Spence and Bear. They just listened and looked at each other, unsure of what was real, and what was not.

Bear gazed at Ernie for a long time. "Stuart? Okay, yeah—Stuart. Nic said Amy had a secret lover; it was him. They were all friends back then."

"My God, he was like a father. He fooled me for years." Angel's eyes were red and tearing. "He sent for Lucca Tuscani to kill Nicholas. Then he tried to kill André, and had Lucca try to finish him."

"Angela, he fooled us all." Bear nodded as the pieces began falling into place for him. "The break-in at his house was faked to throw us off track. I bet it was Lucca you saw at his house the morning after my murder. I bet Lucca was there all along."

"Oh, my God. And Carmen," Angel said. "I told him she was searching for the M.E. report. He thought she had it. It's all my fault."

"No, it's not." Bear shook his head. "I get why he killed the two girls. But why Tuck?"

I knew. I knew it all now. "He didn't expect me to be home. You told him I was working all night." I touched Angel's shoulder and watched the truth surface in her eyes. "You called Bear and he sent me home early. We were fighting again. It's not your fault, Angel—it's not."

"Oh..." Angel burst into tears, sobbing in heavy, deep stutters. Her body shook and Bear tried to wrap his powerful arm around her shoulders but she pulled away and turned to me. All eyes fell on her. "Tuck, he came to our house to get the medical examiner's report and the necklace—he knew they would lead us to the girls. It was supposed to be me, not you."

"I know."

"Ernie was coming to kill me."

"Yes, he was."

"You stopped him—oh my God, you died for me." She came to me, but stopped an arm's length away, looked into my eyes—she could see me again. We were both crying. "Tuck, oh no, Tuck."

I put my arms around her and crushed her to me.

Ernie Stuart. All these years, he had been a part of our family; a friend, mentor, and surrogate father. That was a façade. Beneath it all, he was a ruthless, raging killer—the Diggin' Man. In the past three weeks, every step he took—every violent act—was a failed attempt to hide what he'd done here—right here—at Kelly's Dig over forty years ago.

"What now, Tuck?" Her face was damp and her eyes searching—hoping for the answer she wanted. "You came back because of me. It's all my fault."

"No, it's not your fault, Angel. It never was."

"Yes, yes it is." She shook her head and sorrow rained down her cheeks. "It's my fault you're not, well, that you never moved on. I've been terrified of what would happen after you found your killer—that you might leave me again. Are you leaving?"

It was the guilt—her guilt—that she had been hiding. It wasn't shame for some tryst with Bear Braddock. It was not remorse for a sinister role in my murder. Yet, it was remorse. Remorse for holding me back from the afterlife and the fear that helping solve my murder would send me away to it.

Right then, I looked around, wondering if that evasive, magical light was close and ready to guide me elsewhere.

Nope, not a damn thing. Not even a flicker.

Instead, an old gray-haired, blue-eyed doctor still wearing surgical scrubs stood across the pit. Doc Gilley shook a finger at me.

"Don't even start with me, Oliver."

"What?"

"You idiot, you nearly got all this wrong."

I shrugged. "How do you figure that?"

"Bear." Doc Gilley folded his arms and scolded me with piercing blue eyes. "Your house key? You gave it to him last year before you and Angel went on vacation."

"Oh, yeah. I forgot."

Angel laughed through her tears. "I took it back because it bothered you so much. I gave Ernie one last year, too."

Doc's right eyebrow rose. "Your memory *was* the first thing to go."

Yeah, well, there were still unanswered questions. "Then why was he acting so weird? He searched my house and hid my file on Salazar."

Doc sighed, saying, "You still don't get it. He didn't want anyone seeing that file until he knew what you had in it. And later, searching the house, well, he wanted to make sure that Angel *wasn't* involved. He was protecting you both. Idiot."

"Oh. Shit. Of course." Doc made a good point. He was also making me feel foolish. "What about the emails? Livingston's business card?"

Doc said, "The business card was a clue and he followed it. Detectives detect. That's what he's been doing. Now, those mail-things I don't know. In my time…"

"Emails?" Angel's smile fought through the tears. "They were about Bear and Carmen—she's in the middle of a nasty divorce. They are, well, you know…"

"I do?" Shit, yes I do know, they were having a secret fling. "Ah, I see. Bear and Carmen."

She sighed. "If anyone found out, it would be a big mess for her. And more for him. He begged me not to tell you."

I had been a fool—a jealous, dead fool. Early on, I said that if the roles were reversed—if Bear were dead and I were left behind—I'd tear this town apart looking for his killer. All this time, he was doing that for me, and I was too jealous to see it.

I looked at Doc and hoped for an excuse. "Hey, I'm new to this dead thing. You should have just told me."

He rolled his eyes. "I'm not the detective, you are."

Bear moved closer to Angel and put his arm around her shoulders. All the time, though, he looked anxious and grim, like a parent finding the nerve to tell his child the goldfish died.

"Angela, listen…"

"No, Bear, you listen." She whirled around and faced him. "He's here, right here. Can't you hear him? Can't you see him?"

"I want to, I do. My God, he was my partner." Bear started to cry. "My best friend. He's gone, Angela. Please, don't make this harder than it is."

Doc touched my shoulder. "Oliver, you can fix this. You know how."

"I do?" Something tingled in my head and I understood. I pulled my gold detective's badge off my belt and looked at it. Of all the things that bonded Bear and me together, it was our love of this job. From the academy to just now, we were cops to the bone—partners … brothers. "Yeah, I guess I do."

I reached out and pushed my badge into Bear's hand. When our fingers touched, I felt that sparkle of power and life. But this time it was different, like a warm wave of morning sunlight running over me. He felt it, too—I know he did. He lifted his hand and his eyes exploded when he saw my badge in his grasp. He looked up, right into my eyes, and behind them, grief erupted.

"Oh my God. All this time … Tuck. I'm sorry. I never should have sent you home."

"No, no, then Ernie would have killed Angel." I hugged him and we both cried. "It's all right, partner. I'm sorry—me. With all that's happened, all this insanity, I forgot the rule. You and me—partners to the end. And longer. It wasn't your fault."

He turned away so no one would see him melt. All the while, though, he held onto my badge while his hulking frame trembled. His fingers tightened on it as his grief flowed out, escaping from whatever crevasse it was buried, cleansing away the guilt of sending me home early to my death.

Doc said, "Good for you, Oliver."

"Tuck?" Angel looked at Doc. "It's over now. Are you leaving?"

"I don't know."

"You ass." Doc threw back his head and laughed. "I can't believe any great-grandson of mine is so stupid. I told you, I've been around nearly sixty years. Do you think you can solve one or two little murders and poof, you're home free?"

"Great-grandson?" Ghosts are hereditary?

Doc winked at Angel and ignored Spence's stunned face staring at him. "No, Angela. You're stuck with him. At least for a while."

"Oh, thank you." Her face lightened and the tears—good ones I think—poured out again. "Thank you."

As Doc faded, it struck me that everything I feared as a child was real. When I was six, I believed in monsters—they were in my closet, the attic, and waiting in the dark. Later, my third-grade teacher, Mrs. Young, told me they were imaginary. She was wrong. Ernie Stuart was a monster. He became one when he slayed Amy and Caroline all those years ago. Later, he fed his macabre hunger on Salazar, McCorkle, and me.

Perhaps there were others, too. I fear that.

Yet, in the end, Ernie's victims stopped him. Each of us played a role. Because when there are monsters, there are ghosts. And we all want something—peace, justice ... revenge. After all, he made us. He answered to us. So, if my death is for anything, it is to stop monsters like Ernie Stuart.

I really don't have a choice, do I?

THE END

ACKNOWLEDGMENTS

So many to thank, so little room…

First, I learned so much about writing from Melanie Rigney—Editor For You—who helped me focus my characters and kill off those despicable adverbs. For oh-too-many rewrites goes my thanks to Nic Davis—Editor Extraordinaire—for finding time to do "just one more draft." Endless thanks to Wally Fetterolf for his equally endless wisdom and his mantra "good enough is not good enough." To my readers who gave counsel and encouragement, and demanded more books—Laurie, Jean, Lindsay, and Natalia. Now, I've finished another book…all of you get back to work!

My biggest appreciation goes to my amazing agent, Kimberley Cameron, for giving me a chance and believing in my work. Your advice and support has been invaluable. You said you'd find Tuck a home and you did.

And thanks to all the great folks at Midnight Ink for giving *Dying To Know* a home. Each of you has been a pleasure to work with and has made this experience everything I hoped it would be.

There are others, too, but I'll save them for the next book.

© TJ O'Connor

ABOUT THE AUTHOR

Tj O'Connor is an international security consultant specializing in anti-terrorism, investigations, and security programs—life experiences that drive his novels. With his former life as a government agent and years as a consultant, he's lived and worked around the world in places like Greece, Turkey, Italy, Germany, the United Kingdom, and throughout the Americas—among others. He was raised in New York's Hudson Valley and lives with his wife and three Lab companions in Virginia where they raised five children. *Dying To Know* is the first of his novels to be published.

WWW.MIDNIGHTINKBOOKS.COM

From the gritty streets of New York City to sacred tombs in the Middle East, it's always midnight somewhere. Join us online at any hour for fresh new voices in mystery fiction.

At midnightinkbooks.com you'll also find our author blog, new and upcoming books, events, book club questions, excerpts, mystery resources, and more.

TM
MIDNIGHT
INK

MIDNIGHT INK ORDERING INFORMATION

Order Online:
• Visit our website www.midnightinkbooks.com, select your books, and order them on our secure server.

Order by Phone:
• Call toll-free within the U.S. and Canada at
  1-888-NITE-INK (1-888-648-3465)
• We accept VISA, MasterCard, and American Express

Order by Mail:
Send the full price of your order (MN residents add 6.875% sales tax) in U.S. funds, plus postage & handling to:

> Midnight Ink
> 2143 Wooddale Drive
> Woodbury, MN 55125-2989

Postage & Handling:

Standard (U.S. & Canada). If your order is:
> $25.00 and under, add $4.00
> $25.01 and over, FREE STANDARD SHIPPING

AK, HI, PR: $16.00 for one book plus $2.00 for each additional book.

International Orders (airmail only):
> $16.00 for one book plus $3.00 for each additional book

Orders are processed within 12 business days. Please allow for normal shipping time.
Postage and handling rates subject to change.